The Strange Valley

Lil & Joe,
   It was good
fun!!!!.

            Mildred Nidds
                   2015

The Strange Valley

Mildred Nidds

Copyright © 2006, 2009 by Mildred Nidds.

ISBN: Hardcover   978-1-4415-1344-1
                  Softcover   978-1-4415-1343-4

All rights reserved. No part of this book may be reproduced or transmitted in any form or by any means, electronic or mechanical, including photocopying, recording, or by any information storage and retrieval system, without permission in writing from the copyright owner.

This is a work of fiction. Names, characters, places and incidents either are the product of the author's imagination or are used fictitiously, and any resemblance to any actual persons, living or dead, events, or locales is entirely coincidental.

This book was printed in the United States of America.

To order additional copies of this book, contact:
Xlibris Corporation
1-888-795-4274
www.Xlibris.com
Orders@Xlibris.com

DEDICATED TO MY FAMILY

KYRA, CASEY, CONNOR, TREVOR MATTHEW AND BOBBY

RAYMOND AND CHRIS

DIANE AND ROBERT

A special thanks to Robert who gave me a great amount of help in the preparation of this book.

Of course, thank you and all my love to my husband, Raymond Nidds.

CHAPTER ONE

John Hurley had just picked up the key to his new property. He had just signed the final papers of purchase and he now had full and clear title to his new home and it had all been recorded in the local County Clerk's office. So now it was official, he could start on his new adventure.

He had decided not to go up to the property till the next day as it was now five o'clock in the afternoon.

After picking up some take-out at the local Chinese restaurant he headed to the local hotel.

Jackson, California was a quaint little town. John Hurley had much to discover about this gold mining area in the foothills of the Sierras and the people who came to live here.

He was a little nervous—no, he was *very* nervous. For some reason he had fallen in love with this "fixer upper" in an area called Elk Horn. It was definitely going to be a challenge—a huge challenge! But, he reasoned to himself, to ease his jittery nerves, *You don't have to live here forever. You haven't closed off your past entirely.* And he hadn't. Yes, he had retired from the police force in San Francisco as a twenty-year veteran, but he had not sold the family home in the outer Sunset area of San Francisco.

He would never sell that house. His paternal grandfather had bought it when he came to San Francisco from Ireland many, many years ago. It had been passed down to John's parents and then to him.

The Sunset area, way back then, was full of Irish immigrants. Now it is an eclectic area of Chinese, Koreans and every other nationality you could think of. That is what John loved about his San Francisco neighborhood. That would always be his real home.

Now at the age of thirty-nine, he was retired. He decided long ago to do his twenty years and then get out. His father and grandfather who had also been with the San Francisco Police Department, had stayed on the job too long and were the worse off for it.

Recent events, as a San Francisco detective, had reinforced his decision to retire. Although he was thirty-nine years of age, he looked twenty-five. A handsome man! Six feet tall, full head of jet black hair, blue eyes and fair skin. A "black Irishman," he was often told. He was also in great shape. He worked out often and ran on Ocean Beach in San Francisco every morning before work. John always felt he had to be in the best shape he could be in to do the work that he did.

Being a detective in San Francisco was tough—but it was in his blood—he loved it—most of the time. He had seen every type of crime you could imagine. He still had nightmares about some of the crime scenes he had witnessed. The job took its toll on everyone. You could not help but be affected by the violence that one human being can commit upon another human.

After retiring, John knew he could not stay idle for any length of time, so he decided to try his hand at restoring a property. It was something he had always wanted to do. Contracting might be a field he would go into in the years to come, depending on how this latest project turned out.

John was very handy. He had worked with his Scottish grandfather who was a magnificent wood-worker and electrician. John had paid attention when he worked many summers with and for his grandfather.

He had started to look for the right property in the right place a couple of years ago. But nothing ever seemed quite right.

Then the real estate agent took him to a magnificent property. He knew before he exited the car that he would buy this property.

Just driving up Route 88 to view the property got him excited. When the pine trees came into view he knew he would love this area and hoped the property would be half as good as the description the real estate agent had related to him. He knew some real estate agents puffed up properties and then it was a major disappointment when the property turned out to be a dud.

But then, there it was—a quaint Castle amongst the pines. Something an English Lord would have built—with turrets and spires and little nooks and crannies that John had no name for. To top it off there appeared to be an old dried out moat surrounding the property.

If all that was not enough, The Castle was surrounded by a twenty acre forest of pine trees.

The Castle was almost out of place amid the surrounding houses which were log homes, alpine looking homes and the very plain modular homes. But he loved it! *I'll restore it to be like an Irish Castle—or a Scottish Castle*, he quickly added, as his mother was a MacGregor.

He could hardly sleep that night. The hotel was fine; it was just that he was so excited to get on with this new adventure.

John knew his parents would think that he had lost his mind when they discovered he had bought a huge castle with more bedrooms and baths than you could count on both hands.

For many reasons, he decided not to tell them about the property. He would not tell them about the property for a very long time.

CHAPTER TWO

Stopping at the local supermarket for some groceries the next day he noticed the variety of residents that lived in this area of Elk Horn.

Certainly there were a lot of retired people like him, only thirty years older. He was delighted to see children. Children always meant life to John. There were some cowboy looking men and women in their casual dress and then there were some men and women dressed in business attire. There were people of all shapes, sizes and colors. *This is great*, he thought—a *great diversity of humanity*.

Everyone was so friendly. Everyone wanted to start a conversation. But John was anxious to get started on his new project. He had no time to be friendly and to socialize. Besides, he had very good reasons not to socialize at this time!

John had vowed to keep to himself. He wanted privacy. He *needed* privacy! A hermit's life is what he desired at this point of time. San Francisco had all the friends and family that he needed. Now he just wanted time to think, wind down, be private and restore his Castle.

As he rode towards his Castle, he had just managed to avoid hitting two deer that had jumped into his path. It left him a wee bit rattled. He looked at the local speed sign that said 25 mph. Forever after, John drove that road at 25 mph. He did not want to injure *any* animal that roamed in the Valley.

As he finally turned into his driveway he felt a mystical and magical feeling come over him. John did not understand what this feeling meant, but he liked it.

It was a very, very long driveway, lined by hundreds of flowering bushes. He drove very slowly just seeping in the majesty of the old pines and the serenity of his own forest.

Finally, The Castle came into view. *Magnificent!* thought John. "I feel like a King!" he shouted. *I must find a suitable name for my estate*, he whispered to himself.

The front door key was huge and heavy. It was the type of key that you would use in castles of old or in some of the old local jails. You would almost need two hands to hold the key and open the lock. John found it difficult to turn the massive key in the lock. It was no wonder, as this property had been vacant for many years. Someone overseas had owned it, but rarely, if ever, used it. When the previous owner passed away, relatives just let it rot away to what it was now. But that was fine with John—he could and would fix anything that needed fixing.

He was grateful that it had come up for sale at a time when he was ready and was looking for a property. He felt so lucky. *I LOVE IT!* he shouted to himself. Then realizing no one could hear him he shouted out loud, "I LOVE IT!"

The door wouldn't budge. It had not been open for many years—the weather had swollen the door so badly it could no longer open easily.

He tried to push it open with his shoulder—but that didn't work. Then he gave it the old detective type of push—he backed up and then with all of his weight and might he ran his shoulder into the door. He had seen this done many times—but this time it did not work. All that he achieved was a sore shoulder as the door still would not open.

He stood back and looked at the huge door and rubbed his shoulder that hurt like hell after running full force into the door. He did not know that the door was not like any normal door. It was about a foot thick—and built to keep the owner from any danger from the outside. No arrow of old or bullet could pierce that door.

John decided to try to kick the door open with the heavy boots he was wearing. He backed up and then ran full force and gave the door a mighty kick with his heavy boot. As he limped backwards and howled with pain, he thought he had definitely broken his leg—or at the very least he thought he had a stress fracture.

John was so frustrated that he turned around and gave it a strong push with his "bum" and again all he got for his efforts was a sore bum.

Rubbing his "heinie," his leg and his shoulder, he pondered as to what to do next. He was so frustrated that he even had a fleeting thought of using a bomb to open the bloody door—or ramming his car into the door.

He calmed down and he knew he would not give up and he started to walk towards his car to get the tools that he had just bought. A screwdriver and a hammer just might do the trick.

As he walked towards his car he heard a creaking sound coming from the direction of The Castle.

He slowly turned and looked back and saw that the huge, heavy wooden door that he had tried to open had just swung wide open.

How the hell did that happen? John thought.

It frightened him. He ran and took shelter behind his car door and reached for his pistol. He forgot that he no longer carried his pistol since he left his job as a policeman.

"Is there someone there?" he shouted. There was no response.

"Who is there?" he again shouted. Again there was no response.

He thought he saw movement! "Come out or I will call the Police!"

He waited, what seemed like an eternity, and then slowly walked towards The Castle door. He had finally convinced himself that it was all of his kicking and shoving that had finally opened the door and that his eyes were just playing tricks on him. What other reason could there be?

John suddenly started to shiver and chills ran up and down his spine. The anticipation of finally opening the door and entering his Castle was now a little overwhelming.

As he slowly entered The Castle it felt like he was entering "the inner sanctum." When John finally stepped through the wide open door, the first words out of his mouth were "Good Christ! What have I done?"

He could not see very well as it was very dark inside. But the little light that came through the open door illuminated an awful sight.

He fumbled along the wall looking for the light switch so he could get a better look at the house. "Oh, damn," he said out loud, "I forgot to have the utilities turned on."

The day was not going too well—but he would not give up and he turned to get a flashlight out of the car.

All of a sudden, every light in the house went on simultaneously.

Maybe the utilities were turned on after all. He could think of no other reason.

What a sight! With the lights now illuminating the interior of The Castle, John felt sick. John had bought the property without even going inside. He did not have to, he believed, because the price was so low that no matter the condition, it would be fine. He would be able to fix anything that was wrong with the property. The real estate agent did not, at that time, have the key when she first showed him the property. It was not even properly listed. The agency was waiting for the listing paperwork and the key to be sent by the overseas owners.

There was no peeking through the windows as they were boarded up on the first level. So they just walked the property lines and around the exterior of The Castle and the small guesthouse adjoining The Castle. The huge barn on the property was also tightly boarded up.

John, at that time, could not wait to put an offer in on the property and after reading all the disclosures and being approved for his loan he still did not insist on seeing the interior of the property.

Now he could see that *everything* was in need of repair. *Good God, how will I ever restore all of this?* was a thought that went round and round in his head. There was dust and cobwebs all over the place. It looked like a scene out of that

The Strange Valley

great old movie *Great Expectations*, only there was no old wedding cake and no rats. But that was about all that was missing!

There were white sheets covering all of the old furniture and even the curtains were covered for protection.

As he tentatively walked through a few of the rooms he thought any minute something or someone would jump out at him.

He suddenly saw movement under one of the old white sheets that covered one of the large sofas and his heart skipped a beat as he started to run towards the front door.

He dared to look back and saw a squirrel scamper over to the fireplace and disappear from view as it climbed its way back up to the safety of the outside world.

John took a deep breath and tried to stop shaking and swore he would board up *that* entry to his house.

As he again started on his inspection of his Castle he could see that the wallpaper was peeling from some of the walls. Water stains were visible on the ceilings. There was warping of some of the old wood floors. There were many broken windows and the banister leading to the upper floors was loose. All this, and he had just barely left the huge foyer. What would he find when he went through the entire house?

The stairway leading to the upper floors was spectacular—just like the stairs that Clark Gable had carried Vivien Leigh in that great movie *Gone with the Wind*. There were red velvet runners on every step. He could just imagine the beautiful women that may have daintily walked down those steps with their beautiful flowing gowns.

John finally sat on those stairs and almost cried as he was so overwhelmed with the work that had to be done in this huge Castle. *Where will I start?* he thought. He then thought to look for the bathrooms where he just might have to throw up after seeing the interior of his house. *I hope there is one,* he thought. The real estate agent had said there were at least ten. "In need of repair," he now remembered her saying.

That was certainly an understatement. Everything was covered with dirt and crud. John spent most of the rest of the day just walking through The Castle—just shaking his head as he walked from room to room, floor to floor. That alone took up much of the day as The Castle was so enormous.

Maybe I should just gut the place, was a thought that came to John, as was, *Maybe I should just resell it right away.*

John decided he had seen enough for one day so he decided to close up The Castle and drive back to the hotel. There was no workable refrigerator at The Castle. There was *nothing* that was workable at The Castle! So he decided to bring the groceries that he had bought earlier back with him to the hotel and eat them for supper.

He tried to turn off the lights in The Castle by the light switches on the wall but the lights would not go off.

He even pulled the master switch but the lights still stayed on.

Oh, hell, I'll just leave all the lights on—I'll be back early in the morning.

There was one last problem. How will he close that huge front door? He went towards the car to try to find some type of tool or piece of wood that would help him seal the door for the night.

As he turned with the tools to go back to The Castle, he saw that the front door had closed. A shiver went through him. There was *no way* that that door could close by itself.

Then, as he stood back, the lights in The Castle went off, one by one, room by room.

This is one strange Castle and a very Strange Valley.

Later, as he was walking through the local department store, he bought so many cleaning supplies that one lady made a comment—"Do you clean houses? I'm always looking for a good cleaning man." Then she gave him a flirtatious wink. John got the wink, paid quickly and left.

The next stop was the local hardware store where he bought all of the extra tools he thought he would need. Every type of tool you could imagine. Good tools! Gramps had always told him to buy the best or it was a waste of money. John thought as he left the store that he would probably return often.

During the evening, John got over the depression that had enveloped him earlier that day after seeing the property for the first time and he again felt energized at the thought of what The Castle could become.

He slept soundly that night.

CHAPTER THREE

On the way to the property the next day, John stopped and opened a local mail drop. He did not want mail delivered to the property. He did not want anyone to know his name. He did not want anyone to know his address. He wanted some solace and quietness for a while. He did not want to be found!!!! It would be disastrous if he were found!

As he began to slowly turn into his driveway, a man with a Collie dog waved at him. John did not want to wave back or to stop and talk to this man—he did not want to get to know his neighbors —he did not want his neighbors to get to know him. But the man was insistent.

"You just buy this place?" the man asked.

"Yes, I did."

"You certainly have your hands full."

"That I do."

"I hope you clean up the place. It has been an eyesore for a long time."

"I'm going to try."

As the man walked away, down the road, John forgot what the man said his name was. John had just said his name was "John" and left it at that. John named the man "The Collie Man" and that is what John called him forever after.

I hope he doesn't come back. I hope he doesn't bother me, thought John. *I want to keep to myself. I want to be alone! Like Greta Garbo!* he chuckled to himself.

The previous day had been overcast and dreary. Now in the light of a glorious sunny day, John's spirits rose as the sun glistened off of some of the upper windows that had not been broken over the years. It was an uplifting sight. He felt like a Knight arriving on his white horse having won a major battle. A fantastic, victorious feeling!

Today the door opened easily, how and why, he did not know. As John again walked through the house, he waved away cobwebs and laughed as he was leaving his footprints in the major dust on the floor.

He heard a knock on the door.

"I'm here to turn on the utilities," said the man from the utility company.

"The utilities are on already."

"Can't be—I have an order from Don Black Real Estate to turn the utilities on today."

John went to turn on the light switch to show the man that the electricity was turned on—but nothing happened. None of the light switches worked.

The Utility Man went down to the basement and yelled up, "Try them now." Sure enough, the lights went on.

"I swear the lights worked yesterday—in every room."

"If you say so, sir," was all that The Utility Man said as he got a signature from John. John did not notice the strange looks that he was receiving from the Utility Guy.

Of course, The Utility Man was thinking, *just another Looney.*

John could not figure out what had happened, so he decided not to think about it, and decided to get on with the cleaning and repair of The Castle.

John had decided to start on the bathrooms first. *They were the most important rooms of the house,* he thought to himself. As he was cleaning away over twenty years of dirt and grime he could see that only the best materials had been put into this home in the era that it was built. The bathrooms looked almost brand new by the time he was finished. The dust had preserved the beautiful tile on the floors and walls. The tiles were all magnificent colors—blue, green, red and every color of the rainbow. Not one had the normal white tile that was used in most new houses of the day.

He started next on the kitchen. To John, the kitchen was the second most important room of the house. It was old fashioned but in good condition. When John was finished he thought, *Job well done, John.* As his mother would say, "You could eat off the floors."

The stove was old but was one of the best that he had ever seen. He knew he would need a new refrigerator as the existing refrigerator was just too small for his needs.

John's spirits were steadily rising as he could see the beauty of The Castle come back to life in front of his eyes. The Castle had not been abused, it was just abandoned. John wondered why!

John had ordered a telephone the previous day and lo and behold an installer was there the next day. *Certainly different from the Big City,* thought John. At the last minute, John decided not to have a house phone installed, and he sent the installer on his way. It would make it too easy for someone to track him down. He would only use his cell phone for the time being.

Browsing though the local telephone book he made appointments with several roofers and plumbers and other workmen that were needed to help restore The Castle.

The Strange Valley

Things are going quite well, thought John. *The roofers and plumbers will be here tomorrow and that will be the major jobs out of the way.*

As he locked up for the night he was happy. He looked at his hands and they were red and raw from the work he had done that day. Tomorrow he would work on the guesthouse and he would probably live there while working on the main house. The guesthouse was in better condition than the main house and John felt he could possibly move in there the next day.

He decided to go shopping that night and buy a small refrigerator and a small hot plate and that would do him just fine in the confined space of the guesthouse. He would also buy a small cot and a small table and chairs. *Then I'll be all set,* he thought. Then he bought some wine to celebrate his first night in his new home the next night.

On the way into town, he spied an older man standing on the side of the road and the man was waving wildly at John to stop his car.

John thought he looked distressed. He stopped and asked, "Do you need help?"

"Give me a lift to the supermarket?"

John did not want to! He did not want anything to do with any of the neighbors. Privacy is what he wanted and needed. "Get in," he heard himself say.

The man's stench took John's breath away. It was like he had not bathed in a year and had just drunk a barrel of beer.

"Where are you from?" asked the old man.

"Just down the road."

"Are you the one that bought the old Castle?"

John did not respond and he put the pedal to the metal. He wanted this old codger out of the car as soon as possible.

"You do know that Castle is haunted, don't you?" asked the old man.

John was surprised at the statement the old man had just made. "Who is it haunted by?" John challenged "The Stinker."

"Lots of different people are what I hear."

"Well, I haven't met any of them yet," John said just to humor the old man.

"You will," responded The Stinker knowingly. "I got the bejesus scared out of me when the previous gent lived there."

"No one has lived there for over twenty years or more," John threw back at him.

"I know. I have been around that long in case you haven't noticed. I think the ghosts killed him," added The Stinker while nodding his head. There was no further conversation after that statement.

As John lay on his cot that night in the guesthouse, he thought of the old man who he had nicknamed "The Stinker." "Just an old senile man—probably just seeing and hearing things after swilling down a pint of liquor," is what John said out loud.

17

What a "Strange Valley" this is! he thought as he was drifting off to sleep. *A beautiful Castle among the pines that was uninhabited for years and now an old man who says it is haunted!*

John decided not to dwell on what the old man had said. He remembered what his grandmother had always told him in times of stress—don't let your mind wander!

CHAPTER FOUR

Two of the four roofers showed up. One roofer spent an hour walking around the house, climbing on some parts of the roof, and shook his head constantly. John's heart sank with every shake of that roofer's head.

When he first saw the roofer exit his truck John thought he looked like "The Uni-Bomber." That was the guy that had lived in Montana or one of those mountainous states; and was on the run for many years, while he bombed the innocent. The roofer's beard flowed down his chest and his moustache was creeping around his neck—if it grew any longer he would be able to tie the ends of the moustache together in a bow in the back of his neck—and his work boots and clothes had seen better days!

The truck he had arrived in looked like it had rolled down some huge mountain and had barely survived the fall. John could not fathom how it could still run with all the dents that had been bashed into the exterior of the truck.

The second roofer was cleanly dressed and had a spiffy truck.

"I won't touch this place," the second roofer announced to John after he had spent hours inspecting the immense roof.

"Why?" John asked, totally surprised at what the man had said. "You spent so much time up on the roof, I thought you were ready to give me an estimate."

"I heard this place is haunted and I get bad vibes just walking around the freaking place."

"That's ridiculous!" exclaimed John.

"Maybe so—but I'm not working on *this place*!" He almost ran to his truck and then he drove off as if in a panic—he drove as if someone was after him. He kept looking back as if to see if someone was following him.

So John had to hire "The Uni-Bomber" to replace his roof.

Only one plumber showed up and he looked like he had just come from working on an old-time chain gang. Fortunately, the plumber felt there was little work to be done to bring The Castle into good working condition.

"Might need a new septic system in the future, but I think you will be all right for a couple of years."

So John hired "The Uni-Bomber" and "Jim the Plumber," and the renovation of John's Castle was on its way. Despite their appearances the two men would do magnificent work. Somehow, John trusted them from the start. A handshake was the only contract that sealed the deal. That's the way it worked in this Valley.

John was to learn that his name among the workers was "The Castle Man."

That was fine with John. He wanted his privacy and he wanted this hideaway to be a secret for as long as possible.

Because of the size of the building, John decided to close off half of The Castle and just use the northern end. In time he would restore the whole Castle, but for now, half of The Castle was big enough for John.

CHAPTER FIVE

The real estate agent who had represented John in the purchase of The Castle came over one day with a house-warming gift. A little sign with his name "Hurley" carved into it. It seemed that every other house had this type of sign on it. "Customary," said the real estate agent. "All agents up here do it—it's a housewarming gift—our way of saying thank you."

"Thank you very much," John said very appreciatively. When the agent left he tossed it into the garbage. He certainly did not want to advertise where he now lived. He later retrieved the sign from the garbage can and vowed he would someday post the sign on the nearest tree. He was proud of his name. But he could not and would not display the sign—at least not now.

It would be hard to explain to anyone why he wanted his privacy and anonymity. Sometimes it was hard to explain it to himself. He had, in his twenty years on the police force and as a detective, sent many people to jail for many years. When he was younger, the threats from these criminals had just rolled off his back. Recently, it struck home more severely. Especially the last two cases that he helped to solve and to help prosecute. These cases came back to him very vividly.

"I'll get you, man! Watch your back day and night because I or my people will get you. Don't ever sleep easy again!" the man had screamed at John.

These dreadful words came from Gerald Jackson who had just been sentenced to death.

Then there were the mouthed words from Jose Perez, after he was sentenced to life in prison—"You are dead!" Jose had mouthed these words over and over as John testified at the trial. As Jose mouthed the scary words he also drew his forefinger across his throat. John knew what that meant. The memory still sent a chill up John's spine. The stare of Jose as he was led from the courtroom was forever etched in John's mind.

Of course there were many others but these two gave John many nightmares.

The criminals of old seemed to be much gentler than the criminals of today. Perhaps it was the drug use or the availability of guns or the courts that had changed the atmosphere of the criminal world. Today you have to handle the criminals with kid gloves or the arresting officer could be the one who landed in jail.

The Miranda Rights had ruined many a case when the officer in the middle of a horrendous arrest forgot to "Mirandize" the perpetrator.

John knew it was time to get out when the criminal had more rights than the officers that were trying to keep the streets safe.

Yes, it was hard for John to admit to himself that this was the major reason he had retired early. He could not admit that indeed he had been frightened. How could he admit that he was now basically in hiding? Hopefully, as time passed, the memories would fade and he would go about living more normally. But in the meantime he would stay out of sight and he would enjoy fixing up his new home, The Castle.

He tried to treat his fear with some sort of a sense of humor, or he would go crazy. He thought back to the events of that very morning as he was working around the grounds of The Castle.

A truck had come rolling down his driveway. He was not expecting anyone at that time and a great fear started seeping up his spine.

When he looked at the driver the fear rose up very quickly and his head went a little light. He wanted to tuck tail and run for his life. But instead, he stood frozen to the spot. He could not get his feet to move.

He finally decided to put up a good fight. He would not go easy! If the man was here to do him harm, he was going to be in for a good fight!

The driver hopped down from the driver's seat and immediately John knew he was dead. He started to say a "Hail Mary" as fast as he could.

The driver looked like he had just come from a wrestling arena, having fought ten men at once, and won. This man was a "Mountain Man."

His red hair flowed halfway down his back and the beard hung long and straggly. The pants he wore bared part of his ass as his waist was just too big to put a belt around.

John grasped the hammer he was working with and was ready to stand his ground. *Should I strike first?* he wondered. *Should I aim for the head, or his legs?* John instinctively knew that he would have to be able to fly in order to hit this man in the head as he was many heads taller than John. The man's legs were so thick that John's strike would be like a bee sting.

John decided that he would try to show the man he was not afraid and he started to walk assertively toward the giant. His heart was pounding as he neared the giant and what he thought just might be his last day on this good earth!

As the two walked toward one another the air was tense. It reminded John of that movie *High Noon*. He inwardly vowed to stand tall like Gary Cooper.

John had a hammer in one hand and a level in his other. They were the only weapons that were handy at the time.

The giant was bare handed. John knew that that giant needed no weapons except his monstrous hands.

Suddenly the giant spoke. "Hi! I'm from the glass company. I'm here to fix your windows."

John had expected a loud, booming voice. But instead he heard a normal and gentle voice.

John's body trembled in relief and then in anger he said, "You are three days late!"

"Sorry about that, but there was an emergency at the local hospital and we had to take care of that first."

"Why didn't you call?" John said angrily, since his legs were still shaking with fright.

"Not up to me, sir. Call the office if you have a complaint."

The Mountain Man turned out to be a very gentle giant and with a great sense of humor. John quickly warmed up to this man, even though he had scared John half to death. John vowed never to judge a book by its cover again.

He should have known. Years ago, his grandfather had taken him on one of his jobs in the Financial District in San Francisco. Gramps always wore a full coverall when working, and at the end of the day he was filthy with the dirt and grime that a good day's work would bring when you were a professional carpenter, dealing with paint and varnish and wood shavings.

They stood outside the building that Gramps was working on one afternoon, on a coffee break, and Gramps was proudly gesturing at all the surrounding buildings he had also worked on over the years.

Gramps was just about to throw away the Styrofoam coffee cup that he had been drinking from, when a passerby tossed in a couple of quarters. The man thought that Gramps was a bum!

Gramps looked in the cup and then looked at his grandson and smiled broadly. "Easiest money I ever made, Laddie."

Gramps never tired of telling that story to anyone that would listen.

It was his wise old grandmother who had told him, "Never judge a book by its cover, Johnny."

John had forgotten those wise words, but he would remember them from now on.

CHAPTER SIX

Mountain Man had just left for the day when John heard a dog give a little bark. John was sanding some of the rungs from the beautiful staircase in The Castle. He loved working outside and of course it meant less dirt in the house.

When he turned he saw an older lady with a poodle.

"Hi, there!" she said.

John decided to be polite despite what he really felt.

"Hi."

"Are you the new owner?"

"Yes, I am."

"I am so glad that someone finally bought the old Castle."

John just nodded.

"It was such a beautiful place in its time."

"I hope to bring it back to its full beauty."

"I spent a lot of time in that house when I was younger."

"You knew the previous owner?"

"I sure did. I dated him for a while."

"You did! What was he like?" John was really interested in discovering what type of man built such a tremendously large castle in the middle of nowhere.

"He was a Sea Captain."

John thought, *It was always a Sea Captain that owned funky houses.*

"Oh, an old Sea Captain, eh?" John asked facetiously.

"No! No, he was a young Sea Captain and quite attractive. He sailed on one of those big cruise ships."

"I see." John thought it would be interesting to find out as much as he could about the previous owner and decided to question the "Poodle Lady" further.

"Were the two of you serious? Any marriage plans?"

"We were serious, but then I left him."

"Why?"

The Strange Valley

"He was too rough. Especially in bed," she added with deadpan seriousness.

John looked at the older lady in surprise. He wondered if she was kidding or trying to get a rise out of him. From the look on her face she was definitely very serious.

But this was more information than John needed or wanted from this older woman.

"Do you know what happened to him?" John continued.

Poodle Lady shrugged. "We think he was killed."

"You *think* he was killed?" John wanted to make sure that he had understood what the Poodle Lady had just said.

"That's what I said."

"Do you know who might have killed him?" asked John, trying to get as much information as he could about this supposed killing of the mysterious Captain.

She shrugged and said very matter-of-factly, "Lots of people wanted him dead."

"Why?" said John, still determined to pump as much information as he could from this woman.

"He was a very bad man!" She hesitated, and then she decided to say no more. "Well, I've got to go. Poochy here needs his walk."

John had a lot more questions that needed answers but he knew he had gotten all the information that he could get that day from the Poodle Lady.

So far, he had discovered that the previous owner was a Sea Captain; that he was rough in bed; he was a bad man and that the house was haunted. He had been there only about a week and discovered that everyone wanted to come and talk about The Castle and its previous owner.

What else would he find out? He was sure that Mrs. Poodle, Mr. Collie and maybe even The Stinker would be back.

How many more residents of this Strange Valley had information about the previous owner and this mysterious Castle that he had built so long ago?

CHAPTER SEVEN

John thoroughly enjoyed working outdoors. He had set up a work table on the front lawn and it was there that he did most of the sanding and refinishing of the small stuff. Of course he had planed down the huge front door that he had had such trouble opening the very first day.

He loved working with his hands and he had turned out to be a pretty good carpenter. He was taught by the best—his grandfather, Ian MacGregor. Ian was one of the best carpenters in the City of San Francisco. He was much in demand for his workmanship and honesty. He was just a wee Scot who had emigrated from his beloved Glasgow, Scotland. Everyone loved him! John had spent many a summer apprenticing for him and enjoyed every minute of it—especially when his Gramps would break out in song as he was hammering away. It was always a Scottish ditty. Eventually John would sing along with him. John didn't really understand the words of the song, but he was happy to be singing with his Gramps.

"You have the gift," his grandfather had said to him many a time. "And you got it from me!" he added proudly.

Ian had been unhappy when John had chosen the police force as his life's path. "The Irish side of the family," is the way Gramps had put it.

Ian and Mary MacGregor lived in the Richmond area of San Francisco and they were slightly over eighty years of age. Of course John's mother was over her parent's house practically every day to check on her parents and John used to stop in often on his way home from work.

He missed those visits. Lately, his maternal grandparents liked to talk of their past. There were lots of family stories. They spoke of their past life in Scotland and their voyage to the land where the streets were paved with gold. John vowed to write down all these stories someday to share with his children, if he ever had any.

Bringing himself back to the present he felt the warmth of the sun come through the pines and settle on his shoulders.

He looked up and saw the sun shining brightly on the stone exterior of his Castle. It looked exquisite. He was so glad that the exterior was all-stone and needed no replacement or repair.

Over to one side of The Castle was a herd of deer munching away on the feed that John had spread out for them.

John knew that this was probably a bad idea but he was living alone and he needed some other form of life around him.

The birds were gently flying to and fro and stopping for a little refreshment from the many bird feeders that John had put around the property.

The resident cheeky squirrel spent his day trying to find a way to get back in the house or a way to ravage the bird feeders.

This place is finally coming back to life, he thought to himself and it brought joy to his heart.

John was happy that he had decided to restore only half of the monstrously large Castle at this time. If he had to think of restoring the entire Castle at one time it would be too overwhelming. Restoring The Castle little by little was acceptable to John's mind, talents and his bank account!

Mountain Man arrived for work with a cheeky look on his face. He handed John a muffin his wife had just baked and coffee he had bought at the nearby Martless Supermarket.

"Guess what I just heard?" said Mountain with a slight grin.

"What?" John said, deciding to just play along.

"Scuttlebutt is that the previous owner might have killed his own parents."

John put down his tools and crossed his arms on his chest and waited for what might be a joke or some truth. With Mountain he never knew.

"Go on!" he said.

"Apparently the parents were here one day and gone the next and nobody ever saw them again."

"Did the parents live with The Captain?"

"Scuttlebutt says they did. They watched the property while he was at sea. But one day they went missing."

"Were the police notified?"

"The Captain *did* call the police. But the police could not find anything; there was no sign of The Captain's parents. Rumor says The Captain acted very strange during the investigation and showed no emotion at all. It is said that The Captain only called the police to cast suspicion off of him. He went on with his life showing absolutely no grief."

"You know Mountain, people in this Strange Valley like to talk and speculate. I would not pay much attention to it if I were you. Some say "he" was killed and now you tell me "he" killed his own parents."

Mountain laughed and said, "Yeah, you're right, but it's fun to hear these stories. It breaks up a monotonous day."

"You don't like your work, Mountain?"

"I like it well enough. I like working with my hands." Mountain paused, he continued, deciding that he could share his past with his new friend, John. "I had studied to be a priest at one time. I spent four years in a seminary in upstate New York."

John was taken aback. He didn't want to show too much shock but he could not keep the surprise from seeping into his face.

"Does that surprise you?" asked Mountain.

"A little," responded John.

"It was a wonderful four years. I made many friends, and I will always cherish the time I spent with the other seminarians. We became fast friends. I am still in touch with many of the men that studied with me. Most of them went on to be ordained and are now serving all over the world."

It was strange to hear these gentle words come from such a massive man.

"Why did you leave the seminary, Mountain?"

"My father died suddenly, leaving my mother with my seven younger siblings, I had to go home and help support them."

"That's too bad. What kind of work did you do when you came out of the seminary?"

"I worked with juvenile delinquents. That was the hardest job that I ever had. But my year studying in Rome helped me with the Spanish kids. I had studied Italian, Spanish and French while I was in Rome, in preparation for my missions when I went into the field after ordination."

"You amaze me, Mountain!"

"You confuse me, Mr. Castle!"

They had both accepted the names that they called one another.

"How so?" asked John.

"You don't talk much about yourself. Where you come from! Where you get the money to renovate this place without a job! You say you are retired. You are the youngest retiree I ever met."

"Someday I will explain it all to you Mountain, but for now, I can't divulge my past. There is nothing sinister about me, I promise you that! I am on the up and up. I just need secrecy and privacy at this time. I need your promise that you won't discuss anything we say or do here with anyone."

"You got it, Mr. Castle."

They shook hands and John knew that Mountain could be trusted. He knew his handshake was his bond.

They worked well together, and John felt comfortable and safe with Mountain on the premises. And he always brought a muffin or other goodie that his wife had made for them.

Mountain's smile and goodness came through like a guiding light. Mountain shined!

CHAPTER EIGHT

Mr. Collie came strolling down the driveway and scared the hell out of John. *I've got to put up gates or get me a dog,* John thought to himself.
"Hello, Mr. Castle."
"Hello, Sir." John couldn't call him "Mr. Collie" to his face.
"Just thought I would stop in and see how you are doing."
"It's coming along."
"I would like to see it when you are done."
"I'll be happy to show it to you," John lied.
"Strange place isn't it?" said Mr. Collie as he looked at The Castle.
"Why do you say that?"
"It is just so full of mystery," replied Mr. Collie as he continued to gaze at The Castle.

John decided to try to get some additional information from this man as long as he was there and willing to talk.

"I heard that some think that the Sea Captain was murdered, and that he killed his mother and father even though they are just listed as missing." John wanted to hopefully coax Mr. Collie to divulge more information about The Castle and its previous owner.

"I guess the neighbors have been talking to you Mr. Castle."
"Some have stopped by."

Mr. Collie just stood silent for a minute while composing his thoughts. He was wondering how much he should tell this new owner of The Castle.

He decided to tell it all. "It's my personal opinion that The Captain *was* killed. He was found in the woods yonder—dead. A huge limb was lying next to him and his head was split open. They say it was an accident. But I know better. The limb had been sawed off and there was a saw in The Captain's hand. It was staged to look like an accident, but he was murdered. That man never handled a saw in his life. There were no tools in The Castle. He would not lower himself to personally repair anything in The Castle. Whenever there was a problem he would call a workman to fix it. And yes, the brother and sister did go missing, too. I think they were murdered as well. I think The Captain did them all in!"

"The brother and sister were murdered, too!? I thought it was just The Captain's parents," John said, shocked at the thought.

"They all went missing!"

"The whole family went missing?"

"Yes—one by one they all went missing."

You mean they were living here one day and then the next day they were gone? One by one they went missing and no one knew why?"

"That's right."

"No one saw or heard from them ever again?"

"That's correct."

"You were around when all this was happening?"

"I was living up here part-time at that time. I came up on weekends. After retirement I moved up full time."

"So you knew The Captain?"

"We played chess often."

"So you think he was a murderer?"

"I think he was capable."

"Why?" John asked, still shocked at the abundance of information that Mr. Collie was giving him.

"It's hard to explain. But he was moody and depressed much of the time and a very sore loser; I know that from the many chess games that we played. I've also seen him do terrible things to animals. If a stray cat or dog came on the property they were dead ducks. No one ever saw them again. There were always signs posted by owners looking for their pets. I personally saw some just thrown in the woods. I believe The Captain killed them."

"You never said anything?"

"Do you think I wanted to go missing too?"

"You really think he could kill his whole family?" John asked in amazement. He had to ask the question again just to make sure he understood the answer.

"I saw how he treated them. I saw him raise his hand to his mother more than once. I witnessed his terrible temper."

"Yet you came over and socialized with him." This was not a question, just a statement.

"I finally came to my senses and when I put all the pieces together I never came back again. I also triple locked my door."

"The police found no evidence of any wrong doing in the death of The Captain and his family going missing?" John, having been a detective, found it hard to believe that the police would not have found something suspicious in an entire family going missing and the sudden death of The Captain.

"They ruled The Captain's death an accident and the missing family is now just a cold case file," continued Mr. Collie. "While he was alive, The Captain was a very persuasive and charming character—butter would melt in his mouth. The police would and did believe anything he said."

"Do you have an opinion of who you think murdered The Captain?"

Mr. Collie shrugged his shoulders and said, "Could be one of many. He had lots of enemies."

"Like who?"

"Just look around this Valley and stop at any house and any one of the residents could be a suspect. All of them could tell you an unbelievable story about their interaction with The Captain."

"What kind of stories?" John was getting a little tired of asking questions but the answers he was getting were so unbelievable.

Mr. Collie just shrugged and started walking down the long driveway. He threw over his shoulder, "I'm sure they will fill you in one by one" and he waved his arm in a circle indicating the whole Valley.

John sat sipping a beer after Mr. Collie left. He just scratched his head in bewilderment. A so-called bad man was killed, although it was called an accident. A bad man! Rough in bed! He might have killed his whole family! He was abusive to animals and killed them when they came on his property. And everyone in this Strange Valley was suspect of being the killer of The Captain. At least according to Mr. Collie!

John had thought he was going to live in the quiet country, with the serenity that he needed, where all the natives were innocent and kind. Instead he might be living in the middle of a hell hole.

He just shrugged his head and decided that it was all rumor—it had to be. People are want to gossip when they had nothing better to do. He was not going to let it cloud his love of The Castle and his desire to enjoy living there. He would not listen to any of the junk that he was hearing. Perhaps he was a stranger to them and they wanted to scare him off. So he put it out of his mind and went back to work with a vengeance.

But he was very wary when he dug up the ground on the property to plant a tree or flowers—he hoped he would not dig up a body of one of The Captain's relatives. He laughed to himself; *The Captain would not be stupid enough to bury someone on his own land.*

Although he had decided not to believe all the stories he was told, it was apparent that it *had* made an impression on him—damn it!

He decided to get back to work and not think about all the weird things he had heard. "Now what the devil happened to my screwdriver?" he said, searching the area where he had been working.

CHAPTER NINE

John went to the Sutter Creek address where they were selling a St. Bernard dog. He had seen it advertised on the local supermarket's display board.

He continued to tell himself that the stories of The Captain "murders" had not bothered him and that he was not frightened. He just wanted a dog! His mind accepted that lie.

"Why are you selling him?" was the first question John asked. He did not want a problem dog. He wanted companionship and a good watchdog.

"We are moving overseas and he would have to be quarantined for six months in the country that we are moving to. We could not bear to do that to him. He is too good a dog."

"Is he a good watch dog?"

"Yes, he barks at the slightest noise. But he is gentle."

"What's his name?"

"Butter!"

John bought Butter and on the way home renamed him Sutter from the area that he came from. He could not think of calling any animal, *especially his*, Butter! Sutter was a slobbery St. Bernard and lovable. That night he slept at the foot of John's futon. John had tossed out the cot and bought a Queen sized futon. The next night Sutter slept on the futon with John, side by side—with his face on the pillow. Sutter was very much at home.

Strangely enough, John felt better with Sutter beside him. He had to admit to himself that some of the nighttime noises in his personal forest were a bit scary for a city boy.

Sutter was a quick learner. John taught him not to run after the deer. The birds were a different story. Sutter loved to chase them. But he soon learned it was a losing battle as the birds were too quick for him.

Sutter loved Mountain, since he always brought him a bone or leftovers from his last meal.

The Strange Valley

And there was always a muffin for John from Mountain's wife.

One morning as they both sat eating a muffin and some coffee that John had provided, John related to Mountain the information that he had learned from Mr. Collie. He just could not keep it to himself any longer.

"People like to talk. Everyone likes a mystery. I would take it with a grain of salt."

"You always make me feel better, Mountain! You would have made a good priest."

"I think I would have too."

"Why did you not go back and continue your priestly studies after your family got on its feet after your father died?"

"I met Maggie."

"Your wife?"

"Yes. She changed my life's path. I have never regretted marrying her. I believe I was meant to leave the seminary because I was to meet and marry Maggie."

"I hope that someday I find someone special as well."

"You will! I am still very much involved with the Church, John. I am a Deacon and a Sunday school teacher." After a pause, Mountain asked, "Are you Catholic, Mr. Castle?"

"I was the best altar boy in old St. Mary's in San Francisco," John said proudly, meaning it.

"Good for you."

"I did spend a lot of time in the local Presbyterian Church as well. My grandparents made sure I got a taste of their religion, too. They are proud Scottish Presbyterians. I think they were heartbroken when my mother converted to Catholicism when she married my Dad. I haven't gone to church lately," John added with a slight bit of guilt in his voice.

"You will return to the Church when you have a family," prophesized Mountain.

"Oh, I still believe in God, and I do pray often—but somehow the politics of some churches turn me off."

"I know what you mean. But you have to understand, the congregation of a church is like a family, and they will have disagreements just like some families."

"You sum things up very well, Mountain."

"It's easy when you love people as much as I do—especially children!"

"Do you have any children?"

"Not yet. We are trying."

"I'm sure you will have a baker's dozen."

"That would be like heaven to me. I loved growing up in a big family."

"I missed all that," said John sadly. "I was an only child. But I had lots of cousins that were like my siblings. My MacGregor cousins were a wild bunch and I got my bumps and bruises many a time from all of them. I learned how to stand up for myself and to give as good as I got. I had a good childhood."

Mountain grinned and gathered his muffin and coffee. As he headed back to work on the glass windows of The Castle, he told John, "By the way, I have about a week's worth of work left here. I will miss coming here." As he looked at The Castle and the surrounding grounds he said, "I have enjoyed the work and the company." Then off he went to continue with his window repair.

Walking away, he turned and said, "By the way, Mr. Castle, I can't find a few of my tools. I must have left them somewhere here on the grounds. Did you happen to find them?"

"No, Mountain, but I will keep an eye out for them."

Mountain leaving? thought John. He was stunned! He had felt comfortable with Mountain nearby. He wanted privacy but he would really miss Mountain.

John and Sutter did not sleep well that night. Sutter kept lifting his head thinking he heard something outside. He would give a little growl now and again.

"You are scaring me, Sutter. Go to sleep!"

It was not just Sutter's actions that kept John awake. He kept thinking about Mountain. He had only met the man a few weeks ago, but there was a good connection between the two of them.

That night, John formed an idea, and rehearsed it in his mind. He had a proposition for Mountain.

While eating the daily "Maggie Muffin" the next day, John gave the proposition to Mountain. "Come work for me full time, Mountain."

Mountain looked up in surprise. "The windows are almost done."

"You could help me with other things. I need a lot of help with the rest of The Castle and I need to clear some of the grounds. There is a lot of work to be done here, Mountain. When I am finished restoring the northern part of The Castle I am going to start on the southern end. I could really use your help."

"I have a loyalty to my company, Mr. Castle. They gave me a job when most would not."

"I guess I should have known you would say something like that. I guess I understand. It was just a thought." John felt crushed.

"It was a good idea, Mr. Castle," Mountain said, seeing the disappointment in John's face. "Let me mull it over."

John looked at him hopefully. "Give it good thought, Mountain."

"I will do that!"

Mountain did not take the offer. John somehow knew he would not. He was an honest and loyal man and he would not leave the glass company holding the bag. But Mountain said he could come over on the weekends and help out if John wanted that.

"I want that!" said John quickly, and gave a silent sigh of relief.

It was true that he did need help with the restoration of The Castle. But in his heart, John knew that it was Mountain's company that he enjoyed and needed more than anything.

"By the way, Mountain, did you borrow my screwdriver and my wrench?"

"No."

"It's probably that pesky old squirrel! I'm always missing a tool here and there."

"Me, too! They'll show up, we probably just misplaced them. It's probably just old age setting in—senior moments."

"Thanks Mountain—very funny!"

CHAPTER TEN

John was constantly going to the local lumberyard for supplies. The renovation of the old Castle was costing him a fortune—The Castle was turning out to be the proverbial money pit.

As soon as John stepped into the warehouse, the owner of the lumberyard came running over.

"How's it going?" was the normal start of their conversation.

"Going good!" John would always reply.

"Have you heard the latest?"

"What is the latest?" John said wearily.

"It's a long story."

"I'm ready," said John with a slight smile.

"Well, a young couple that lived about half a mile from where you live was having marital problems. The husband beat her up and hurt her badly. The wife that is! He was sent to jail. While he was in jail the wife took up with a new lover. The husband got wind of it while in jail and spread the word that when he got out of jail he would find the lover and chop him up into a million pieces and no one would ever find him. Then when the husband got out of jail the lover went missing." Mr. Lumber waited for a reaction from John.

"Was he related to The Captain?" John asked facetiously.

"What?"

"Nothing, please go on."

"That's it. The lover is missing and probably in pieces somewhere in these here mountains. So don't eat any local sausage. The husband is a butcher."

John cringed at the thought. "I'll keep that in mind" he said as he tried to keep from gagging at the thought of it.

On the ride back to The Castle, John decided to order material by telephone from now on and have it delivered. He didn't want and didn't need to hear about

The Strange Valley

any more murders, or love triangles. This Strange Valley has more alleged crimes than San Francisco!

"Just a good story," said Mountain after John relayed the story to him.

John felt at ease again. Mountain always made him feel better.

Sutter had jumped all over John when he got home. He did not like to be left alone and John would not leave him tied up outside. First off, John did not like to see *any* animal tied up or caged. Secondly, he was told there were mountain lions, coyotes, foxes and bears in these here mountains. He believed the mountain lion, coyote and foxes story but not the bears; but he did not rule it out in this Strange Valley.

"Okay Sutter, I got the message." John went shopping the next day and bought a big, big truck. He said he needed it for Sutter. The truth was that John had always wanted a truck, and now he had one and it was even big enough for Sutter to sit beside him in the passenger seat or ride in the open back, which the dog loved. The dog loved the wind blowing through his beautiful coat of fur.

Sometimes John took the truck to far off lumberyards to pick up material for The Castle, just for the long ride in the big new truck. Especially when he was not in the mood for any more gory stories!

It was good to get away from The Castle for a while. It cleared the cobwebs from the old noggin and his thoughts became very clear on the long drives to and from the distant lumberyards.

"Where you from?" asked the cashier at the Lodi lumberyard.

Not here too! John thought. *Why do people up here insist on talking to me?*

"Nowhere in particular," John said, as he paid in cash and left in a hurry.

In San Francisco, he thought on the way home, *I could meet a hundred people in a day and no one would stop and talk to me. I could go a whole day and no one would start a conversation. But up here people will seek you out from a mile away and start up a conversation.* Everyone *liked to talk. And they* all *had a story to tell.* He wondered if he would get like that if he lived up in the mountains for a long time.

Mountain stated it well. "San Francisco is a city of transient people. Up here most people were born and grew up here and they treat everyone like family. Get used to it, man!"

"I guess I'll have to. But I just wish everyone would mind their own business and leave me alone, at least for now!"

"Pretty sad world if that happens."

John just shook his head and went to empty the truck.

"I'll give you a hand," offered Mountain.

Mountain could lift three pieces of lumber at one time while John struggled with just one. *I had better start working out again,* thought John.

John had lots of work to do on his old Castle and he would need all of his strength to complete the renovation that was needed.

He would also need lots of money—the way things were going.

CHAPTER ELEVEN

John was just falling asleep when Sutter's head went up sharply and he gave a heavy growl.

"What's the matter, boy?"

Sutter crawled under the blankets and went back to sleep.

"Oh sure, wake me up, scare the hell out of me and then go back to sleep. You are some watch dog!" Sutter just snored in response.

Just to be sure, John grabbed a large stick he kept by his bed and walked to the door and looked through the security hole. It was a moonless night and he could not see anything from his vantage point in the guesthouse. He heard a noise from behind him, and quickly turned to look back at his bed—Sutter was sound asleep and peacefully snoring away.

Settling back into bed he felt a little uneasy. Was there something out there? Was it an animal or someone that was after John? Could "they" have found him? He decided to retrieve his police revolver that he left at his parent's house and keep it next to his bed. He had turned in his badge, but not his trusty revolver.

John was still not use to the quiet and the darkness of this Strange Valley that he now lived in. He was still a City Boy at heart and it would be a while until he was a Country Boy, if ever!

It was about three in the morning when John rose with a start. He felt for Sutter who was usually right on top of his feet at the bottom of the bed, or sleeping with his head on the pillow right next to him, but the dog was not on the bed.

He glanced over at the window and there was Sutter standing on his hind legs with his front paws resting on the window sill. Sutter was slowly moving his head from side to side as if he were watching a tennis match.

Probably just some deer moving around the grounds, thought John, trying to calm himself. *Damn it! I wish I had my pistol here, right now!* He was afraid that the men he had put in jail had found him and he felt defenseless without his trusty gun.

John again grabbed the nightstick and walked to the window and with his arm around Sutter's shoulder he looked around the grounds to see what the dog was looking at.

Again he could see nothing! But then John's eyes went toward the direction of The Castle and it was then he saw the glow, as if by a muted candle, gliding through the downstairs of The Castle.

It definitely was not a flashlight and it did not move as if carried by a human. It just appeared to glide. The light went from the downstairs, to the upstairs, then up to a turret at the very top of The Castle.

The light appeared to mesmerize John and Sutter. They were frozen to the spot at the window. They could not take their eyes off of the light and their heads moved in unison, back and forth, back and forth, as they gazed at the mysterious light.

Suddenly, the light just floated through the stonewall, then glided to the back woods of the property.

John rubbed his eyes. He could not have seen what he saw. He had thought at first that it *might* be a human light. Perhaps Mountain, looking for his tools, but after seeing it float through the stonewall of The Castle—he knew it was "not of this world."

Sutter jumped down from the window and ran to the front door and barked to get out.

John was not going near The Castle *that* night. Nor was he going to the back woods. "Sorry, Sutter—I'm not about to chase after you tonight. It's much too scary out there." John and Sutter got no sleep that night. *What the hell was that?* was the thought that raced through John's mind all night.

The next morning John rose early and walked around the property to see if there were strange footprints or any evidence of what he had seen the night before. There was nothing!

"Your vivid imagination," was Mountain's opinion when he heard the story.

This time Mountain did not make John feel better! He vowed that he would get his police pistol or buy another one at a local gun shop. He did not feel totally safe in this so called Shangri-La. This was a *very* Strange Valley!!!

CHAPTER TWELVE

John had finally bought a cell phone that would work in these mountains and called his parents to tell them he would be coming home the next day, and not to tell anyone.

"Why won't you give us your home phone number, John?" asked his Dad. "And why can't we know where you are?"

"It's easier this way, Dad." John did not want to tell his Dad that it was for their protection as well as his that "they" did not know where he lived and that "they" could not reach him by phone.

"Are you going to stay awhile?" asked his Dad hopefully.

"No Dad, I will be coming back up here the same day."

"When are we going to see your new place? Wherever it is and whatever it is?" his Dad asked with a wee bit of sarcasm in his voice.

"It's a work in progress Dad, and I want it to be near perfect when you see it. By the way, I will be picking up my pistol. Will you have it ready for me?"

"Why do you need your pistol?" asked John's father suspiciously.

"There are mountain lions up here," was the reason John gave his Dad. Somehow his Dad knew that to be a lie.

John felt the natural "air conditioning" of San Francisco hit him as he crossed the Bay Bridge. Oh, how he had missed the fog! No one could understand how he could love the fog, but he did! He loved to see the fog rolling down the hills of San Francisco as the fog left the safety of the ocean.

He loved the feeling of the fog as it enveloped his body and he loved when he could not see a foot in front of him as he walked—that was the best of times.

He realized he really missed San Francisco. *When I feel safe again I will come home for awhile,* he thought. *But right now I still feel threatened by the past.* He was embarrassed to admit it, but he was afraid!

John's parents met him at the door. They missed their only son. When he lived in San Francisco they could see him as often as they wanted. Or they could call him and chat for a time.

"I check your property every day, John."

"I have a security system, Dad. You don't have to check it so often. I would prefer it if you didn't."

John could see the hurt look on his father's face.

But he could not put his Dad in harm's way if his enemies were hell bent on getting to him to kill him.

John's mother, Laurie Hurley, made his favorite meal—Scotch pies with peas and mashed potatoes. The pies were really meat pies. Meat with a crust! As a child he would mash the peas and potatoes and make a face out of it. First he would eat the eyes and then the mouth and a fork dab would make the nose. Then he would start all over again. He had seen his mother do it herself, many a time. It was only when he got older that he realized it was his mother's way of getting him to eat. But at the time, to him, it was a game. When he got older he just loved the taste of the meat pies.

John's father kept giving his son strange glances. Michael Hurley could not figure out the life his son was now leading.

His mother was just happy to have her only son there for dinner. "I miss you, Johnny," she said.

"I know, Mom. I'll come and visit more often."

"Where is this house of yours?"

"It's way up-country, Mom."

"Why can't we see it?" she further questioned him.

"You will Mom, when I'm finished."

"Why can't we help you fix it up?"

"Mom, I'll have you up real soon." John got up and said, "I'll help you wash the dishes." He could not answer his mother's questions and he did not want to irritate her and spoil the visit.

"Mother can handle the dishes, Johnny—let's go out for a smoke," broke in his father.

"I thought you gave up cigarettes, Dad."

"I have little enjoyment left in life; leave me at peace with my cigars!"

As Michael Hurley lit up his beloved cigar, John said, "Dad, you should get yourself a hobby."

Michael Hurley had just retired a few years ago. He had served forty years in the San Francisco Police Department. John always thought his father had stayed too long. Michael could not understand how his son could retire at the early age of thirty-nine.

They would discuss and argue that for hours on end and no one ever came out the winner.

The difference was that Michael loved his job as a policeman. John did not love it quite as much toward the end of his career. The job never affected Michael. It had definitely affected John.

"I'm not handy like you and Grandpa MacGregor," Michael explained. "I guess that is why Gramps is living so long. He is still working around his house and building little things for his grandchildren and great-grandchildren. All that I know how to do is to be a policeman." Michael's last words came with a little quiver of his lips.

"Maybe you could volunteer at the church or something."

"Your mother is kept busy with her parents. Mine are gone," continued John's father.

"I miss Grandma and Grandpa Hurley," said John.

"Not as much as I do," said Michael Hurley, with a touch of melancholy in his voice.

"There's lots of clubs you can join," continued John.

"My father should still be alive! You know that, don't you Johnny?" John's father seemed to be ignoring all of John's suggestions of how to keep busy.

"Don't go into *that* again Dad, it's too painful for us both."

John's paternal grandfather was shot to death in the Mission District. Matthew Hurley and his partner, Steve Murray, were cruising that area; as they approached 24th and Mission they saw a group of suspicious characters. Young thugs by the looks of them and they were hanging around together on the southeast corner of the street. It looked like they were drug dealing.

Matthew Hurley exited the police car and walked towards the crowd of hispanic, white and black youths. He was just going to talk to them and disperse the crowd. His intent was not to arrest anyone that night. But they suddenly surrounded him, then they all ran like hell. After they disappeared, Matthew found himself on the sidewalk bleeding to death; stabbed in the stomach. He laid there for a long while. His partner called for help, but did not go to Matthew's aid. He said he did, but witnesses say he did not leave the police car until others showed up. By then, Matthew was dead.

"That bastard Murray helped to take my father's life. A policeman should be willing to give up his life for his partner. Murray was a coward! He was just as responsible for my father's death as the drug dealers and the gang that took his life." Tears were welling up in John's father's eyes.

"Let it go, Dad—or it will bring you to an early grave."

"Maybe it was good you retired early, Johnny—I could not bear to lose you as well." Michael grasped his son's shoulder and gave it a squeeze. It was always hard for Michael to show emotion to his family so that little grasp was like a bear hug to John.

Laurie Hurley held onto her son for a long time as she was saying goodbye. She had absolutely no problem showing love and affection to her husband and to her son.

"Come more often, son."

"I will, Mom."

John was a little sad waving goodbye to them. He wanted to tell them all about his Castle and the area of Elk Horn where he lived, and he wanted to have them with him while he fixed up the place. He also wanted to tell them why he was so secretive. But he could not bring himself to do it, at least not yet! He did not want to endanger them in any way.

John had called his old partner, Calvin Wong. They had been partners for a very long time when John was on the police force. They had agreed to meet for coffee near the Cliff House.

"Hey John-Boy, you look great," said Calvin to his ex-partner.

"You don't look so bad yourself—for a Chinaman," joked John.

"I will always look better than a dumb Mick like you," Calvin joked back.

They settled back and continued with the usual small talk. Then Calvin startled John by saying very seriously, "There's a contract out on you, John."

John's head jerked up, and finally he asked, "How do you know?"

"It's the word on the street."

"Perez or Jackson? Which one put out the hit?"

"Not sure, but it is ten grand to anyone who knocks you off. It's a wonder the Irish and Russian Mafia don't have contracts out on you as well, seeing you put so many of them in jail. But it's probably Perez or Jackson."

John nodded. He was a little shook up—he knew the word on the street was usually right. "You would think my life would be worth more than ten grand," responded John, trying to bring levity into the conversation.

"I see it as nine thousand too much."

John smiled. "Thank you, my friend."

Cal and John knew how to lighten the situation. All during their careers together they had worked this way.

"Why isn't there a contract out on *you*, Calvin? You were my partner. You helped put them behind bars as well."

"I didn't testify, John."

John thought back and remembered Calvin always hid in the shadows during the court trials. John always took the high road—openly testifying for the prosecution. He knew the perpetrators had to be put behind bars and taken off the streets of San Francisco.

"I guess you were the smart one, Calvin," John said staring at him.

"You should have been more low-key, John."

"Bullshit!!" John said, suddenly angry. "I couldn't let those creeps back on the street."

"Was it worth your life?"

"I couldn't have done it any differently!" John shot back.

"I guess that is why we were so different, John. Detective work was just a job to me. To you it was a passion. A mission! I wanted to go home every night to my family. You worked fearlessly, I worked cautiously."

John's thoughts went back to his grandfather, Police Officer Matthew Hurley; he hesitated, then asked, "Would you have covered my back if I was in danger, or hurt?" John immediately regretted the question as soon as it was out of his mouth!

"I ALWAYS DID, JOHN!" Calvin shot back. "Think back, you got us into many a dangerous situation. I would have turned my back on a lot of things. But not you! NOT YOU! The Crusader! You had to rush in and put yourself in harm's way. To be truthful John, I was glad when you retired." Calvin stopped short before he said too much.

John looked sadly at Calvin.

After seeing the look on John's face, Calvin said, "Oh, I didn't mean that, John. It's just that you accused me of not covering you. You were my friend! You were my partner! You were and are my brother. Please forgive me for saying that."

They sat in silence for a while.

John decided to change the subject. He did not want to lose this friend. He knew he might need him sometime in the future. Besides, Calvin was like a brother to him. At one time John thought Calvin might become his brother-in-law.

"How is Susan, Cal?"

"She's good. She loves her job as Assistant D.A."

John and Susan Wong had been an item for a couple of years. John had once thought of asking her to marry him. She was a beautiful Asian woman. Taller than most Chinese women and with the most spectacular eyes and legs he had ever seen.

John's parents liked her very much. Of course Grandpa MacGregor had said, "Could ye no find one of your own kind?" But Susan eventually charmed Gramps as well.

"Tell her I said hello, and give her my love."

"You gave her your love and then took it away. You broke her heart!" Calvin responded curtly.

Suddenly, John was sorry he had come to meet with Calvin. He knew this last comment could start another argument so John just said, "Some day I'll explain it to you." He grabbed the bill, and they both left the restaurant.

"Are you and I okay, Calvin?" John was a little afraid that they had both said too much at this meeting.

"Of course," said Calvin. "We are brothers. Nothing can change that."

"I may need your help someday."

"There is no doubt about that, John! I will keep my eyes *and* ears open and keep you up to date. I have to keep you alive so that someday I *can* be your best man."

"You are my only brother, Cal."

"Maybe someday you will still be my brother-in-law?" Calvin said hopefully.

"You never know!"

They shook hands and gave each other that half hug that men do, and they both turned and walked towards their cars.

Halfway to his car, John turned, and trotted back to Calvin.

"Calvin, would you do me a favor?"

"Of course man, what is it?"

"I'm worried about my parents and grandparents. Would you have police cars ride by every once in a while. Sort of keep an eye on them and their homes?"

"Done," said Calvin.

"If you have any news, overnight a message to this box number." John suddenly withdrew the note and said, "That's too close to home." He then gave Calvin his cell phone number and said "Memorize it, then throw it away."

"Are you *that* scared, John? We don't know where you're now living. We don't have a real telephone number for you. We never see you. How is anyone else going to find you?"

"Wouldn't you be scared, Calvin?"

Calvin thought a second and replied, "I sure would."

"I'm just being real cautious until I feel things have calmed down and the danger is over."

"I've got your back, partner."

John gave a thumbs-up, and walked to his car.

John looked back at Calvin as he entered his car. He knew this man was closer to him than a brother. When they worked together in the police department, Cal had saved his life many a time. John hated himself for even questioning his friend about covering his back when they were working together.

John would recklessly run into a bad situation and Cal would stay back and cover him and keep John's parents from mourning the death of their only son.

You rush in where angels fear to tread, is what Calvin had said to John many a time.

He was glad that Calvin had remained his friend even after he had left the police force. Yes, they had been more than partners, they were indeed brothers.

CHAPTER THIRTEEN

It was very late when John arrived home. Mountain had come over to The Castle to feed and walk Sutter. Sutter went crazy when he saw his master. He slobbered all over John. John did not care, he slobbered all over Sutter in return. You can't duplicate the love of a dog.

John had not been sleeping very well lately, and after hearing of the threat on his life, he got no sleep at all that night.

He called Mountain the next day and thanked him for taking care of Sutter.

"It was my pleasure, Mr. Castle. The neighbors say the dog looks like me!"

"They flatter you, Mountain."

"Well, I couldn't have chosen a better living thing to look like."

John laughed. Mountain always made him laugh.

John was beginning to feel a little confined in the guesthouse and after walking through The Castle he felt he could possibly move in and still work on different parts of the house.

He drove into town and shopped in all the furniture stores in the area, all two of them.

But he was happy with the bedroom set and the kitchen set that he had purchased. That was all he needed for now; a place to eat and a place to sleep in The Castle.

He also bought a couple of rifles at the local gun shop. With them and the pistol he had retrieved from his parents' house he now felt more secure.

He stashed one rifle in each of the lookout turrets. He wondered why The Captain had these turrets built into The Castle. Had the Captain been afraid for his life as well? John was afraid of criminals he had helped to put in jail. The Captain was probably afraid of the people in the Valley that he had hurt. God knows what The Captain had done elsewhere.

As he was glancing out one of the turrets he saw a Doberman Pincer running down the path toward The Castle. John made sure Sutter was in the house. Then

The Strange Valley

he went to meet the older man that was running breathlessly after his dog. The dog had gotten away from him.

"Sorry," the older man said.

"That's all right." John helped the man, who was gasping for breath, re-leash his dog.

The old gent looked around the property and sadly said, "This place holds very bad memories for me."

These statements no longer bothered John. He was getting immune to them.

"Why is that?" he asked the man. He recognized the fact that the man was dying to tell his story.

"That bastard, The Captain, raped my sister!" and the man had to stop and turn away from John as the tears were starting to flow down his cheek.

John just waited for him to go on with the story. He gave the man time to compose himself.

Mr. Doberman turned again toward John after he settled himself down. "My sister was just a kid. She was selling candy for her high school swim team. She knocked on the door of this Castle and that was the end of her virginity and her life as she knew it."

"Did you call the police?" John asked, as Mr. Doberman again wiped away the tears.

"We didn't know what had happened until much later. He also hired her to do some work around the house. So for a long time he had his way with my sweet sister."

"How old was she?"

"Fifteen, maybe sixteen—she was just a baby!"

"Why did she go back after being raped?"

"I think she thought she loved him. He was a charming, handsome man. He looked and talked like Michael Rennie. You know that actor from the movie *The Day the Earth Stood Still?*"

John was surprised that he actually knew who the man was talking about for it was one of his favorite movies. So now he had a face and voice for The Captain.

"How did you finally find out about the rape?"

"One day, The Captain told her never to come back again. My sister was distraught. She cried for weeks. Finally she told my mother. When I found out, I was a kid myself; I grabbed my father's rifle and went to kill him. I can still see him up there in that turret, yelling "Get off my property or I'll shoot you dead."

"Did you call the police then?"

"My parents and my sister were too ashamed."

John wondered inwardly why The Captain had spared the life of the young girl—he seemed to kill everyone else that was close to him.

"I'm really sorry about that, sir," John said with great sympathy in his voice. Then, after a pause, John asked, "Do you think The Captain's death was an accident?"

"HELL, NO! Thankfully someone killed the bastard!"

"Are you sure?"

"Yep!"

"Do you know who?"

Mr. Doberman just smiled and tugged at his dog. "Come on, Dobbie. Let's go home."

John watched Mr. Doberman walk back down the path. So The Captain was a rapist as well! The list of horrors this man had perpetrated was growing.

No one liked this Captain. The Collie Man, the Poodle Lady, the Stinker and Mr. Doberman; they all had bad things to say about The Captain. One of the roofers didn't even *know* The Captain, but couldn't bring himself to work on The Castle.

John placed a call to Mountain. "Mountain, I need you to bless this house before I move in!"

"Getting religion all of a sudden, are you?" laughed Mountain.

"I think I'm going to need all the blessings and prayers I can get."

Mountain laughed, thinking John just meant the stories of The Castle. But John meant much more than that—he could not get the thought of the mysterious gliding light out of his mind, and the contract that was out on his life.

If a Catholic house blessing would help, he was all for it. Hell, he would take the prayers of the local Rabbi. And the prayers of the local Presbyterians, Methodists, Baptists, and any other church or temple that could help rid any evil that still existed in this house. Jesus, Allah, Buddha—this Castle needed all the help it could get.

CHAPTER FOURTEEN

John was working around The Castle when his cell phone rang, startling him. He could not remember who he had given the number to, then recalled he had given it to Calvin.

"John, it's more serious than I thought," said Calvin Wong. "Perez wants you dead TODAY! He has his henchman out for your blood. He has upped the ante to twenty-five thousand for your life."

"Now *that's* more like it," said John, trying not to show his anger and fear.

"Do you think the info is good?" he asked, more seriously.

"It's more than good. Our undercover policeman said Perez is on a mission and *you* are his mission."

"Watch yourself, Calvin," John said, then pressed "off" on the cell phone.

John felt it was time to alert his Dad about the threats on his life, and the contract that Perez had put out on the street for the life of his only son.

He chitchatted with his mother for a while and then his Dad got on the phone.

"Is Mom within earshot?"

"No, she left to check on Gramps and Grandma."

"Good!"

"What's up, son?"

"Dad, the reason that I have been so secretive is that one of the last perps I put away for life has put a *contract* out on me."

"Is that why you ran away, John?"

John cringed at that. He did not want to admit that he had left San Francisco because of threats on his life and because he was afraid.

"I didn't run away, Dad." He continued, knowing what he had just said was a lie. "I was looking for property way before I put that creep in jail. I am just keeping out of sight until the danger is past. I don't want you to tell Mom yet.

Just be extra careful. If you see anything out of the ordinary, notify the police. Dad, do you still have your pistol?"

"Does Paddy have pigs? I will never give *that* up!"

John realized his Dad's voice sounded excited—he seemed to respond with authority in his voice. His Dad now had an important job to do.

"What else can I do, son?"

"I'm going to give you my cell phone number. Please memorize it and burn it. Don't give it to anyone—not even Mom, Grandma or Grandpa. Call me if you suspect anything. Anything at all!"

"Do you want me to call up any of my old cronies or stoolies? They will respond in a minute, John."

"No, Dad!" he almost shouted. "I just need you to keep your eyes open. And just be very careful. Don't go near my house any more. These thugs are ruthless."

"I'm not scared, John!"

"I know, Dad, but please promise me you won't get involved—that you will just be vigilant! Keep your eyes open and report to me anything that looks suspicious."

"All right, Johnny. I promise. Be careful yourself."

"I will, Dad."

"I love you, son."

"I love you too, Dad," he responded and as John put the cell phone back in his pants pocket, he broke into tears. His dad had never said that to him before.

His father did not hear the tears as John had hung up hurriedly.

John wondered why his dad had felt the need to tell him he loved him! Why now? He decided he did not care about the reason; it was just great to hear him say it. His mother was always telling him that she loved him, and he always "knew" his father loved him. He had felt it all during his lifetime.

But his dad had never verbalized it before. It was the Irish in him John had always thought. It was hard for him to show emotion. But his dad was always there when John needed him. He was there when he was on the swim team; cheering him on. He was there when he played baseball with the Little League, giving him good advice. He was there to watch him play basketball in high school. There are many ways to show love and that was his dad's way.

John knew his mother was disappointed when he did not go straight to college. His father was delighted that John had decided to join the police force.

He kept his mother happy by getting a college degree by taking classes in the evening.

It was difficult to work all day and then go to school at night. But it kept him focused on a life after he left the SFPD.

He could get a law degree right now and easily pass the bar exam. He was not ready to do anything right now except to save his own life, protect his parents and grandparents, and of course to enjoy rebuilding his Castle.

John now wished he had some brothers or sisters.

What if something happens to me? he thought. *My parents would never get over it.*

Well, he thought, *I must not let anything happen to me!* And he was working very hard at that.

John had hung up the phone with the feeling of his parents' love surrounding him.

CHAPTER FIFTEEN

John was backing out of his driveway when suddenly the sight of a horse and rider appeared in his rear view mirror. He stopped short and could see the horse rear up on its hind legs and he could see that the rider was fighting to stay in the saddle.

John hurried out of his car, rushed to the rider and her horse and tried to grab the reins.

Instead of finding an irate rider, she was laughing.

"That's the fastest Rocket has moved in a long time," and she gave another hearty laugh.

"I'm sorry, I was not paying attention. I didn't know there were horses in the area."

"That's okay, no harm done." She leaned over her horse and stretched out her hand. "I'm Carol Lang."

As he grasped her hand he said "John." He noticed she had a very strong handshake.

She stood up in the stirrups and looked over the apple trees that bordered John's property. "The place looks great. You've done a lot of cleaning up."

"It's a hell of a lot of work. Nothing has been done to the property for years."

"Someone should have burned it down years ago."

John looked up at the rider, very surprised. "Why do you say that?"

"A lot of misery occurred in that Castle."

"I've heard that, but I am still going to fix it up to be a place of joy and laughter."

Carol Lang looked down at John and said, "I believe you will. I'd like to see it when you are done."

"You and the whole neighborhood," he laughingly said.

"Have they been dunning you?" she said with a smile.

"Not really. But everyone wants to stop and tell me something about the previous owner."

"There's a lot to tell," she said knowingly.

"Do you live around here?" John asked hopefully. He had noticed that this woman was a real beauty and he wanted to find out more about her before she rode off. He immediately wondered if she were married.

"I used to. I'm just up for a week, visiting my folks."

"Where do you live? The Bay Area?" he asked, hoping that she lived nearby.

"Redwood City."

"Oh, not too far away—just a short driving distance."

"Far enough."

Carol reared her horse around to return home.

"Can I invite you in for a drink?" John asked hurriedly, not wanting her to leave just yet.

"Not in there!" she said, nodding towards The Castle.

"Then, can I take you out for a drink? After all, I almost killed you and your horse."

"There aren't too many places around here where you can sit and have a quiet drink."

"Then how about dinner as well?" he quickly added. John was not going to give up until this beautiful lady consented to meet with him.

Carol turned in her saddle and looked at John. She thought he looked awfully cute and he looked pretty safe.

"Okay, I'll see you at seven." She turned her horse around and the two of them started to trot away.

John yelled after her, "I don't know where you live!"

"I'll pick *you* up," she yelled back.

Smart girl, thought John. *She doesn't know me and she is going to have the control. Smart and beautiful!*

Carol Lang *was* beautiful. Long blonde hair and the brownest eyes you have ever seen. And from where he stood, she had the body of a model.

At seven o'clock sharp, Carol Lang beeped her car horn and John went trotting out the door and ran down the long path to the front gate.

"Why didn't you come up to The Castle?" he asked her.

"No way! Too many memories!"

"You too?"

"I'll tell you about it sometime."

John loved Carol's choice of a restaurant in Sutter Creek. They were given a quiet and cozy corner and quickly ordered a glass of wine while reading the menu.

"Here's to us," she said while raising her wine glass.

"And them that's like us," John added as he clinked her glass with his.

"What? What did you say?"

"It's just something my grandfather always says. A Scottish saying, I think."

"So tell me, have you found anything of interest in The Castle?" she asked, while sipping her wine.

"Like what, for instance?" John knew there were lots of things that he had found in The Castle. He did not know what she might be looking for in particular.

"Well, he was such an evil man. I thought you might have found vials of poison, a devil's pitchfork or a torture chamber."

"No, nothing like that—but I will keep an eye out." The memories of all the gory stories he was told kept rolling around and around in his brain.

"You just might find them," she said very seriously.

"What did he do to your family?" he asked softly.

"He poisoned one of our horses!" She almost yelled this reply as her heart still ached at the loss. "Cricket" was the first horse that was exclusively Carol's.

"Why would he do a thing like that?" he softly probed as he could see she was upset.

"Because he was evil! My horse liked to nibble at the apples on the trees bordering your property. The Captain saw us one day. The next day the horse was found dead in his stable. The veterinarian found poison in his system. She was our best horse. She was part of the family. She was *my* horse. We were heartbroken."

"Did you call the police and report it?"

"No. We could not prove it was The Captain that had done it."

"He did *that* just because your horse ate the apples from the trees?"

"Yes," she said and her eyes brimmed with tears.

"What type of man was he?" John asked, getting the conversation off of the horse and to discover more about the mysterious and evil Captain.

"He was a tall, thin Welshman. He could charm the pants off of anyone he met. Underneath, he was a dark soul. I would say he was a psychopath and a narcissist."

"It surprises me that he was a Captain on a cruise ship. When you captain a ship, you have to be very social, mix with all types of people and be smart enough to command a large vessel."

"That's what a psychopath is. Two faces. Like Jekyll and Hyde," replied Carol.

"Did he live alone?"

"Much of the time he did. Oh, please, let's change the subject for now. There! Our food is coming."

The rest of the evening was pleasant. John discovered that Carol was an attorney. *Just like Susan Wong,* he thought.

Carol was easy to be with and very, very easy on the eyes.

"Are you married?" Carol asked suddenly.

"I wouldn't be here with you if I were."

"Are you?" he shot back.

She got the inference and said, "No. Close once or twice, but no cigar. I was too engrossed in getting my career started."

"Are you a lone attorney, or are you with a large company?"

"I needed to pay the rent after college, so I decided to go with a major law firm. Clonnon, Bonno and Pismo."

"I've heard of them."

"Who hasn't—they are one of the biggest firms in the Bay Area."

John recognized the name of the law firm as they had represented Perez. The man John had helped to put away for life and who now was trying to kill him.

"What do *you* do?" she asked.

John had to think fast. "Security" is what he came up with.

"What company?"

"I'm in business with my Dad."

"How is it you have all this time off?"

"I'm on sabbatical." John was surprised that he came up with that—he was usually not so quick at coming up with lies. Even as a kid he usually told the truth because he could never think up a good story.

Carol just nodded and seemed to accept that John was in security.

John felt it was all true. Not really a lie. Except the sabbatical part!

He *was* in the same business as his dad. They *did* work to keep the public safe and secure. He again searched Carol's face to see if she had bought it.

"You are very lucky," was all she said.

"Why am I lucky?"

"It must be very satisfying to work with your father."

On the way home they almost stopped at the local Indian Casino, but Carol and John decided to leave that for another night as it was getting late and John had to get back to take care of his dog. He had not expected to be so late in getting home; he and Carol had talked the night away.

John was sad when the evening came to an end. Carol stopped the car at the entrance to The Castle. John leaned over and kissed her on the cheek. "Thanks for a great evening, Carol. Now let me pick *you* up tomorrow and go to *my* choice of restaurant."

Carol hesitated for a long minute, and just as John's heart began to sink she said, "I live in the blue house three doors down on the left. What time?"

"Seven seems good."

She honked goodbye as she drove off.

John added horse killer to the list of mysteries involving The Captain. He wondered and dreaded what else he would be adding to the list.

But for now he was intrigued with this beautiful and intelligent woman that he had begun to date. He had not been with a woman for a long while and he enjoyed the company. In the back of his mind he hoped for more!

CHAPTER SIXTEEN

The next night brought more revelations. Eating spaghetti and feeling a little giddy from the wine, Carol went into detail about her experiences with The Castle and The Captain. John was getting a whole new story, and it turned out to be one that he really did not want to hear.

"You asked me if The Captain lived alone. At one time he had a housemaid who took care of the house and the little girl that lived there. I went to school with that little girl; she was so sweet. We were pals. We would walk home from the bus stop arm in arm, just chatting away. When "he," The Captain, wasn't home she would come to my house to play. The housemaid gave her some freedom and fun when "he" wasn't around. When The Captain was home she never came out. My parents would not let me go near The Castle. Apparently, they had heard some awful stories about The Captain, but did not want to scare me, so they did not tell me what they had heard. One day he was standing at the end of the driveway by the big gate and he invited me into The Castle, and stupidly I went in the house with him and my little friend—disobeying my parents. I thought it was safe as he gave me a great big smile and he took my hand so gently."

As she continued her eyes brimmed with tears. "After a while he started acting very strange and I bolted and ran out the door. I ran so fast to my house that I could hardly catch my breath when I reached home. I couldn't tell my parents that I had gone into The Castle. I just told them that the little girl and I were having a race."

Carol hesitated, than continued. "Shortly after that, the little girl was found dead. She fell from one of The Castle's turrets." Carol began to sob.

John was stunned. "She fell? From the turret?" he asked with disbelief in his voice.

Carol nodded and wiped her eyes with her napkin. "That's what The Captain told the police."

"Carol, there is no way a small girl could easily *get* to the turret. There are no stairs, you have to climb a rope ladder to get to it, and it's a *long* way up. It's a climb you would make only if you *had* to, and I seriously doubt that a little girl could *ever* climb up that ladder."

"I know," she whimpered. "I'm sure he carried her up there, then pushed her off. I'm sure he murdered her."

"What did the housemaid say?"

"She disappeared right after the incident. No one ever heard from her again. Her family in Ireland came over to the States looking for her but she was nowhere to be found."

"Who was this little girl?"

"I believe she was the housemaid's daughter. I also think she was *his* daughter as well. I think he raped the housemaid when she came from Ireland to work for him and he got her pregnant. He kept them both until he was sick of them and were of no further use. Yes, I think he killed the maid as well." Carol started to cry again.

"Let's go," said John. He quickly paid the bill and they drove to a local McDonald's, had some coffee and more conversation while sitting in the car.

John put his arm around her and she laid her head on his shoulder. "She was such a sweet little girl, John. She was too young to die; especially like that."

John just held her tightly. She was beginning to stop shaking and he loved the smell that emanated from her hair. Her perfume was intoxicating. He bent down and kissed her hair.

Surprisingly, she lifted her face to his and they kissed gently at first and then passionately.

"I can't believe I did that," she said as she sat up and adjusted her hair. "It must be the wine."

"I'm glad you did," replied John with a smile.

She looked at his face and she too had to smile. "Don't get cocky John-Boy! I'm not easy."

"That's too bad," John said facetiously.

They both laughed so hard they almost spilled their coffee.

"Where do we go tomorrow night?" asked John.

"You want to go out again?"

"You are only here for a week. I have to make the most of the time I have to spend with you."

"I was going to take a ride up to Carson City. There are some antique stores I wanted to go to. Can you take a day off from your labors?"

"That sounds great! I need to get some furnishings for The Castle and I thought some old antiques would go well with the decor."

"Then it is settled. I will pick you up at ten."

After calling Mountain and asking him to watch Sutter, he had time to think about the little girl who fell from the turret. He went to the gun turret and thought of the rope ladder that was there when he first bought the house. He had not been able to climb it without great effort. He had to make a special ladder that was tall enough to reach the top. Even *that* was difficult to climb. No child could have gotten up there without assistance.

The bastard was probably a child murderer as well. What kind of monster could kill a little, innocent child? How could he kill a little girl that may have been his own child? And where are all those missing people? His family and now the housemaid, were the thoughts that went round and round in John's mind.

CHAPTER SEVENTEEN

It was a beautiful ride up to Carson City. They passed beautiful lakes! Far away mountains still had a slight dusting of snow nestled on the summit of these beautiful mountains. John felt the tension fall from his shoulders. His worries for the day were on the back burner.

They were both light-hearted that day. They even stopped to do a little gambling. She won! He lost.

John felt he was a winner at the antique store. Sconces and old chairs that would fit so grandly in his Castle were some of the treasures that he bought. They had decided to drive up in his truck just in case they found some large treasures—and they did!

The ride home was just as beautiful. The shadows floating in and out of the mountains, in the twilight of the day, gave a different view of the beauty and nature of the area.

"Let's stop for a bite by Kirkwood. I'm starving," Carol suggested.

John had never been to the Kirkwood ski area but he vowed to go there as soon as there was enough snow.

Dinner by a glowing fireplace was grand. It was a little too warm by the fire as the weather was not yet cold, but the ambience could not be beat.

He reached for her hand and brought it to his mouth and kissed it gently.

"Trying to seduce me are you?" she said laughing.

"Is it that obvious?"

She reached for his hand and kissed it as well.

"Are you trying to seduce *me*?" John cheekily asked.

"If you are, let me warn you, it won't take much. I think I'm falling for you, Carol!"

"After only three dates?" Carol asked with surprise in her voice.

"My mother always said it would happen when I least expected it," John said lightheartedly. "And *my* mother is never wrong."

As they were driving back to Elk Horn, she turned to him suddenly and said, "Do you want to park?"

"What do you think?" he answered quickly.

She giggled and they pulled off into a little spot overlooking a valley. A vista lookout! They were the only car parked there. He realized he could not see anything from their vista spot as it was getting very dark.

Carol wasted no time as she turned to him and took his face in her hands and gently kissed him on the mouth. Her mouth then flew open and she kissed him with a passion John had not experienced for a long time.

John gathered her in his arms and pulled her closer to him. His hand instinctively went under her blouse. She was not wearing a bra. He leaned back and looked at her in surprise.

"I come prepared," she said with a cheeky look on her face.

John let her take the lead. He would in no way be too forward with this gentle but forward kitten. He had seen her soft side talking about her horse and her little friend, but now he was seeing a little tiger.

She took his hand and led it to her breasts. She kissed him again with her tongue examining every inch of his mouth. She then drew herself away from him and John thought it was over for the day. She quickly, but very seductively, tore her blouse over her head; not waiting to undo the buttons.

"You are beautiful!" John said as he looked appreciatively at her glorious breasts that were full and round and compact; almost pointing to John and inviting him to enjoy them.

"Want to try them out?" she whispered in his ear.

"It would be my pleasure," he responded as he gently bent to caress one breast and then the other.

She moaned with pleasure. "I haven't done this in a long time," she again whispered, "It feels so good."

"That's good to hear," he said still keeping the air a little lighthearted. He didn't know what to expect from this woman! He didn't know her that well!

She laughed and lay back upon the seat. "Just keep doing it, John. It feels *so* good and *so* relaxing."

"You don't have to ask me twice." He went from one breast to the other and then to her mouth, then back down again. Her nipples became taut and ready for him. He wasn't sure if he would be able to stop at just her breasts. He had not been intimate with a woman since Susan Wong and that was a long time ago; so he was more than ready.

Carol opened John's zipper on his pants and lay on his lap and gently caressed him and he came quickly and easily. He kissed her again as she was slipping her blouse back over her head.

"That's enough for today," she announced as she straightened out her clothes.
"Enough for whom?" John responded hoarsely.
"Enough for me today—thank you!"
"You are thanking me for what?"
"For being so gentle with me, for not pushing it further when I asked you to stop."
"You're the boss," he added while zipping his pants.
"And don't you forget it!" she laughingly said.
As he stopped the car to let Carol out at her house, he asked, "Where to tomorrow?"
"How about antiquing in Placerville?"
"Where is Placerville?"
"It's not too far, and a very nice ride."
"I'll drive again," he said. "I don't want you taking advantage of me again."
"Don't hold your breath, Johnny."
He leaned out the window and pinched her breast gently.
She laughed and ran into her house.
Lying in bed that night, he thought about the lovemaking at the vista spot that afternoon. He was not ashamed—after all they were adults—and they were attracted to one another. But he vowed to take it slow!

CHAPTER EIGHTEEN

As John drove the winding roads to Placerville the next day, Carol started to ask him some strange questions.

"Was there anything left in The Castle when you bought it? Were there any furnishings?"

"Yes, there were. The attorney for The Captain's estate asked me to store the stuff that was left in The Castle in the old barn at the back of the property and they would pay me for the storage. They told me that if no one came to claim it in six months I could dispose of it."

"What was left?"

"Just lots of old dressers and chests—nothing of great value, I think. Mountain helped me haul all the stuff and store it in the barn."

"You never went through it??"

"No. Why should I?"

"Aren't you the least bit curious?"

"No."

Carol sat quiet for a while then out of the blue she asked, "Do you know the family with the Great Dane dog? They live down the road from you."

"No. They haven't stopped by yet."

"Their little boy attended Sunday School at the local Catholic Church. And guess what? The Captain was a Sunday school teacher when he was in town. Little George was only five when it started. For years The Captain abused him. He was a pedophile as well."

Again John asked, with a tone of disgust in his voice, "Why did they not call the police?"

"George did not tell anyone until much later. It had gone on for years. It was his word against The Captain's."

John just shook his head as he drove on. "I hope it really wasn't an accident, that someone really killed the bastard." It was an awful thought, but John really meant it. He wondered why Carol had told him that story *now*! He didn't want anything to spoil the day. He supposed she had a good reason to do so at this time—at least he hoped so. Perhaps it had been on her mind for a long time and she had finally found a "kind ear" to tell the story to.

Placerville was fun. He bought more antiques, they stopped at every coffee shop they could find, and they wound up suffering from a sugar and caffeine high from all the great pastries they had with all the coffee.

Carol was easy to be with. They both had the same sense of humor. *Mother always said that was important,* John thought.

She had a beauty she did not have to work at, not like other women he had known. He thought of her actions the previous day and got excited all over again.

Could she be the one? he thought. Then reality set in and he remembered the contract that was out on his life and realized his life was at a standstill—for the moment.

As he drove down the road towards her house that evening to drop her off, out of the blue she said, "Pull in your driveway and let's pet, John. It has been such a perfect day and I just don't want it to end, as yet."

"Like teenagers?" he asked cheekily and hopefully.

"I never petted as a teenager."

"You didn't? Then you have a lot of catching up to do," he cheerily said as he turned into his driveway, with great anticipation.

"That's far enough," she said. They were only a car length into the driveway.

In no time at all she was on his lap and he was gently caressing her breasts. He was looking forward to going further in their lovemaking tonight. His excitement was beginning to show.

She suddenly sat up straight and brusquely pushed his hands off of her breasts and asked, "Did you pet with a lot of girls, John?"

"As many as I could," he truthfully answered.

"How old were you when you started?"

"As soon as I reached puberty and I felt the urge, I knew I was ready, and off I went—full speed."

She laughed as she kissed him hard on the lips. He loved her laugh! He followed her directions and gave her the pleasure that she asked for and seemed to need and desire greatly. It made him happy just to satisfy her.

She suddenly sat up straight and stared at The Castle. She screamed—in total terror!

"Is it your parents?" he whispered, mentally sliding back to his teenage years.

"LOOK AT THE CASTLE!"

John's focus went straight to The Castle and there was that *strange light* that he had seen a few nights ago. The light was going from room to room, as it had done before.

"Do you have a guest?" she whispered.

"The house is empty, I have no guests."

"Could it be Mountain?" she again whispered knowing that Mountain was helping John with the repairs to The Castle.

"Wait here!" John said, as he moved her from his lap, annoyed with whoever it was that was taking him away from lovely Carol.

John was gone for about fifteen minutes. "There's no one there! The doors are all locked. No sign of Mountain. Besides, his truck would have been parked in the driveway."

"Then it *is* really haunted—just like everyone says." Carol started to shiver.

"It was just the moon playing tricks with the old windows," John replied, trying to keep her calm. He did not tell her of the night when he and Sutter had seen the light come through the stonewall of The Castle. He shivered, too!

"Take me home, John!" she demanded.

"Scaredy—Cat!"

"Are you going to sleep there tonight?" she asked, ignoring his smart remark. She could not believe that anyone in their right mind would sleep in that Castle.

"Maybe! Unless you want me to come and sleep with you," he added hopefully. "Your bed would be much more comfortable than this old truck."

"Stop joking, John. I'm scared."

"Don't worry," he said as he dropped her off at her blue house. "But if I should go missing . . ."

She interrupted him abruptly. "Don't even joke about it, John."

John did not sleep well that night in the guesthouse. *I wonder if Mountain knows how to get rid of ghosts?* he thought and indeed he hoped that Mountain just might know how to do that, since he knew how to do everything else.

CHAPTER NINETEEN

John woke that next morning, having had just a few hours of sleep, with a feeling of peace and a longing for Carol. He did not sleep in The Castle that night. He would not sleep there until the mystery of "the light" was solved. The sun was shining through the window of the guesthouse, warming him and Sutter, who was gently snoring by John's side.

John laughed to himself. *I'm one poor specimen of a man if I can only have a dog by my side when I wake in the morning.*

The past week with Carol had been wonderful. It had taken his mind off of his troubles, at least for a little while.

While dressing, he peeked out the window and saw what a glorious sunny day it was. He loved the sight of the herd of deer grazing and the wild turkeys strutting their stuff across the lawn.

A wonderful day to do outside work, he thought as he put on his work clothes and looked around for his missing garden shears.

John was working in the back of The Castle when he heard a car coming down the driveway. A peek around the corner of the building showed a police car slowly coming down the drive.

John's hand instinctively went for the pistol that was strapped at his right hip. Criminals posing as police officers was a tactic that he had seen used many times in his long career.

As the policeman exited his car, John advanced slowly toward the officer. The feel of the pistol by his side emboldened him—it always did.

"Hello, sir. I'm Officer Robert Chesney."

Immediately John's instincts kicked in. He had seen some very talented imposters, but there usually was *something* that would be off in their performance that a real cop would pick up on. John had seen this officer's eyes go to his holstered gun and then the surroundings as he approached, which *he* would have done if their positions had been reversed. He also knew a hit man wouldn't get out of the car.

So he decided to go with the direct approach.

"Hello, Officer. What can I do for you? Why are you here?"

"We had several complaints last night regarding your property."

"What sort of complaints?"

"People heard a child screaming."

"There are no children living here, Officer. What time did they hear this noise?"

The officer looked at his notes. "I believe it was about eleven o'clock last night."

"I arrived home sometime around eleven, but I did not hear any noises." John did not mention the lights in The Castle that he and Carol had witnessed.

"Where were you yesterday?" asked the officer.

"I drove to Placerville to do some shopping."

"Can anyone verify that fact?"

"I was with a friend who lives down the street."

"What is your friend's name?"

"Carol Lang."

Suddenly the officer's demeanor changed. "I know Carol. We grew up together."

"Why the questioning, Officer—is there someone missing?"

The officer cringed, then quickly gained composure. "No. It's just that there were several complaints from your neighbors. They thought they heard the screaming of a child. You are new in the area, and this place has a miserable history."

"So I have heard."

"Have you found anything of interest here since you moved in?"

"No." There was *that* question again. A lot of people were asking that question. *What did they think I could find?*

Shortly after the officer left, Carol came galloping down the drive on her horse, Rocket. At least that is what Rocket thought he was doing. At the horse's advanced age it was more of a fast walk.

"What's the matter, John?"

"Nothing," he said, trying to sound nonchalant.

"Why were the police here?"

"Come down off your horse and let's have a cup of coffee."

She dismounted, and tied Rocket's reins to a post just off the driveway. They went into the guest cottage, since Carol would not set foot in The Castle. John didn't mind being in The Castle during the day—it was the nighttime that freaked him out.

"Okay. Now why were the police here?"

"There were complaints of a child's scream coming from this property last night."

Carol looked intently at John and asked, "What time were the screams heard, John?"

"The officer said about the time we were parked in the driveway."

Carol started to shake. John got up and sat beside her and put his arms around her in an effort to stop her shaking.

"What's the matter, Carol?"

"Remember the light in the window, John? Maybe it was the little girl who died—maybe she is trying to tell us something."

"That's ridiculous and you know it. Besides *we* didn't hear any screams."

"We were preoccupied," she said blushing.

"Drink your coffee and let's go for a ride. Let's get out of here."

"Who was the officer?" she asked.

John took a card out of his pocket that the officer had given him.

Carol looked at it and started to sob and shake all over again.

"What?????" John asked.

"Robert Chesney!"

"Yes, that is what the card says—so what?"

"You don't know what happened to his family, do you?"

John settled back for the latest horror. He was getting a wee bit weary of it all.

"Robert's father had been a police officer, too. Robert's mother was a stay-at-home Mom; and very beautiful. Robert's parents had married very young. One day, after The Captain had lived here for a long while, the family found a note from the mother. It said she was going away with The Captain. He was taking her on one of his cruises and then she would live in his house in Spain. Apparently he had homes in Wales, Spain and the South of France. She apologized to her husband and family but she said she could not bear to miss the chance to finally live and see the world."

"Did she ever come back?"

"Her husband tried to locate her, but The Captain said he did not even know her—and she was not on the passenger list of any of the other cruise ships The Captain was involved with. She was never heard from again."

"That woman was Robert Chesney's mother?" John asked softly.

"Yes!" Then the sobs began again.

John now knew why the officer had cringed when John had asked if someone was missing.

"Come on! Get on your horse and go home—I will pick you up in twenty minutes."

Carol was very upset riding home after telling John about Robert Chesney's mother, breaking down into tears several times as she rode home. *Some vacation I'm having,* she thought. As she was putting the horse in the stable she thought about her recent time with John and she felt somewhat better. She did like him very much and he was very comfortable and easy to be with.

Carol and John spent the last few days of her vacation together. They spent most of the time looking for furniture for The Castle. It was such great fun to have someone's opinion on the purchases and to have someone you care for by your side.

They had one last day to spend together, and John couldn't bear the thought of her leaving.

CHAPTER TWENTY

They had planned a glorious last day together. They would picnic in the high mountains; Carol would pack a delicious lunch. After lunch they would visit some of the local wineries. It would be a day to remember!

John's thoughts were interrupted by a ringing cell phone. The ringing of that phone never meant good news.

"John, it is Dad. I think you had better come home. Mother has been hurt."

John's pulse quickened. "What happened?"

"Just come home," and John's father disconnected the call.

John dressed quickly. He called Mountain to come and get Sutter and then he headed to Carol's house to tell her he had to leave.

She was disappointed and she didn't really understand why he had to leave—but she didn't make a fuss once she saw how distressed he was.

"I don't have a number where I can reach you after you leave," he reminded her. "You'll be gone when I return."

She quickly ran into the house and got a pen and paper and wrote down her home and cell numbers.

"How do I reach *you*?" she asked.

He felt it safe to give her his cell number since she had no connection to him in San Francisco, since she hardly knew him at all. She didn't even know his full name. Strangely enough, she had never asked him what his last name was.

"I hope everything is all right," she said as she kissed him goodbye. She saw the worried look on his face.

"So do I."

The ride back to San Francisco was brutal. His dad did not reveal how his mother was or how she had gotten hurt. He was worried sick.

The fog was just lifting from The Marina area where his parents had bought a two family home many years ago. John was happy when his parents bought this house on Beach Street, until the earthquake came in 1989. There was some damage to the house, but it was easily repaired. His parents loved living there—the earthquake would not scare them away. They could walk to Marina Green and Lily, their Yorkshire Terrier, loved to prance down Crissy Field where everyone would stop to pet her.

Once he arrived, John sprang from his car and ran up the front steps to his parents' apartment on the lower floor of their two-family home.

As he entered the apartment, he immediately noticed his mother lying on the couch with her arm heavily bandaged. He was relieved to see she was not very badly hurt.

"What happened?"

His mother started to talk but his dad interrupted. "The bastards grabbed her when she opened the garage door. She was going to her parents' house. They dragged her into the garage, roughed her up and told her to tell you that this is only the beginning."

John's heart sank. They had found his parents!

"You have got to leave this house, Dad."

"They won't chase me out of my home, son."

John looked at his dad and knew that to be true.

"They are cowards, John; they went after a poor defenseless woman. If they had attacked me they would have been in for a good fight."

"I know that, Dad. But we must protect Mom!"

John's Dad looked at his wife with fury on his face. "Yes, we have to protect your Mother" he finally conceded.

"Can she go to Scotland to visit her cousins?" John suggested.

"Who would take care of Gramps and Grandma if she went to Scotland?"

"Can't they go with her?"

"They are too old, John. They would never go."

"What about Mom living with her parents for a while. I don't think *they* know about the MacGregors. What do you think?"

John's dad thought for a minute then agreed that that would be best for now. He was not frightened, but he could not let anything happen to his bonnie Laurie. So John's mother was told the entire story and what danger there was to her son and the whole family. She was a trooper, a policeman's wife through and through! "But we cannot let them dictate our lives, son," she warned John.

"We won't, Mom," John promised. "But for now I need you to be protected. Please trust me!"

John was so furious about the attack on his mother that he could hardly contain himself. But he knew he had to keep his emotions in check. If his father saw how upset his son was, he would get so riled up there was no telling what he would do. His dad was like that.

So Laurie MacGregor Hurley went very unwillingly to live with her parents. The lie they used was that they were repainting the interior of their house. It was all she could do to keep Gramps from going over to help with the paint job. The cheeky wee Scot!

The transfer of Laurie Hurley was performed in the middle of the night, with about ten of John's policeman friends supervising the move. John zigzagged through the streets of San Francisco to confuse anyone that might be following them. A direct run would have taken about ten minutes, but John drove through the Financial District, then up through the Potrero area, through the Civic Center, up Bush St., Divisidero, then Geary, then California, Pacific, Union Street, through the Presidio and on and on it went. When John was fully satisfied that he was not followed, he pulled directly into his grandparents' garage on Lake Street and closed the garage door.

Many of his friends had gotten into their cars at the same time and all drove off simultaneously, in all different directions; hopefully confusing "the bastards."

CHAPTER TWENTY-ONE

Once John got his mother settled, he headed back to Elk Horn and his Castle. There was nothing more that he could do in San Francisco. His mother was settled in the Richmond/Sea Cliff house with her parents. His father, the old retired cop, got prepared for a possible assault—making sure his guns and ammo were always close by and ready to use.

Calvin Wong and the rest of John's policeman friends were going to continue to be vigilant. There would be security twenty four hours a day. All of the time would be volunteered by John's friends. They would stand guard, out of sight, when they were off duty.

John did not take the normal route home. He again zigzagged and got on and off the highway. If anyone was following him, they would have to be damn good. John was sure no one could have followed him the way he was driving.

It was a sad drive home. He was stymied—he did not know what to do. How could he end this horrible situation with the Perez Brothers? His mother would not be able to identify her attackers as they wore masks.

John could not be sure if it were the Perez Brothers who had physically hurt his mother or if it were other criminals that they had hired to do the job. Either way he knew it were the Perez Brothers that were somehow involved in the attack on his mother. He would have to find a way to stop the Perez Brothers—he and his family could not continue to live in fear.

It would be useless to report it to the police as he had no evidence—he needed more than just a hunch that it was the Perez Brothers.

It was about now that he wished that he had become a priest or a carpenter instead of a police officer.

He vowed he would find a way to stop the insanity—he just had to!

By the time John turned into his driveway in Elk Horn, it was getting very dark. He was exhausted—he couldn't wait to just flop into bed and sleep for hours.

As he was turning his key in the lock of the guesthouse, he noticed that the lights were on in the old barn.

There is no electricity in the barn, John remembered, reaching for his pistol.

He turned off his car lights and withdrew his pistol from its holster and crept from tree to tree toward the barn, hoping he could not be seen or heard.

The barn windows were still covered with decades of dirt and grime. John could have kicked himself for not cleaning them, but he could see *some* slight movement within the barn.

His heart was racing. He wondered how "they" had discovered where he lived. It *had* to be the Perez Gang! *Maybe I should just shoot through the window!* he thought in a panic. He wanted to kill the bastards and get rid of the fear once and for all. *Maybe I should wait until they come out and then shoot. There may be more than one.* His mind was running rampant with outrageous thoughts. He was almost out of his mind with rage and fury. They had hurt his mother—IT HAD TO STOP!

He decided to confront the bastard, *then* he would shoot him. Either way he was going to kill whoever was in that barn, and who was probably there to kill him.

They had hurt his mother—now they were after him. He could not fathom how they had discovered where he lived. He had been so careful.

John stood by the door to the barn and tried to calm himself so that he could shoot straight. Then he backed up about 10 feet from the door, made a running leap and kicked open the door. "Come out you swine, or I will kill you where you stand."

He was taken aback when he heard a familiar voice say very meekly, "John, it's me—Carol!"

John's arm fell trembling to his side. The pistol almost dropped from his sweating and now shaking hand.

He cautiously stepped in, and the lamps that Carol had arranged around the barn illuminated the scene.

"What the fuck are you doing here? I ALMOST KILLED YOU!" he yelled at the top of his lungs.

"Let me explain," she sobbed. She didn't know where to start—she was so embarrassed. "I didn't think you would be coming home so soon."

"That's pretty obvious," he yelled as his eyes roamed around the barn. Every dresser, every chest, every suitcase, every type of furniture there was, was ransacked. The drawers of all the chests were still out and the contents were strewn about.

John was devastated. He grabbed Carol's arm and literally dragged her across the yard into the guesthouse and roughly threw her on the couch.

The Strange Valley

She was crying and rubbing her arm that had hit the arm of the couch. "LET ME EXPLAIN!" she yelled.

"No need! It's all very clear to me now. All that wining and dining and the enticement of a little sex was all an act—so that you could get into the barn and steal or whatever the hell you were doing in there."

"No! No! NO!"

"You even gave me a blow job to seal the deal."

She rose in a fury and slapped his face.

He grabbed her arm and threw her down again. "You bitch! I mean absolutely nothing to you. It was all a bloody act—just a game! You are nothing but a lying slut!"

She just sat there shaking her head back and forth slowly.

"And to think I almost gave you my heart!" he said with a slight tremor in his voice.

"I care very much for you, too!" she sobbed.

"BULLSHIT!" He ran to the door and while holding it open he said, "Get the fuck out of my sight. I don't want to hear any of your shit. If I never see you again it would be too soon! Never darken my doorway again!"

She didn't move. She couldn't. She was frozen to the spot. "Please give me a chance to explain!" she begged. "Just calm down and let me explain and please put the gun away. I'm deathly afraid of guns."

Finally, John grabbed a chair and placed it before her and he sat with his arms folded tightly against his chest. "Go ahead. Let me hear more bullshit!" He was so angry he could hardly see or think straight. Every part of his body was still tingling with the fear and anticipation he had felt when he first saw the lights on in the old barn.

She knew he had a right to be angry. But to say the past week was an act was almost too much for her to bear.

She had very deep feelings for this man. She hadn't known him very long, but he was very special to her. Their lovemaking had been spectacular. It had moved her.

There was a connection between them. She had had this with no other lover.

"Listen with an open mind, John."

"I'm listening," he half shouted.

"It's a very long story."

"I have lots of time."

"It all started a very long time ago."

"Sounds like the start of a fairy tale."

"John, if you are not going to listen, I may as well leave right now."

"Go on! Go on!" he said angrily.

"Back then," she started, "The Captain was acting at his worst. People were missing; animals were missing; girls were raped; boys were abused and God knows what else. When the little girl fell from the turret, we all knew it was murder. We knew The Captain must have killed her. The people of the neighborhood decided to take matters into their own hands since the police could or would do nothing. One by one, each of the neighbors called The Captain and threatened him and told him to leave town. Some even wrote threatening letters."

When she continued the story, her eyes filled up. "Remember when I told you I had gone into The Castle to play with the little girl—that wasn't the whole truth. That day, the little girl and I were in The Castle playing by ourselves—she had told me "he" was not due back for a few hours. When The Captain arrived home unexpectedly, a look flashed across the little girl's face that kind of scared me. But The Captain was quite pleasant and very charming—and my guard was down. I was just a little girl, I thought the look on my little friend's face was because she had been caught doing something that she was not supposed to." Carol's voice caught in her throat. She struggled out, "I did not suspect anything evil."

As the tears were now streaming down her face, John became uncomfortable enough to get up and find a box of tissues, which he angrily tossed to her.

"The Captain sent the little girl up to her room for some made up reason and when she was out of sight he dragged me into one of the bedrooms. He undressed me quickly and began to feel me all over and he started to sodomize me. I was petrified. I was so scared. I tried to scream but he put his hand over my mouth so I could not make a sound."

John's folded arms slowly dropped to his knees. Carol started sobbing and shaking at the memory of what The Captain had done to her so many years ago. John rose, got a blanket, and gently placed it around Carol's shoulders.

"Finally," Carol continued, "for some reason he left the room for a minute. The little girl came running in the room with her forefinger on her lips, telling me to be quiet and she pointed to the window. She had placed a chair outside the window. I quietly climbed out and she threw my clothes after me. I grabbed my clothes and ran like hell!"

"She was a brave little girl," added John, now with a more sympathetic and calmer voice.

Carol looked at John with the most pathetic expression he had ever seen. Finally, Carol yelled, "SHE WAS FOUND DEAD THE NEXT DAY!"

John sat with his hand covering his mouth and just shook his head in horror.

"And you feel responsible?" he finally asked, with a touch of sympathy in his voice.

"I don't know how to feel about that. I guess in a way I do. Perhaps if I had told my parents what he had done she would be alive today."

"You never told your parents?"

She shook her head. "Not right away. When I finally told my parents, my father grabbed his gun and ran out the door ready to kill him."

She was still shaking, but she continued. "The Captain saw my father coming and stood way up in the turret with a rifle. My father did not care; he kept walking closer and closer. The Captain fired a warning shot over my father's head and shouted to him, "I have taped all the threatening telephone calls and saved all the threatening letters that you all sent. If anything happens to me the police will have them the next day. My attorney knows where they are."

"My father left, knowing it was a futile situation. He later met with all the neighbors and told them what The Captain had told him. They all knew that if anything happened to The Captain, either he or his estate could drag them all into court and bankrupt them all, or worse. So they backed off."

She seemed to be regaining her composure and she almost happily reported, "A few months later The Captain was dead. Everyone held their breath waiting for the tapes and letters to come out. But apparently his attorney did not have them. No one knew if they really existed or if it had just been a scare tactic."

John sat still, just listening and letting her vent years of pent-up emotion.

"When the house was unoccupied for all those years, we all just seemed to enjoy the calm. After you moved in and told me there were things left behind I became petrified. What if those tapes and letters were in the barn somewhere? If they were found, they might exhume his body. When they did they would find he was one bloody mass of humanity. I was told that when they found him he was almost unrecognizable—it looked like he was beaten to a bloody pulp. It was no accident. I don't know who killed him, but I'm afraid to find out. All the people here don't need to go through all of that fear again. They are all afraid the finger would be pointed at them."

"You say he was badly beaten, Carol?"

"I heard it took a long time to identify him. It was his dental records that proved it was The Captain."

"Why was it reported as an accident?"

Carol just shrugged her shoulders.

"Do you think your father did it?"

She sighed and said sadly, "I don't know."

"Well, if a man killed my horse, I would definitely kill him," John facetiously said, hoping that some of his cop's gallow's humor might bring the smile back into Carol's face.

"Very funny! It's no joking matter, John."

"I know." John got the whole picture now and he could appreciate the fear that drove Carol into his barn. She was protecting everyone in this Strange Valley and most of all, her father. Perhaps, that is why she told him awful stories at inopportune times.

"Do you forgive me?" Carol asked through her tears.

"If you give me another blow job, I might" he joked and he grabbed Carol's arm as she went to slap him and he pulled her close and kissed her with all the forgiveness and love he could muster.

As he led her to his bedroom he asked gently, "What was the little girl's name?"

Carol thought back. "Emily. Her name was Emily."

Carol stayed the night and they made love passionately and with great tenderness—the way only lovers who really love one another can. He could see she was pulling back at first. Then she let go with a passion both had not experienced in their lifetime.

When they woke in the morning, John held her close and said, "I guess I'll have to marry you to make an honest woman of you."

"Do you think I'd marry a black Irishman like you?"

"You had better." They made love again and again. John had needed this diversion. He had been wound so tight he was ready to spring at the slightest sound or word.

Holding Carol and caressing her, he could forget a little of what had happened to his mother and he was grateful that Carol had held nothing back and they were as one that magnificent night!

CHAPTER TWENTY-TWO

As Carol was leaving that morning, after the loving, she turned to John and asked, "Can we please finish looking in the barn? If nothing else, to put right the mess I created."

Carol could see John stiffen. "No! I did not sleep with you so I could continue my search. If that is what you think, you stupid son of a bitch, then I will step out that door and disappear from your life forever."

John just looked at her in amazement. One minute she is so loving, and the next minute she is so willing to leave him. She was a bit of a mystery!

As he gazed at her he could see she did not mean it. Her eyes were pleading.

"Carol, you have to stop thinking like an attorney. You think the tapes and letters definitely exist and that they will be found."

"Stranger things have happened."

"Okay. Let's go and search the barn if that will ease your mind. Before we do, if your parents don't know where you have been, shouldn't you call them and let them know you are still alive?"

"They've been in Oregon for the past few days, visiting my aunt."

"You mean I could have been ravaging you for the past few days and your parents would never have known?"

"In your dreams, Buster! In your dreams!"

They spent the better part of the day going through every nook and cranny of every piece of furniture that had been owned by The Captain. They did find some odd things that they put to one side. Handcuffs, lots of them! Whips! Lots of unmentionable magazines! Porno movies—lots of them, too!

John joked, "Put those to one side for me. If you are going to go home today, I might need them."

Carol threw them at John.

"Thank you," he said while catching them and tossing them into a dresser drawer. One or two missed the drawer and fell to the floor of the barn.

In the end, nothing was found that would incriminate the Elk Horn residents. "Happy now?" he finally asked.

"What if they are hidden in The Castle?"

"Carol, I have been through every inch of The Castle while renovating it. If I haven't found anything by now, it does not exist."

"I guess you are right." But Carol knew the worry would not go away. She wondered if she would ever have peace of mind in her lifetime!

CHAPTER TWENTY-THREE

John walked Carol home and when they reached her door, she invited him in.
"Nice house," he said while looking around the living room and dining room.
"My parents have done a lot of work on it lately. They want to fix everything now so they won't have to worry about it when they get older. Peace of mind, I guess."
She took his hand and led him to her bedroom. "I always wondered how it would feel to make love in my bedroom in my parents' house."
"Let's give it a go," John said with his usual sense of humor.
He watched her undress. He had not seen her full body in sunlight. She undressed with no embarrassment, as if they had known each other for years. She was breathtaking! From her full round breasts to her curving hips and her strong long legs—she was perfect.
"Your turn," she said.
So with a little embarrassment John took off his clothes a little at a time. To keep the moment a little light, he started to hum the strip tease song as he took off one piece of clothing at a time, and tossed them aside.
Carol had not seen a man so handsome before. Not that she had known many men. Her eyes went from his dark wavy hair, and bluer than blue eyes, to his muscular chest. She thought he was perfectly formed. She passed quickly from his private parts to his legs. She thought that his legs were better formed than hers. *So unfair*, she thought.
She grabbed his hand and quickly led him to her bed.
"Make yourself comfortable, John. I am going to ravage you!" She meant it. The sight of him had excited her so, that she almost had an orgasm just looking at him.
"Oh," John said—taking on a weak, feeble voice—"I feel so helpless, I don't know if I can resist you," he joked.
Carol eased into the bed beside him. They lay on their sides just looking at one another and smiling.

He reached over and gently massaged her breasts. He knew what pleased her. She responded by bringing his mouth to her taut nipples. She reached down and gently massaged him. She knew the right spot. It did not take long. She guided him into her and they were one, once again. The passion took them both to new heights.

"I didn't know it could be so sweet," she said after the loving and after they finally tore themselves apart from one another.

"And we didn't even need the handcuffs," he added.

That was it! He had ruined the moment and any further hope of more sex that day. The mention of handcuffs reminded her of The Captain and the porno tapes they had found in the old barn.

"Some times you can be such an idiot, John."

"I know," he said apologetically. "But otherwise I'm perfect," he again joked hoping to see her smile again.

She gave him a strong slap on the stomach and without any anger said, "I really have to pack and go home."

It suddenly dawned on John that she did not live here full time. "Will I see you again soon?"

Carol looked down at John's naked body and smiled. "I don't live too far away."

"Come up next weekend, Carol."

"I can't. We have a major trial starting next week and I may have to work over the weekend preparing the case."

"Are you the prosecutor or the defense?"

"Defense."

"Murder trial?"

"Yes."

"Another Perez?"

She turned quickly and asked, "How did you know my firm handled that case?" He quickly caught himself and said, "I read it in the newspaper."

"I didn't try that one, but I did a lot of research."

"Your firm lost that one," he said knowingly.

"We are appealing."

"Too bad!" he said strongly.

"Why do you say that?"

"From what I read, he was guilty."

"Well, don't tell anyone I said so, but he *was* guilty."

"I know."

"What?"

"Nothing." John tried to get her to lay with him again, but she adamantly insisted she had to pack and go back to her home in Redwood City.

CHAPTER TWENTY-FOUR

She was only gone a few hours, and he missed her already. How could he get so involved with a woman he knew for only a few weeks was a thought that roamed constantly through his mind. His time with Susan Wong had been good, but after a year he was unsure if it was a life partnership. He thought he could be reasonably happy with her, but was that enough? They mutually agreed to part for a while and Susan had moved out of John's house. John had realized he didn't miss her that much after she left. But after a few hours he was lonely without Carol. Maybe it was the sex that he missed. Well, he certainly missed that, but he thought it was more than that. They were alike in so many ways. She understood his sense of humor. They were easy together. He liked the total package. She might be the one! The family would like her. Gramps would adore her, he would love her feistiness.

But coming back to reality he remembered he still had a problem to deal with in San Francisco and he would not put Carol in any danger.

John was busy thinking of Carol's bedroom and all that had transpired that morning. He was giggling to himself and reliving the wonderful moments over and over.

He answered his buzzing cell phone, thinking it was Carol who could not live without him. She was one of the few he had given his cell number to.

"Hi, Sweetie!" he answered with a smile on his face.

"It's Dad, John."

John held his breath.

"I think they have killed Calvin!" his father said hoarsely.

John's head dropped to his chest. "How, where and when?" was all he could say.

"They ambushed him in Chinatown."

"How did you find out?"

"His sister called me and asked me to call you."

"Where is he and how bad is he?"

"San Francisco General! Susan said you should not come to the hospital. She feels they may be waiting for you there."

"How bad is he?" John asked.

"It's bad, John."

"Okay, Dad."

"Be careful, Johnny." John's father knew that his son would spring into action. He would not sit back and take this type of treachery.

"I'll be careful, Dad, don't worry."

John's heart was racing as he closed the lid on his cell phone.

It was only days ago that they had attacked his mother and now Calvin. They were working very quickly in their endeavors to get to John. How far would they go to get to him? How many people would get hurt?

CHAPTER TWENTY-FIVE

John patted the trusted pistol that hung on his hip and felt for the rifle he had put under the seat of his truck as he began his frantic drive to San Francisco. Mountain agreed to have Sutter live with them for a while as he seemed to be with Mountain and Maggie more than with John lately.

John didn't even remember crossing the Bay Bridge. The cold air woke him out of his reverie.

He dialed Susan's cell phone. He still knew it by heart.

"How is he, Susan?" he asked when she said hello.

"He's hanging on, but he is hurt very badly. The doctor isn't too optimistic." She choked back a sob.

"Susan, I need your help!"

"What can I do?"

"I need doctor's scrubs, or whatever they wear."

"John, you must *not* go to the hospital. They beat up Calvin, hoping to get to you."

"Get those clothes for me, Susan!" he demanded.

Susan begrudgingly agreed.

"Meet me at Potrero and Sixteenth. I am in a blue Ford truck."

"What time?" Susan asked, still hoping that somehow she could still change his mind about going to the hospital.

"NOW!" he yelled.

"I don't know how long it will take me to get the doctor's scrubs, John."

"Use your D.A. influence."

"I don't like it, John."

"Calvin is my brother, Susan."

"I know! But he is my *real* brother, and I don't want any further harm to come to him—or you."

Susan arrived one hour later. She looked worried, but still lovely. John's stomach jumped. He realized that he still had feelings for her. But not the same feelings that he had for Carol!

The lovemaking with Susan Wong had been good but the passion had not been there all the time. She always held back. Maybe her heritage had something to do with it. Then again, he really didn't think that a person's race had anything to do with it. That was just Susan!

"Hello, John."

"Thanks for helping me, Susan. It's good to see you again."

She smiled at that—then grew serious. "I don't like this, John. Calvin would not want you to jeopardize your life."

"I've got to see him, Susan."

She handed him the doctor's scrubs. "Come over tonight, John, so we can talk."

"Where are you living now?"

"I'm still at my Ocean Beach condo. Call me when you are coming and I will meet you outside."

John drove to San Francisco General Hospital. It was one of the best trauma hospitals in the Bay Area, and Calvin was still in the ICU. John hoped by wearing the doctor's scrubs the nurses on duty at the monitoring station would pay no attention to him as he walked through to Calvin's room.

His plan worked—once he knew what room Calvin was in he walked across the floor unchallenged.

Once he got there, he found the cop on guard duty outside the door was a guy he knew from his old precinct, who recognized him and let him in. He and John had been to this hospital many times to pick up injured prisoners.

"I'm here on the Q.T.," he threw at the guard.

"My lips are sealed."

When John saw Calvin, his knees almost buckled. His head was swathed in bandages, he was wearing a plastic mask that John knew was there to reshape a badly beaten face. He was unrecognizable. John did not speak as the tears were streaming down his cheeks. He slowly drew up a chair and sat beside his friend's hospital bed, and took his hand in his and gently stroked it.

He spoke in a whisper to his friend so that he would not startle him. He told Calvin how much he meant to him. He told him he loved him and that Calvin was the brother he had never had. He sat for hours, just talking to Calvin.

John had heard that you should talk to comatose patients. It was thought they could hear you even if they were unconscious. So he rambled on and on.

John talked and talked until his mouth was dry. As he finally stood up to get some water, Calvin's hand tightened ever so slightly over John's hand.

John sat back down quickly. "Can you hear me, Cal?"

The Strange Valley

There was a slight pressure on John's hand.

"You can, you can! You big, yellow son of a bitch!" he half shouted to his friend.

"Who did this to you, Bro?"

No pressure on John's hand. He had to establish some sort of communication between him and Cal.

"Okay Cal, one squeeze for yes, two for no." John had seen this in some old movie—it sounded hokey, even to him, but he hoped it would work. It had to work!

"Do you know it's me, Cal?"

One weak squeeze.

"Do you still love me, Cal?"

Two squeezes from Cal.

John laughed out loud.

"Couldn't you at least have lied about that last one?"

Two squeezes.

"Are you in pain, Cal?"

One squeeze.

Just looking at Cal, John knew that that was one stupid question.

"Cal, was it the Perez Gang?"

John waited for a squeeze. With all the strength that Calvin could muster, he squeezed John's hand.

JUST ONCE.

"Did you recognize the one that did it?"

One squeeze!

"Was it the Perez Brothers themselves?"

It came quickly and again very strongly.

ONE SQUEEZE.

The bastards, John muttered to himself.

Apparently, Calvin heard him and he gave another squeeze in agreement.

"I'll get the bastards, Cal. But you must get better. We need you to testify against them. Most of all, Susan and I need you, Bro. Don't let go. Don't let them win."

Just before he left, John gave Cal's hand an encouraging squeeze, then bent over him and gave him a gentle kiss on his forehead before he turned to go.

If he remembers that I kissed him, I'll never live it down. And that's OK!

CHAPTER TWENTY-SIX

John called Susan and told her he was on his way to her condo. She was at the front door of the condominium complex to meet him, knowing that he would be very upset after seeing Calvin.

"Let's take a walk on the boardwalk for a while. I need to clear my head," John said, taking Susan's hand.

She felt the same way, and the ocean breeze usually helped to clear the cobwebs from her brain as well. That was just one reason why she loved living down by the Pacific Ocean.

"Do you think he will be okay, Susan?" John suddenly asked.

"Only God knows, John."

"What do the doctors say?"

"He has a fifty-fifty chance," her voice breaking as she reached for her handkerchief to wipe the tears from her eyes.

"Then he will be all right. I know Cal, he is a fighter." John put his arm around her and they continued on their walk, leaving the boardwalk for the beach.

They walked very slowly arm in arm. John took off his shoes and socks and walked in the water. He liked the waves coming in and drawing out, the cold of the water jolting him out of his weariness. They walked all the way down the southern area of the beach, and then turned back towards the Cliff House.

"You look awful. Let's get a bite to eat." Susan motioned towards the Cliff House.

"I don't think I could stand to be among the public right now."

"Then come up to my apartment. I'll cook you something special."

Sue Wong made the best Chow Mein in the world and the delicious vegetable dishes she would fry up in her wok could not be beat. He secretly wondered if Carol could cook.

They had a pleasant evening with wine and great food and conversation about Cal.

"I know who did it to him," blurted John.

"Who?" asked Susan incredulously, surprised that John could know who did it!

"The Perez Brothers! But unless Cal pulls through we will never be able to prove it."

"Cal told you that?" she urgently asked in surprise.

"Yes, he did."

"How?"

"He can hear us talk, he squeezed my hand in assent when I asked him if it was the Perez Brothers. When you visit him keep talking to him and get him to respond. It is good for him."

Susan sprang to the phone. She ordered double security for Cal. If the Perez Brothers knew that he had survived and that he had recognized them they would try to kill him for sure.

"Good idea," said John. Calvin had to be protected at all costs.

Once she got off the phone, they went into the living room, to get comfortable and enjoy some after dinner wine.

She gazed at this man that she still loved with all her heart.

"Go and lie down, John. You look beat."

"I should be getting home."

"Just rest awhile. You're exhausted, and I'm afraid to let you drive like this. Besides you had entirely too much wine."

John had to admit that that was true. He let her lead him to the bedroom and cover him. All he took off was his shoes; he was too tired to undress completely. Besides, he was only going to take a short nap.

John woke with a start. *Where the hell am I?* he thought. He looked at his watch. It was two in the morning. He turned to see who was next to him in the bed, and there was Susan.

As he went to get up, she grasped his arm and pulled him back on the bed.

"Stay, John!" she said pleadingly. She drew the covers from her body and he could see she was naked.

"For old times sake, John."

John realized at that moment that he had no clothes on. Susan had undressed him without his knowing it. He must have really been under the influence. He wondered if Susan had put something in his drink to make him sleepy.

She pulled him toward her and he could not resist. He was still very groggy and he did not need much coaxing.

Suddenly her hand was stroking him in all the right places. John could not believe this was Sue. When they were living together, John always had to take the initiative. Then she kissed him with urgency and passion. John had to blink to see if it was really Susan.

Yes, it was really Susan, but this is not how he remembered her. She had never been like this when they were together. He looked at her body. She was so much smaller than Carol; but she was beautiful as well. He could not hold back.

She was responding, as was he, as she stroked him again and again. Then she got on top of him and eased him into her, gently and lovingly. She was taking the initiative!

They both came at the same time. Susan did not disengage herself from this man that she loved with all her heart. She had missed him. They were connected now, and that is how she wanted it to stay—at least for a short time.

They lay in silence for a while after the loving.

"Where is my friend Susan?" John whispered. "What have you done with her?" John joked. Then, "Have you been taking lessons?"

Sue laughed. "I thought perhaps the reason you left was because of the sex."

"So you took lessons?"

"No! It was always there, I just never let myself go."

"Too bad," he joked.

"Can we put it all back together again, John?"

"Now is not the time to talk about it, Sue. Cal is in the hospital and the Perez Brothers are trying to kill us all."

"What is there about me that you don't like?" she said impatiently as she pulled the covers off of her body. "Tell me and I will change it. Should I get implants? Should I lose weight?"

John just drew her close to him to comfort her and to rock her to sleep. "You are perfect, Susan. I did not leave because of the sex." He rocked her gently until she fell asleep. Then he quietly dressed and left.

He had had two women in just a few days. Both were so totally different. He liked them both. Which one did he love? Time would tell. Right now he was totally confused!

His only mission at this time and place was to find a way to stop the Perez Brothers; to get the contract off of his life and the danger away from his loved ones.

Those were the only issues that were tops in his mind at this time.

Oh, yes—and the mystery of The Castle and the Strange Valley were also weighing heavily on his mind.

CHAPTER TWENTY-SEVEN

There was no sense staying in San Francisco, John thought. Cal could not physically identify his attackers at this time. When he could, maybe they could have all the Perez Brothers behind bars. Would John then be out of danger? He thought not. Jose Perez would just find someone else outside of the prison walls who could and would carry out the contract. At this time he could not think of a good way for all of this to end.

The week passed slowly back at The Castle. He missed Carol. Hell, he even missed Susan Wong. *Maybe I should become a Mormon and have two wives,* he joked to himself.

John was confused. Susan's plan had worked. He had enjoyed spending the evening with her and the sex after was great. *And she is a great cook!*

But Carol was fantastic as well. But in a different way!

It's a great problem to have, he thought, *I wish it was my only problem!*

The next morning he went to the barn to get a scythe to work on the back property. He wished The Captain's attorney would call so he could get rid of all the junk that was stored in the barn. Probably good junk, but junk, nevertheless.

His foot kicked something, and it scooted across the barn floor. He bent to see what it was. It was one of the pornographic movies that he and Carol had found.

John smiled cheekily. *I haven't seen one of these since those good old teenage parties,* he thought.

John found the scythe and shoved the film into his pocket. *Let's see if they are better than Carol and Sue. You are soooo bad, John!* he laughingly thought.

He tossed the video tape cassette on the table and prepared himself some soup and a grilled cheese sandwich. *Where is Sue when I need her,* he thought as he prepared his own meal.

The tape was staring at him all through lunch. *What would Father John Fitzpatrick say about this?* he thought. He answered his own question—*The*

Priest will forgive me; he always did. A few Hail Marys and I will be back in God's good graces. I hope!

John put the film into the old VHS player and he settled back to have a few laughs.

A man in a Naval Uniform came into view. John looked intently at the screen waiting for the naked girls to come into the scene as well.

The man started to speak. "I am Captain Timothy Henson. I make this tape in case anything happens to me. I have been threatened by the horrible people that live in this Valley. My neighbors! I will now play all the telephone calls that I have received and recorded and I will also read the horrible letters that I have also received in the mail."

John sat back with his hands behind his head and his mouth wide open.

Captain Henson had held the microphone to the answering machine and there, one by one, every neighbor in the vicinity threatened his life. He then held the letters up so you could read the writing and then read them out loud.

The Captain ended by saying, "If I should be found dead, I accuse everyone in this neighborhood of being the murderer. I want them prosecuted and punished. EVERY LAST ONE OF THEM!" That last sentence was said in the most evil voice and tone that John had ever heard. That Captain could outperform Boris Karloff in the scariest movie ever produced—he looked and sounded like evil itself personified.

John could not believe what he was seeing and hearing. The Captain had accused everyone else, but he did not admit to what *he* had done. He did not apologize for the rapes, murders and God knows what else. He was one *son of a bitch!*

John played the tape over and over. He thought he recognized several of the voices, but Carol would certainly recognize them all.

Should I tell her I found the tape?

He decided he would not tell her just yet. He had to give the situation a lot of thought. Carol would want to dispose of the tape right away. He did not know why, but he could not bring himself to destroy this tape. He would stow it away in a vault that he had opened at the local bank.

Carol's intuition had been right. There *was* a tape and it did point the finger at all of her neighbors. Her father was the strongest voice on the tape. Her father had even mentioned the death of his horse and his accusation that The Captain had done it.

John stopped the tape at the picture of Captain Henson. He had known the name. He had seen it on the final papers when he bought The Castle. Now he saw the face. He was a very handsome Welshman, tall and thin, with a charming Welch brogue. It was easy to see how he was able to entice young girls to be snared in his web, and to get the police officer's wife to run away with him. The officer's wife was taken in by him and was probably murdered soon after she moved in with The Captain.

But where did all these missing people go?

The detective in him started to try and solve the mystery.

Perhaps he put them in a trunk and loaded them on his ship and then dumped them in the cold Atlantic Ocean.

John knew from the real estate agent that The Captain had several homes; in Wales, Spain, the south of France and Switzerland. The attorney had told her that The Captain was a very wealthy man.

John's imagination continued to run wild. *Maybe he put them in a trunk and buried them in Wales or one of those other countries.* The Captain had lots of options.

But then John thought maybe he had nothing to do with the missing people at all. *Perhaps I should give him the benefit of the doubt. He should be considered innocent until proven guilty.* All these thoughts, and more, ran through John's head.

The thought that bothered him the most was the thought of The Captain sodomizing Carol. To do that to a young girl was evil. He then thought of the bravery of the little girl who planned Carol's escape. It had probably cost her life.

John remembered Carol telling him what her dad had said. *When that man moved here, darkness descended on the Valley.*

How sad, that one man could bring such grief and sadness to an entire community. He brought such suffering; the loss of life, the loss of innocence.

John was suddenly glad that someone had murdered this miserable piece of shit. He wished he could tell the world how horrible and guilty this man was!

He went to the bank immediately and put the tape into his safe deposit box. Little did he know it would not end there—many other items would eventually be put into that safe deposit box.

CHAPTER TWENTY-EIGHT

John stopped at Mountain and Maggie's house to see how his dog Sutter was getting along.

Mountain was just finishing with his lunch.

"Say Mountain, not only do you look like Sutter, but you are beginning to slobber like him."

"You flatter me, John."

Mountain looked at himself in the mirror and then at Sutter. "You're right, John!"

"I think I'll take Sutter for a few days if you don't mind, Mountain."

"He's your dog."

"I think at this point we have joint custody."

"He's a good dog. He is fun to have around and Maggie feels safe with him in the house when I am gone."

"I think he likes you better than me."

"I take him for long walks and I play with him. He likes that."

"Okay. I got the message. I'll start spending more time with him. But I may have to leave again at any moment. May I leave him again if the need arises?"

"You can leave him anytime, John. Maggie and I both feel safe when Sutter is with us."

Mountain looked curiously at his friend and part-time employer. "You seem troubled, John. Can I help?"

John thought for a minute, but realized there was no way that Mountain could help him in San Francisco. And he was not ready to share with anyone what he had recently discovered—The Captain and his accusations.

"Believe me, you are the first one that I will call if I need help, Mountain."

"I'll be there before you hang up the phone."

Sutter left unwillingly with John. With Mountain and Maggie he ate and played very well. This was no dumb dog.

CHAPTER TWENTY-NINE

John was getting some of his energy back. When he returned from San Francisco, he had felt drained, emotionally and physically.

He was constantly on guard just waiting for bad news from San Francisco. He called every day to check on Calvin, but there had been no noticeable change.

Today he felt like he needed some physical exercise.

"Come on Sutter. Let's go!"

Sutter trotted out after John and chased some birds and just looked at the surrounding deer. He was used to them at this point and he no longer chased or bothered with them.

John decided to clear some of the high grass by hand rather than use the mower, and soon was swinging his scythe back and forth, breaking out in a good sweat.

"Move over, Sutter—or you will get your head chopped off."

Sutter did not move.

John picked up a small branch and tossed it into the woods for Sutter to fetch.

Sutter was gone for a long while and John finally whistled for him. He did not come.

"Sutter, come! Sutter, come! SUTTER—COME!"

Finally, Sutter came trotting out of the woods with the branch hanging from his mouth.

"Say Buddy, come when you are called. Oh, you want to chase the branch again." He reached for the branch and then recoiled in horror. It was not a branch. It was a human bone.

"Sutter, where did you get that? Come on, show me boy." John's hand was shaking—he could not bring himself to touch the bone.

Sutter just sat on his butt, panting and drooling.

John finally got a leaf and put it over the bone so he could pick it up and examine it. It was a leg bone, and definitely human. John had seen enough bodies in his career as a detective to know that this was a human bone.

John walked around the back woods for a while, as Sutter recuperated from his run. But there was over twenty acres. He could not cover it all. He called for Sutter, went into The Castle, sat at the kitchen table and examined the bone more closely.

John wondered to himself, *Should I call the police? If I do, then every piece of this property will be dug up. Every tabloid cable news channel in the country would be parked on this lawn.*

At that point, his life would be over, with the publicity putting a spotlight right on him. The Perez Brothers would find him in a New York minute.

From the look of the bone it had been there for a long while. A little longer would do no harm.

He sat drinking a cup of tea and just stared at the bone. Finally, he started talking to it.

"Now who are you? Are you The Captain's parents, siblings, the Nanny, the officer's wife or God knows who?" An adult he thought, after looking at the bone closely. Probably a woman, from the looks of it! He had seen enough bones in his career to have a pretty good idea what the gender of this victim was.

John placed the bone very gently into a box. He believed all life was sacred and he would treat the bone with respect until it got a proper burial.

Could this have been a killing field, he wondered as he looked around his property. *How the hell did I get involved with all this? Then again, maybe I was meant to buy this Castle to help bring all the mysteries to an end,* were the philosophic thoughts that John suddenly had running rampant through his mind. He always believed there was something to "God's Plan."

He knew he could not mention the tape to Carol. He knew he couldn't call the police and tell them about the bone and the tapes. He was left in a quandary.

"I'll think about it tomorrow," he said, much like Scarlett O'Hara. Now he knew how she felt. *I just can't face it today. My mind is just too tired and weary.*

That night he had terrible nightmares, dreaming about The Captain and all the horrible crimes that he had allegedly committed. How God had allowed such a miserable creature to walk on this earth was beyond him.

His grandmother had told him as a youth that God allowed evil to happen because all humans had free will. But it allowed the "good" in Man to come forward to overcome that evil. She said there was "more good" in the world than evil.

John had to agree with that, as he had seen much heroism in his years as a policeman. He and his fellow policemen had rushed into dangerous situations, not giving a thought to the danger involved. Even if it was to save the life of a miserable drug dealer or killer—it made no difference—it was a human life!

CHAPTER THIRTY

Carol wasn't coming up for a few weeks. A major trial was going to take up much of her time. "Why don't you come here?" she asked.

"I have workmen coming," he lied. "I have to keep an eye on them."

"Have you turned up anything?"

"Like what?" John asked, knowing full well what she meant.

"You know what!!"

"I thought we had settled all that."

"How can I rest knowing that that information might be out there somewhere?"

"Don't worry!" John said, knowing he had the information, but had decided not to share it with Carol.

"Easy for you to say, John!"

"I miss you," he said to change the subject and to take her mind off of her worries.

"I miss you too."

"I liked your bedroom," he whispered sexily.

"I bet you did."

"Now we should try out my bedroom in The Castle," he suggested, hopefully.

"Not in *that* Castle!"

That night he hid the bone in the attic of the barn. Way up in the hayloft. No one would find it there.

He was still sleeping in the guesthouse. He worked in The Castle during the day, but until he could figure out what the mysterious light was, he would not sleep in The Castle.

That night, at about two a.m., he heard a sort of moan. He looked for Sutter to see if he was having a dream, but he was sleeping peacefully at John's feet.

Grabbing a lantern, John went outside to investigate. Perhaps it was an injured animal. The does had been dropping their babies lately and John feared one was hurt.

Then he saw it again. The light! It was again floating through The Castle. It appeared to go from room to room, from floor to floor, then up to the turrets. Finally it exited through the stone exterior. A heavy moan came from the direction of the light. When the light disappeared into the woods there was a loud cry; then horrible weeping. Then, what seemed like a child's hysterical scream came like thunder to John's ears.

John ran like buggery back into the guesthouse and locked the door. He put his hands over his ears so he would not hear any other terrible sounds that were coming from his back woods.

"The bloody house IS haunted," he panted. *There are things going on here that I don't understand,* he muttered to himself. *Maybe I need an exorcist!*

A little while later, after calming down, he laughed at how ridiculous it was to lock the door. If the ghost wanted to get in it could just float through the walls.

One awful thought crossed his mind. *What if the ghost is The Captain? What if he too, is after me?*

Like a child, he hugged his dog, and Sutter seemed to be fearful as well as he wrapped his paws around his master in return. John pulled the blanket over the two of them as they huddled in bed together. Each drew comfort from the other!

CHAPTER THIRTY-ONE

The next morning John called Mountain. "Mountain, can you come over after work?"

"I'm not working today, I can come over now. Have you got some work for me?"

"There is plenty for you to do here," John said, not really meaning physical work, but there was plenty of that as well.

John decided to walk down the path to pick some apples from the trees fronting his property. Sutter trotted after him, happy to be going somewhere, even if it was only to the end of the driveway.

Sutter started to growl as he they neared the trees. John finally saw what the dog was growling at. A man with the biggest bird he had ever seen started walking towards him. The bird was happily sitting on the man's shoulder.

John nodded at the man, hoping the man would not stop and talk. No such luck!

"Hi there," said "The Bird Man."

John just nodded again, hoping that would be enough.

"Have you found anything unusual in that place?" The Bird Man asked, motioning towards The Castle.

"Like what?" John asked already knowing the answer. It was the same question that Carol and others had asked.

"Like animal bones."

John was surprised at the answer. Usually the others were just fishing for information about the tape that The Captain said he had.

This was the first time anyone had asked about something specific.

"Did you lose an animal?" John asked.

"I lost many. I lost about five dogs and ten cats."

"How did you lose them?" John asked in disbelief.

"I believe The Captain killed them."

"Why do you think that?"

"A few of my animals had their throats slit and they were left on my doorstep. Up to then, I thought that perhaps the animals had been attacked by a fox or coyote. But it was The Captain who killed them."

John just nodded his head. He knew The Captain was capable of doing something as awful as that. If he could kill humans, then killing animals would be very easy for him.

"That's when I finally bought a bird. They don't wander off. And they live a long time. Now I have five of them. They are good company and some of them talk to me. I appreciate that more and more since my wife died."

"I'm sorry to hear that your wife died."

"The Captain killed her."

"You know that for a fact?" John asked, wondering if the Bird Man's wife was actually killed by The Captain and how the Bird Man knew, since the others were killed secretly.

"My wife mourned terribly for the animals, as they were our children. They were all we had and we had them for many years so they were part of our family. It broke her heart when they were killed. And she was so frightened of The Captain that eventually she would not leave the house. She felt he was after our whole family. You see, we had guinea pigs, a monkey, and a few snakes, plus chickens, turkeys, goats and a llama. She thought he would come and kill them all. She basically had a nervous breakdown and was never the same again."

John just shook his head from side to side in a sympathetic gesture.

The Bird Man turned and started walking away with tears streaming down his face.

"If I find anything, I will let you know," John yelled after the man.

The Bird Man gave a backward wave, not turning around, ashamed he was crying.

John just shook his head constantly as he walked back to The Castle. What a miserable fiend The Captain had been.

He looked at Sutter, and knew that if he found him dead on his doorstep he would be shattered.

As he was nearing the house, he saw a herd of deer eating the feed he had put out. He suddenly wondered what The Captain did about all the deer that wandered on the property. If the Captain hated all animals, then what did he do about the deer, since there were so many roaming around the Valley? He would have to ask Carol about that. That was a mystery!

When Mountain arrived, Sutter jumped all over him.

"He doesn't act that happy when he sees me," pouted John.

"It's my charisma," responded Mountain. "More and more people tell me that Sutter looks like me."

"They just flatter you to get Maggie's muffins."

Mountain just laughed.

"Have a muffin for me?" John asked hopefully.

"If you have the coffee, I have the muffins. You know Maggie would not forget you."

The muffins were always warm and delicious.

"You should sell these muffins, Mountain. They would go over big."

"Funny you should say that, John. Maggie and I have often talked about opening a little coffee shop. But it is a very expensive proposition."

"Maybe I can stake you, or go into business with you."

"Would you do that for us?"

"For you, yes."

"I'll talk it over with Maggie. See how she feels about it." Mountain would love to go into business with this Castle Man and do something that he really loved.

"Good. Discuss it with Maggie and get back to me."

John had not gotten it straight in his mind how he would approach Mountain with what he had seen and heard the previous night.

"Mountain, do you believe in ghosts?"

"Spirits maybe, but I'm not sure about ghosts. I believe spirits are around us all the time. Ghosts, I have been told, have something to settle on earth before going to their final home with God."

"Can you do an exorcism, Mountain?"

"What the hell are you talking about?"

"The bloody Castle is haunted!!" John almost shouted.

Mountain looked at John and chuckled, then realized that John was dead serious. "Why do you think it is haunted?"

"I see lights floating through The Castle. I hear moans and screams. And I bet you that sometime this morning, the police will come driving down that path to investigate complaints about the screams of a child."

"You have been working too hard, John."

"It's not just in *my* mind, Mountain. Carol saw it too. Sutter saw it as well; I saw him react to it. I wish he could talk. One night Carol and I were sitting in the car in the driveway and we saw the same thing that I saw last night. I also heard the moans and screams of a child."

"Maybe the light was the aurora borealis?"

"What the hell is that?" John asked.

"The Northern Lights—they appear over the North Pole or something like that."

"I don't know what the hell you are talking about Mountain, but these are real lights and real screams."

"John, I don't know what to tell you. And what makes you think I could do an exorcism?"

"You studied to be a priest once, didn't you?"

"Yeah, but that doesn't mean I can do what you are asking."

"At least spend the night, Mountain."

"John, this is so sudden."

"Please, Mountain!!! I need you to see what I am seeing, so that I know I'm not crazy."

Just then a police car came rolling down the drive. Mountain remembered John mentioning that a police car would be coming down the driveway sometime that day. It was then he knew there was some validity to what John had said.

Sure enough, the police had come to investigate strange sounds coming from the property. After receiving no information from John, they left, and Mountain said "Okay, okay, I'll spend the night—but I *don't* believe in ghosts."

"Mountain, I love you."

With a twinkle in his eyes, Mountain said, "You won't take advantage of me, will you?"

"The size of you! NO!"

"Pity!"

They bantered back and forth like this for most of the day. Mountain was easy to be with. John was glad to have him around. Mountain was truly a gentle giant.

They had decided that when it got dark they would sit outside the guesthouse and just watch for movement in The Castle.

Mountain was sure that they were both wasting their time.

CHAPTER THIRTY-TWO

At midnight they settled themselves in comfortable chairs just outside the guesthouse and just waited for something to happen. Midnight seemed to be a good and bewitching hour to begin the watch. It was a dark and moonless night. They could hardly see one another, even though they were only a few feet apart.

"I'm glad the mosquitoes aren't out," offered Mountain to break the silence.

"Sssshh!"

Then after awhile, "My feet are getting cold. How long do you want to sit here, John?"

"Sssssh!"

Time was passing very slowly for Mountain. "I'm getting mighty sleepy, John. It's well past my bed time."

"MOUNTAIN!"

"Okay, Okay."

John was just about ready to give up for the night. He was tired, achy and ready to go to sleep as well. Before he could say anything to Mountain, it happened!

John saw the light first. It was going from bedroom to bedroom and then down a stairway.

John tried to peek at Mountain to see if he saw it as well.

"I see it," Mountain whispered with a slight bit of fear in his voice.

The light continued through the living room, then the dining room, then the kitchen.

"What do you think it is, Mountain?" John whispered.

"Hell if I know," Mountain responded in a hoarse whisper. He did not want to draw the light's attention towards them.

Then the light came through the stone exterior and headed toward the back woods. Suddenly, it stopped. It then turned, and headed very, very slowly towards John and Mountain.

John and Mountain could not believe their eyes. They just stared at the light as it slowly, very slowly, floated towards them. They sat watching the light as if they were paralyzed.

John spoke first. "Mountain, on the count of three!!"

When John hit "three," they rose quickly, knocking over their chairs, and ran like hell to the front door of the guesthouse. They were crashing and falling into one another as they tried to enter the guesthouse door at the same time.

"You first!" yelled Mountain, as he shoved John in the door and followed with a crash.

"LOCK THE BLOODY DOOR," yelled John, again totally forgetting the fact that the light could float through the door if it was so inclined.

Mountain locked the door.

They backed up against the wall waiting for the "Thing" to come through to them. They believed that the end was near. They believed that the "Thing" was going to hurt them. They did not know who the hell this "ghost" was! John was getting ready to say a "Hail Mary" and he was wracking his brain to also remember the prayers that his Jewish and Buddhist friends use to say. He was taking no chances—he would pray to every God he could think of.

Mountain was ready to fall on his knees and say an Act of Contrition. But nothing happened! The light did not come after them! They remained where they stood for a long while. They could not stop shaking.

When it seemed safe, John crept over to the window, he reported that all seemed quiet—the light seemed to have disappeared.

"John!" whispered Mountain.

"What!" answered John, also in a whisper.

"Will you look at my pants and see if I need a change of clothes?"

"Mountain, I may have shit my pants as well. But to be honest, I was scared shitless."

They both fell on the couch with a nervous laughter. They laughed for a long time. But it was not a joyous laugh.

"Believe me now, Mountain?"

"Yep! I'm a believer!"

"What should I do?"

"Hell if I know!"

"You're the priest!"

"Almost! Remember?"

"Do you think it meant to do us harm?"

"I don't think so. When we ran, it disappeared. It was as if it were trying to tell us something. It seemed like it wanted to lead us somewhere!"

"Maybe next time we should follow it."

"I may be big, but I'm not stupid. I'm not following any ghost anywhere."

"Please Mountain, stay again tonight. I need a witness so I don't think I'm going out of my mind."

"My wife will think we're having an affair."

John laughed. "Maybe we should have her stay as well."

"To protect us?"

"Maybe! As a matter of fact, YES!"

Somehow, John was able to find humor in every situation, something he learned on the job as a police officer. Perhaps that is what kept him sane—even with a contract out on his life, and owning a Castle complete with ghosts.

"You know, John, I wasn't really scared," Mountain said looking to see if John believed him.

"Me either," John responded facetiously.

They both laughed heartily knowing that each of them were liars and they had been scared out of their wits.

"I never saw you move so fast, Mountain."

"In the face of danger I am known as twinkle toes."

And so the banter went on to cover the fact that both had seen something otherworldly and could not find an explanation for it.

Again that night, John had weird dreams. But he realized that the ghost had taken his mind, at least for the moment, off of the Perez Brothers and he was thankful for that.

CHAPTER THIRTY-THREE

They talked Maggie into staying with them the next night to witness the apparition.

She was excited. She was not scared. Not one bit. She was interested in the after-life and everything spiritual. Mountain thought that Maggie was a psychic. Maggie was made for Mountain. They were sweet together. She could bully him when needed and Mountain listened. "No use fighting Maggie," he would say.

Maggie had the sweetest singing voice. John felt she could have gone professional, what with her voice and her looks. Curly, flowing dark hair and dressed simply in dresses that she herself had made and in which she felt comfortable. John believed she could have become a famous country singer.

That following night they set out three chairs. They were eating Maggie's cookies and drinking gallons of coffee to keep them awake.

Soon, all the cookies were gone, and still no light.

"Maybe they don't like you, Maggie," Mountain teased.

Maggie just smiled and continued to look straight ahead for any sign of a light.

John and Mountain were nodding off and wearying of the lookout. Maggie was quietly humming one of her favorite songs.

"Boys, BOYS!" she said as she shook them awake.

They brought themselves awake immediately and looked at The Castle.

The light was going back and forth, back and forth. It always seemed to follow the same path.

"She is looking for something," offered Maggie.

"How do you know it is a female?" they asked in unison.

"The measure of her walk," answered Maggie.

"She is determined to find something."

Finally the light came through the stonewall and stood still for a few seconds, as if it were looking around and deciding what to do next.

The Strange Valley

The light suddenly started towards Maggie, John and Mountain. John and Mountain stiffened and were ready for the count of "three" again. Maggie put her arms out against their chests to keep them in their chairs. She did not want the light to be spooked—if a ghost *could* be spooked! They would later laugh at the silliness of the thought.

The light continued in its motion towards the three.

"What is it sweetheart? What is it you are looking for? Show me! I can help!" they heard Maggie say to the ghost.

The ghost stopped in its tracks as if it was surprised someone had spoken to it. The light just floated in place as if it was thinking. Then the light floated towards the woods. Then back towards the seated three, then towards the woods again. Then it stopped and lingered again, as if to say, *Well, I thought you said you would help.*

"I'm coming," said Maggie.

The light continued to the woods with Maggie following.

"Maggie, come back!" Mountain whispered.

Maggie gave him the shrug of her hand as she followed the light. When the light hit the woods it faded and was extinguished. As if someone had turned off a light switch.

"All right, Honey, I understand," Maggie said as she witnessed the light fade.

Mountain grabbed Maggie and hugged her when she returned.

"Don't do that again. You scared the hell out of me."

"I didn't see you running after me!" she laughingly replied.

"Was it talking to you?" asked John.

"In her way she is talking to us. She is looking for something in the house and the woods. I think she is giving us a message. I believe she wants to show us something important."

"Are you really a psychic?" asked John.

"Yes, she is," Mountain answered for her. "She knows things before they happen."

"Oh, Mountain, that's not true," Maggie tossed back.

"She is! She told me to go home and see my mother as she was ill, before we knew she was ill."

"That's enough!" Maggie said very softly. And Mountain was quiet.

"What should I do, Maggie?" asked John.

"I believe it is a little girl, from her stride and the height of the light. She is a gentle spirit, so don't be afraid. Talk to her! She likes that."

"What do you think she is trying to tell me?"

"You know the history of The Castle better than I do, what do you think she is trying to tell you?"

"Did you tell Maggie the history of The Castle, Mountain?"

Mountain shook his head no.

"The community thinks The Captain murdered his parents and siblings, and possibly many others. He also abused girls and boys from the neighborhood."

"Was it proven that he committed these crimes?" asked Maggie in horror.

"No. All these people went missing and no one ever found them. But I have spoken to someone who was abused by The Captain."

"So there is no proof that he killed anyone?"

John almost told them about the bone that the dog had found, but he could not bring himself to do it; not yet.

As John lay in bed that night, he was thankful that Mountain and Maggie had also seen the light, and that he was not going crazy!

CHAPTER THIRTY-FOUR

John was all set to sit out the next night and chat with the ghost with Mountain and Maggie, but the phone call from his father sent chills through his body.

"They got to Grandpa MacGregor!"

"How bad?"

"Come home!"

John went straight to the Presbyterian Hospital. He didn't wait for a doctor's uniform. He was frantic! To think they would go after his old Gramps. These people are animals. He had to stop them, NOW! *I'll kill them with my bare hands if my Gramps dies,* he vowed.

His mother met him in the hall. "How bad is it, Mom?"

"Bad enough."

"What the hell does that mean? Is he going to live?"

"The doctor says he is strong and they think he will be okay after a long recovery."

"I'm going in to see him."

"Grandma is in with him now."

John opened the door slightly and saw the two people he loved most dearly in the world. They had been married for well over fifty years and were devoted to each other.

"You cannee leave me, Ian," John heard his grandmother whisper to her beloved husband. "I cannee live without ye. Remember what we promised one another. When we go, we go together. You cannee break your promise. Don't break my heart, Ian. You are my love. You are my heart."

John could hardly contain himself. The tears started streaming down his cheeks and he silently sobbed. He had tried to enter the room quietly but his grandmother had heard him and rose to greet him.

"Can I talk to him alone, Grandma?"

"Aye, ye can," and she wiped away his tears as she had so often done when he was a child. She kissed his cheek and quietly left the room.

John just stood at the foot of the bed and stared at his Gramps' bruised and battered body. Then he sat by the side of the bed and held his grandfather's hand.

"Gramps, I have never seen you looking better," John said, hoping to get a rise out of the old man.

Gramps' eyes slowly opened. John saw recognition in those eyes.

Grandpa MacGregor was trying to say something but he could not get it out, he was too weak.

"What is it, Gramps?" and John put his ear to Gramps' mouth. He felt that perhaps his grandfather was going to tell him that he loved him and that he would be all right.

"Kill the bloody bastards!" Gramps whispered with all the strength that he had remaining in his body.

John stood up with hope in his heart. He now knew his grandfather would be all right. The old Scot still had a lot of fight left in him.

"We need security outside this door," he said to no one in particular as he exited the room. He called the police station and they sent two men right out. One policeman patrolled the front of the hospital and one patrolled outside the hospital room.

"Where did they get Grandpa?" John asked his mother.

"He was going to his Scottish Clan meeting and they got him when he got off the bus," John's mother answered.

"So they know where *they* live and that you are staying there?"

"I guess so."

"I'll get a hotel for you and Grandma."

"No son—I'm tired of running."

John called the police station again and got a man for outside the MacGregor house. John's father agreed to stay in the MacGregor house as well. As his father put it, "I'll stay, only to watch over your mother and grandmother! I'm not afraid of those punks."

Later that evening John rode past his house in the Sunset District and it looked secure enough. The alarm had not gone off. He decided not to go in. *They probably have a bomb set to go off when I open the front door.*

He next called Susan Wong and told her about his Gramps.

"Come over, John."

CHAPTER THIRTY-FIVE

When he entered Susan's apartment, she went to him and hugged him, and he openly cried.

"They hurt my mother, my old gramps and Cal" he sobbed.

"I know. I know," she soothingly responded.

"I'm going to kill them all!"

"Come sit down, John—and let's talk." She took his hand and led him into the living room.

"Susan, I need your help."

"You've got it."

"How is Calvin?"

"He is coming along. But we have not spread the news that he can now communicate with us."

"He's talking?!" he asked incredulously.

Susan nodded.

"Why didn't you call me?"

"I didn't want to take the chance that the Perez Brothers could discover that I knew where you were."

"I've got to see him. I have an idea of how to stop all of this. I've given it a lot of thought and I think I have come up with a solution."

"We will go and see him after you have rested. By the way, you still look awful."

"Sue, have you seen my Gramps?" he asked sadly.

"Yes, this morning. He's my Gramps, too!"

Susan firmly massaged his back, his taut muscles relaxing as she worked.

"I have missed that, Sue."

"I have missed doing it for you. Now go get some sleep. You are not doing anyone any good by driving yourself into exhaustion."

John took Susan's advice, went to her bedroom, collapsed on her bed, and slept soundly for hours. When he woke, it was dark outside, but still quite early in the evening. Susan was in the room puttering around and trying to be very quiet.

"Damn it!" John said suddenly.

"What?" she asked nervously, thinking there was something wrong.

"I still have my clothes on!"

"Easily remedied," then she jumped on the bed and started to tear off his clothes.

"I'm only kidding," he laughed.

"I'm not," and she kissed him while unbuttoning his shirt.

At the same time, John was pulling her blouse over her head and removing her bra. He took both of her breasts into his hands and lovingly massaged them. She got up and removed his pants and underwear. She forgot his shoes.

"Am I to die with my boots on?"

She laughed and went back to the shoes and then removed her skirt.

"You're not wearing underwear."

"I was expecting you."

John drew her on top of him and just rubbed her from top to bottom. "I love the feel of you, Sue!"

Susan explored John's body as well. She could feel that he was ready for her but she wanted more of his gentle foreplay, which she adored.

She loved his kisses that were so gentle and exploring. She loved his touch as he explored every part of her body. John knew where and how to touch her to give her pleasure.

Susan told John what she wanted and he obliged. He enjoyed her tall thin body. She moved around him like a cat, so agile!

Susan was almost as frantic with passion as he was. "What else can I do for you, Susan?" he asked with a raspy voice.

She gently guided him into her waiting body. They came together as one. Gently moving at first and then in frenzy as the ecstasy flowed in them both. When it was over, he gently kissed her forehead and rolled over in a heap of fulfillment.

"Susan, where were you for the last few years?"

"I got some help."

"From whom?" he laughed. "Who taught you all that?"

"I went to a sex therapist. She helped me deal with a few things that were troubling me."

"You did?" John could hardly believe it.

"Yes. I wasn't going to tell you. Do you think it helped?" she asked hopefully.

"It sure did!"

Susan reached over and turned John's head gently towards her. "Is that why you left, John, because of the sex?"

John rolled onto his back, thought a moment. "I don't know why I left, Sue. I guess I needed some time apart. I don't think it was the sex. I was happy. I didn't know any better. I always thought sex was just sex. But what you do now is spectacular."

"Will it bring you back?"

"I need a lot of time to settle my life and situation, Sue. But don't give up on me."

"I won't." Susan got out of bed, walked around to the other side, knelt down and looked John straight in the eyes. "But don't expect me to wait forever. And don't expect *this* every time. That was just a taste. If you want more you will have to marry me."

He tenderly caressed her cheek. "Then I had better get more while I can."

To his surprise, she responded. They started all over again; when it was over he was spent. They both contentedly fell asleep, when he woke it was daylight.

"And you can cook, too!" he said as he ate the bacon and eggs she made for him. "What a beautiful view," he said as he looked out at the ocean view from Susan's condo window.

"I thought you meant me!" she said laughing.

"You too," he added, bringing her down on his lap and kissing her gently.

She got up and sat on the chair opposite John and asked seriously, "Okay, what is your plan?"

"First, let's go and see Calvin. I'll explain it to you both at the same time. We have to have a strategy to pull my plan off. One more hour of great sex before we go?" said John, enticingly.

She took his hand and drew him toward the bedroom. "Give me that therapist's number," John laughed. "I want to send her flowers!"

They made love—then fell asleep in each other's arms.

It was the soundest and easiest sleep that John had had in a very long time. He felt safe in Susan's arms.

CHAPTER THIRTY-SIX

When they got to the hospital, John filled Susan and Cal in on his plan, told them where he was now living and why he was spending so much time away from San Francisco.

He told them about Carol. John could see the hurt in Susan's eyes, but she said nothing. He supposed that she had decided that now was not the time to make a fuss over the situation, but her silence made him feel very uncomfortable.

When they left Cal's room, Susan curtly told John that she would keep in touch and headed for the elevator. John went after her, grasping her arm once he had caught up with her.

"Hey, I'm going to need your help today—we've got some reconnaissance to do."

The elevator sounded its arrival tone, and as the doors opened, Susan wrenched her arm free, and without a word walked into the elevator.

"Susan," John began, standing in front of the elevator. He wanted to say something about his feelings for her, but didn't know how.

Susan didn't give him the chance—she quickly found and stabbed at the "door close" button on the control panel, and was gone.

John spent the rest of the day in his truck with his camera, fighting city traffic as he went around town getting the pictures he thought he would need to implement his plan. After a few hours, he took a coffee break to stretch his legs a bit—he hoped the caffeine in a good, strong cup of black coffee would get him through the rest of the afternoon.

He sat down at one of the sidewalk tables of his favorite coffee shop, the heat of the piping hot coffee penetrating through the layers of the paper cup, almost burning his hand. He couldn't get the image of Susan's face, as the elevator doors closed in front of her, out of his mind. He thought that he was being honorable by playing it straight with her, that they were all mature enough to deal with the situation. *And maybe I'm just a totally oblivious asshole.*

He needed Carol's help to pull off his plan, now was as good a time as any to get a hold of her. Still feeling guilty about Susan, John dialed Carol's cell phone.

"Well, hello stranger!"

"Carol, can we meet today?"

"When?"

"Now!"

"What's the rush?"

"I have some serious things to discuss with you."

"Oh, a marriage proposal I guess," she said facetiously.

"Not yet," he replied, which gave her hope that he *might* ask her *someday*.

"Where are you now?" he asked.

"The courthouse."

"Can you leave for a little while?"

"I think so. Want to meet at my condo in Redwood City?"

John did not want to put her in any danger, but he needed her help. Vowing to himself to be as careful as possible, he agreed.

He followed her directions very carefully and found her condo without any problems.

Carol greeted him with a big, wet kiss. "I have missed you, my friend."

He returned the kiss and said, "I have missed you too." He had to admit to himself that at this moment he wasn't sure whether he missed her personally or the sex.

"You sounded a little frantic on the phone, John. What's up?"

"Do you have some wine?" John asked. He suddenly needed some reinforcement, and a little time to get up the nerve to ask Carol for the information that he desperately needed.

"I sure do. Sit down and I'll get some. White or red?"

"Whatever you have open."

John sat down on her couch, accepted the glass of wine and began to compliment her on her condo. She abruptly interrupted him. "You didn't come all this way for small talk, John. Get to the point. I have to get back to work," she demanded very curtly.

John raised his glass, clinked *her* wine glass, looked her straight in the eye, and started, "My name is John Hurley. I live in San Francisco. I have a home there. I spent twenty years as a policeman and detective with the SFPD. My last case was the Perez case. I was the one that helped to put him away, for life. He is now threatening my family, and he has put a contract out on my life. His brothers almost killed my old partner, beat up my mother and almost killed my grandfather. I need your help to put a stop to the madness."

Carol plopped down on her sofa, dumbfounded, and confused. All that information was too much to absorb all at once. Finally, after a long pause, she said "Perez is in jail. How can he hurt your family?"

"My partner recognized his brothers as the attackers who almost killed him. After showing the photos to my grandfather, he identified them as well."

"If your roots are in San Francisco, then why did you buy The Castle?"

"I always wanted a getaway home and at this time it served two purposes. I am rebuilding a home which I always wanted to do. Secondly, it gave me a hiding place until all of the Perez threats blew over. But they are not going to blow over. I need to end it, and I need to end it now!"

"Well, at least you're not a murderer. Thank God for that," she finally said with a sigh. There was so much she did not understand. She would need time to absorb everything that John had just told her.

"I might be, if you don't help me."

"How can *I* help?" Carol could not imagine what help she could be to John.

"Your office handled the Perez case, didn't it?"

"Yes, we did."

"I need to find Perez's mother. I know she lives in San Francisco, I have searched all over town—I can't find her. She is not listed in the telephone book—she is not listed anywhere! I know you must have her telephone number and her address, since you handled the Perez case."

"No way!!!" she almost screamed, "and I resent being used like this." *Perhaps he had always just been using her*, she thought. The information he wanted was privileged, her firm had wanted to protect Mrs. Perez by keeping her address confidential. There were lots of people that hated her son and would want revenge.

"Carol, I won't hurt her—I just want to talk to her."

"I would be disbarred if I told you where to find her."

"Does she live in the Bay Area?" he probed.

"She is a sweet old lady," was all Carol could think to say.

"And she doesn't need to lose any more sons," John added.

"What are you planning to do?" she asked angrily.

"I don't want to get you involved. Just tell me where she lives."

"I CAN'T!"

John took out his pistol and made sure that Carol saw that there were bullets in it.

"Are you willing to shoot me for the information?" she said, not believing what she was seeing.

John turned towards Carol and said, "I will shoot anyone I have to, to get the information I need." He had shown the gun to Carol to show her he meant business. He started slowly towards the door, hoping Carol would call him back.

"She lives locally," Carol spat at him. She did not want him to hurt *anyone* to get the information he needed. From the look on his face, God knows if he would go after one of the other lawyers in her firm to find Mrs. Perez.

John walked around the room, saw Carol's Blackberry on a desk. "Is it listed in that?" John said, pointing to it with the gun.

Carol glared back at him, confirming his suspicions.

"So you have what I need, and you won't help me—or my family."

"John, would your family want me to throw away my career? Would they want me to be publicly disgraced or go to *jail?* I have a code of ethics to live with, just as you do."

John headed back to the door, opened it and waved goodbye with the hand that held the gun, just for effect. It was a last ditch effort to get that phone number that he wanted—but it gained no response from Carol.

He was down the hall and ringing for the elevator when Carol's head popped out from behind her door. "Come back."

He came back into the apartment; Carol closed the door quickly behind him, then backed him up against it.

"Do you promise not to hurt her?" she hissed, getting right up into his face.

"I won't hurt her, I promise."

"You promise not to frighten her?"

"Carol, I may have to get her good and frightened to get her help. Without her help she will lose two more sons. I will be as gentle as I can be in this situation; that much I can promise you."

Carol backed away and went into the living room. She went to her desk and picked up her Blackberry, paused for a moment, then turned it on. Thumbing in her password, she pulled up the entry for Mrs. Perez, then placed the Blackberry back on the desk. "Do not take the Blackberry outside this room. Write the information down. Then leave." Carol went to her bedroom, and closed and locked the door behind her.

John went to the bedroom door, raised his hand to knock, then paused as he thought better of it. He picked up Carol's Blackberry, saw the entry for Angelica Perez, scribbled the information that was on the screen onto the back of a business card he had in his pocket, and left.

CHAPTER THIRTY-SEVEN

John sat outside Angelica Perez's house in Crocker Amazon, all day long. Mrs. Perez finally came out to get her newspaper and that was all. No one else came in or out. She apparently lived alone. John wondered where her other two sons lived. He did not want to tangle with them at this point of time.

John spent the night with his parents and grandmother in the Richmond house and in the morning he returned to the Perez house.

Around eleven o'clock in the morning Mrs. Perez came out of her house. She was dressed in black with a black kerchief on her head, a black purse on her arm—like a typical old time Italian or Spanish widow.

John recognized her from the trial. He had felt sorry for her at that time. It is not easy for a mother to believe that a son is a murderer. A bad seed! John did not believe the brothers were as bad as Jose Perez, but they were following his orders. They were going to end up in prison as well if they were successful in murdering John or killing one of his friends or relatives—if he didn't kill them first. The brothers had to be stopped! John would retaliate, kill all of them, if his plan did not work. They had hurt his mother, grandfather and friend.

John left his truck and followed Mrs. Perez. She got on the #43 bus. John got on the bus as well and sat in the back of the bus so he could watch her every move. She exited at Geary Street. John exited as well.

Where the hell is she going?

Then she took the #38 Geary bus towards the Financial District; John joined her.

The bus went a very short distance and again she exited. John was taken off guard, but he hurriedly got off just in time. He didn't want to lose sight of her.

Mrs. Perez entered St. Mary's Catholic Church.

She came all this way to go to church? John thought. They had passed many churches on the way to St. Mary's. St. Brendan's, for one, was on the bus route

The Strange Valley

and just a few minutes from her house. He wondered why this church was the one that Mrs. Perez had to attend.

She sat in a pew halfway down the aisle of the large and beautiful church and John sat in back of her. Somehow she did not notice him.

At this time of day there were very few people in the church. The people that were there were engrossed in their prayers and paid no attention to John and Mrs. Perez.

Mrs. Perez had her rosary beads out and was praying very seriously and diligently. She had a lot to pray about!

John was very nervous. He did not want to upset this old lady. Just because she had three miserable sons, it didn't mean that she had to suffer any more than she already had. He too, took the time to say a prayer. Surprisingly, he prayed for Mrs. Perez and for the success of his plan that would save the lives of her sons.

John let Mrs. Perez pray for a long while—he was in no hurry. When he felt the time was right he slowly leaned over, and gently placed his hand on her shoulder. He whispered, "Mrs. Perez, please don't turn around. I am not going to hurt you. I just want to talk to you."

He could feel her back stiffen as she went to turn to see who was behind her. He placed both hands on her shoulders and said again, "Please don't turn around! I am not here to hurt you."

From his firm grip she knew he meant business. But she, as yet, did not know if she was in danger.

She sat up straight and was perfectly still. There was not a whimper out of her. She was a tough old lady!

Finally he said, "I'm the detective that put your son Jose in jail."

Her back stiffened again. She wanted to get up and run, but she did not.

"Jose is trying to get revenge because I testified against him, and in so doing he is involving your other sons. You are going to lose them as well."

"What have they done?" she whispered. She was alarmed at the news that she might lose her other sons as well.

John held the pictures he had taken of Calvin, his mother and his grandfather, in front of her.

She gasped and put her hand to her mouth. She was visibly shaken.

"They did that? Manuel and Eduardo?"

"They did."

"How do you know?" she asked, still unable to grasp what she was hearing.

"That old man is my grandfather. He recognized both of your son's pictures. He can and will identify them in court if he has to. That Chinese man is my old partner. They almost killed him. He will also testify in court as to their guilt."

"They beat up on that old man?"

"They beat him so badly it will take him a long time to recover."

"That policeman is almost unrecognizable!"

"*Your* sons did that to him."

Mrs. Perez sat silent, thinking about what she had just heard and the pictures she had been shown. She remembered Calvin from the courtroom when her son was on trial; she soon placed the voice coming from behind her. She did not have to turn around; she knew what he looked like.

"What do you want from me?" she finally asked after a long silence.

"I need you to help me to get them to stop this madness. Otherwise, I will probably kill them or they will kill me. Either way, you lose your sons."

"What can I do?" she asked in her "old world" accent. She did not want to lose her other sons, she also did not want anyone else to get hurt. "They stopped listening to me many years ago."

John came forward and sat next to her. Here in the pews of St. Mary's Church, John went over the plan that he had in mind with Mrs. Perez.

There were still very few parishioners in the church that time of day, so they had almost total privacy, and Mrs. Perez felt comfortable while surrounded by Jesus and his Disciples. The Church, at this time of her life, gave her comfort and peace of mind. It was all she had left in life.

The Parish Priest noticed Mrs. Perez and the man she was talking to and approached them.

"Mrs. Perez, how are you today? Do you need any help? I see you have been sitting here for a long while." He asked this while looking suspiciously at John.

"I am fine, Father. I am just praying for my sons and that they will find the right path and will live a good and useful life."

"Amen," John whispered.

After hearing about the plan, she did not have to think too long about her answer. She agreed to cooperate, completely. She saw validity in John's plan, and realized she didn't feel afraid anymore.

She had been through quite a lot in her lifetime. She, like John's grandparents, had made the major leap to come from a foreign country to the "New World." She had raised her three boys by herself after her husband had left them high and dry. She had worked hard to support her children and with the help of relatives she was able to keep her house and put food on the table. The widow garments she wore were to save face.

"I always knew Jose was bad," she said, "but I don't want him to turn his young brothers into criminals. They are not like Jose. Jose was always trouble. Since childhood he has given me grief. Perhaps that was one reason Jose's father left us. His brothers were and are influenced by him. They follow him like a God. In their hearts they are good boys. I know, I am their mother, and a mother always knows. I did not want them to go and visit Jose in prison but he ordered them to come and see him. Did you know his given name is really Joseph?" She continued without waiting for an answer. "He has called himself Jose since he was a very young boy because he thought it sounded tough. In our neighborhood he thought it was better to be called Jose than Joseph."

"If the plan works Mrs. Perez, you will have your sons and they will give you many grandchildren."

Mrs. Perez smiled a little. She desperately wanted little grandchildren that she could bounce on her lap and sing little songs to. To just hold and love! Yes, she dearly wanted grandchildren. She knew that Jose would never give her a grandchild. The way things were going, if she did not help change the situation, then her other two sons would not give her grandchildren either. She wanted a little bit of herself to continue, to live on in her grandchildren. A little bit of immortality.

CHAPTER THIRTY-EIGHT

John picked up Mrs. Perez the next morning, and they headed to San Quentin, where Jose was housed. He had borrowed his father's BMW so that Mrs. Perez would be comfortable.

They rode in silence, each of them consumed with their own worries and thoughts.

As they were driving over the Golden Gate Bridge, Mrs. Perez was the first to break the silence.

"I wish they had put Jose on Alcatraz. It is such a pretty place and the prisoners would be surrounded by water and they would have a beautiful view of San Francisco."

John looked quickly down at Alcatraz as he was driving and it did not look as appealing to him as it did to Mrs. Perez.

"The authorities are not interested in making things pleasant for the prisoners, Mrs. Perez. Besides, Alcatraz has not housed prisoners for many years. It is now a National Park and Rangers take care of the island. Thousands of tourists pass through this beautiful city of ours and they like to visit Alcatraz and see how the prisoners of long ago used to live."

The conversation again went silent. They had practiced over and over what she would say to her son when they arrived at San Quentin. They had sat for hours drinking Mrs. Perez's coffee and eating her delicious cakes. They had gone over the scenario that they would carry out when they got to San Quentin and faced Jose Perez. John liked this woman; it was a shame she had a murderous son.

They finally arrived at the prison and they were both nervous. They got out of the car, and as they did, John remembered Carol's fury at him for involving Mrs. Perez. He couldn't be sure that her sons wouldn't retaliate against her once they found out she had cooperated with him. She had willingly placed her life in his hands. Even though he still had the images of the beaten faces of the ones he loved burning in his mind, her fortitude was enough to cause John to reconsider what he would do if the plan failed.

John went to Mrs. Perez and said, "If you don't want to do this, I will understand. I will find another way if you feel you cannot go through with it."

Mrs. Perez straightened her clothes, adjusted the hat she was wearing and stood straight and tall. Looking John straight in the eyes, she said, "I am doing this not only to help *you* but to save my other two boys. If I don't do this, I will lose them all."

"You are right Mrs. Perez, you will lose all three of your sons, because Jose has to be stopped one way or the other. Unfortunately, I would probably have to kill Jose myself to stop this vendetta that he has against my family."

Mrs. Perez was taken aback, but she was a smart woman; she understood what the future would be for her and her sons if the plan did not work. She felt she had no choice, this was the best option. There was no other way!

Mrs. Perez went in to visit Jose first. He was very happy to see his mother—she came often, his brothers came rarely. Other than those three, no one came to visit him.

Who would come to see this murderous bastard? *Much like The Captain,* John thought.

Jose was a tall, muscular man, with long black hair flowing down his back. His eyebrows were so thick they almost covered his evil dark brown eyes—eyes that bore right through you. If you met him in a dark alley, you would immediately run the other way.

There was some small talk between mother and son. The window that was between them was not very clean, but the barrier, today, was welcome. Mrs. Perez knew very well how her son would react today after he received her news. He always had a violent temper.

Each asked the other how they were and she asked him if he was eating well, the ages-old mother's question.

"Are you reading the bible, Jose? It will give you strength and peace of mind."

Jose ignored the question and asked if his brothers were coming up to see him today. He needed to talk to them.

She then, very quickly, took out the pictures that John had taken of his mother, grandfather and friend and held them up to the window for Jose to see.

"Mama! What's that?" Jose's eyes were beginning to bug out in incredulity! What was his mother up to? This was not like her. What was she doing with these pictures?

"That's what your brothers did, Jose! What you told them to do!" Her voice quivered, but she did not cry. Today she would be strong—she would not cry!

"No, Mama!" Jose protested.

"YES!" she yelled in frustration. "Your brothers were recognized. They will be prosecuted. I will lose them too! I have lost you—I cannot bear to lose another son. You must make them stop and you must remove the contract that is on the life of that cop."

"No, Mama!" Jose again protested firmly. He couldn't understand where his mother had gotten all that information. If his brothers had ratted on him, he would have the shit beaten out of them.

"YES, JOSE! You *must* make them stop."

Jose slumped back into his chair and sat there, stunned. For once he was at a loss for words. This was not like his mother. She was usually so gentle, supportive, loving and kind. He could not understand why she was acting so strange.

His mother quickly got up and left, as planned.

Jose just sat there, watching as his mother left the room. He could not believe what he was seeing.

"MAMA, please come back," he begged.

Mrs. Perez hurriedly walked away without a glance back at her son. She was playing her part very well.

Her heart was broken, but she would play her part as well as she could.

"You have another visitor," announced the guard, interrupting Jose's pleas for his mother to return.

"Who?" he asked, hoping it was one of his brothers who had come to see him! He would curse them out for being so sloppy in carrying out his orders and ratting on him.

"JOHN HURLEY!" was the reply from John as he sat down hard and faced his nemesis.

"GET THE HELL OUT OF HERE!" Jose shouted as he rose, crashing his chair to the floor.

"LISTEN TO ME, JOSE!" John said loudly and forcefully. "You have a sweet mother! I am telling you right here and now, from this day forward, if just one little hair on my family's head is hurt because of you and your brothers, I WILL KILL YOUR MOTHER!" John shouted the last five words. He did not care who heard. He had to make sure that Jose understood the threat.

Jose's face was contorted in anger and rage.

"I SWEAR, I WILL DO IT!" John yelled, reinforcing his position.

John did not give Jose time to respond.

"Back off now, and *never bother me or my family again*, I will not prosecute your brothers for the attacks on my family and friend."

"YOU CAN'T PROVE THAT MY BROTHERS DID IT!" Jose shouted in a rage and started to pound on the glass wall that separated them. He pounded the glass with his fists, even with his hands in handcuffs—and then with his head. The guards rushed over to restrain him, but John motioned for them to stay back.

"Calvin Wong is conscious and talking, and he recognized Manuel and Eduardo, as did my grandfather! Attempted murder—that's what I'll have them prosecuted for, and they will be great company for you, Jose. I'm sure your mother will be very proud to have all of her sons in the same prison at the same time."

Jose's face was now beet red, and if looks could kill, John would be dead!

"It will kill your mother! If *I* don't kill her first!" he added, just for effect.

Jose just stood there in stunned silence. You could almost hear Jose's mind working hard to find a way to break through the barrier between himself and John so that he could throttle that lousy detective.

"The detective, your mother, and the old man survived the beatings?" Jose finally asked with a hiss.

"YES! No thanks to you."

"SHIT! My brothers never could do anything right."

Jose righted his chair and sat down facing John. They sat staring at one another, for what seemed like hours but were really only minutes. Neither of them would blink.

"Do we have a deal?" John finally asked while still staring into Jose's steely, evil eyes.

Jose spat at the visitor's window and again grabbed his chair and threw it at the window that separated him and John Hurley. The guards stopped him from picking up the chair and throwing it at the window again, grabbing Jose's arms and putting a choke hold on him to restrain him. Jose did manage to give the glass window a mighty kick before the guards began to forcefully escort Jose out of the room. The visit was over.

"THE HELL WITH YOU!" he screamed at John as he was being led from the room.

John's heart dropped. He knew it was now all out war. It was going to be "kill or be killed."

He sadly watched as Jose was being led out of the room. The guards were each holding an arm to lead him out. They knew he was trouble. There were always two guards accompanying Jose wherever he had to go.

Suddenly, Jose stopped and shrugged the guards' arms off of him.

He turned sharply and stared at John.

John waited for more expletives and threats. He stood up—straight and tall—and returned Jose's evil stare. He wanted Jose to know that he was now in for the fight of his life and that John was not afraid to carry out his threats.

They stared at each other for again what seemed like eternity. Again neither of them blinked.

"DONE!" is all Jose yelled as he turned to go out the door.

"WE HAVE A DEAL?" shouted John after him.

Jose again stopped at the door, and as John held his breath, Jose nodded his head in assent before he started to exit the room. John saw Jose's head slump to his chest—he knew he was beaten, and by a cop. Word would spread fast—he would pay a heavy price once they returned him to the general population of the prison.

"SAY IT JOSE! SAY THE BLOODY WORDS! DO WE HAVE A DEAL?"

Jose did not move.

John jumped up and left the room, and returned dragging Mrs. Perez by the arm.

Mrs. Perez had thought her part was over. She did not know what to expect, but she was willing to participate until the end.

As John put his arm around her neck and held his gun to her head, he was able to whisper to her—"It's not loaded."

"Do I blow her head off now or later, Jose?"

Jose turned to John and was suddenly panicked at the scene in front of him.

"How did you get that gun in here, you bastard?"

"The guards know me very well, Jose. They didn't even search me when I entered the prison." Inwardly, John hoped that Jose would believe that lie.

Jose could not know that the guards were in on the deal, with the approval of the Warden.

"Make up your mind fast, Jose—I'm sick of the whole situation. My trigger finger is shaking, I would hate for your mother to die before your eyes. It won't be a pretty sight! Believe me, with no hesitation, I WILL BLOW HER HEAD OFF!"

With his steely, evil eyes, he looked at John, then his mother. "WE HAVE A FUCKING DEAL—YOU LOUSY BASTARD!" He then turned quickly to the guards and said, "GET ME THE HELL OUT OF HERE!"

John was relieved and he slumped down quickly in his chair as his knees were suddenly weak. His unloaded gun fell to the floor as his hands went weak as well.

"Is it over, Mr. Hurley? Is it finally over?" Mrs. Perez asked as she picked up John's gun and handed it back to him.

John rose, put his arm around Mrs. Perez' shoulder and as they walked out of the prison he was able to say, "It's over, Mrs. Perez. You don't have to worry any more. Nor do I," he added with a sigh.

As bad as Jose was, John knew that he would keep his word, it was part of the criminal code. Jose didn't want his mother to be killed; he had that *one* saving grace. He had given his word before his mother. Jose also knew that if he did renege on the deal, Hurley could get together a bunch of his cop friends and go "visit a sick friend," which was the cop term for what *he* did from his prison cell to John's family. The cops would find out where his brothers were and beat the living shit out of them, then falsify the evidence to make it look like his brothers attacked the cops first. He knew guys who were found dead after they got this kind of visit, and if the cops were ever brought to trial, the case was *always* ruled a "justifiable homicide."

Jose had gone after a cop, and even worse, a cop's family. That would get him a lot of respect in prison, but meant that there would be police officers who would show no mercy to his relatives on the outside. As far as Jose knew, Hurley could be capable of having Jose and his family killed and get away with it—especially now that his brothers were recognized as the thugs who had beat up John's family and Calvin Wong.

John had promised Carol he wouldn't hurt Mrs. Perez. But Jose did not know that! That was the major reason the plan worked. The one saving grace that Jose had was that he did not want his mother hurt!

"He did agree, didn't he?" Mrs. Perez asked quietly.

"Yes, he did. He loves you."

"You didn't tell me you would point a gun at me."

"I didn't think I would have to go that far—but knowing Jose I knew I had to do something outrageous. I do hope I didn't scare you too much. I'm fortunate the Warden allowed me to have the gun. I had to go through a lot of red tape to do so."

"I guess the end justifies the means. I can endure anything as long as I can save my other two sons."

"You have saved them, Mrs. Perez."

"You won't prosecute Manuel and Eduardo?"

"You make sure they call Jose right away so that they don't do any further damage."

Surprisingly, Mrs. Perez was so grateful that she kissed John on the cheek.

John drove her home, and as he helped her up her front steps, he said as gently as he could, "Jose *was* guilty Mrs. Perez. I *had* to testify against him. He would have killed again."

"I know. I knew it all the time. I was relieved in a way when he was sent to jail. I didn't want him to kill anyone else. Thank you for not seeking the death penalty at the trial."

"After seeing you in court, I could not bear to ask the attorneys to seek death. I knew it would have killed you."

"You would not have really killed me if Jose had not agreed, would you Mr. Hurley?"

"Mrs. Perez, in my darkest hours, I thought I would do anything to protect my family. I often wondered "what if that meant choosing between my family and you and your family?" He paused, in thought, then said, "No, I would not have killed you, but I think I could easily kill your sons or anyone that threatened my family. But before I took such desperate measures, I would have given it very grave thought. I was raised to respect all life."

John paused, then continued. "Many times, during my lifetime, someone very close to me reminded me about the consequences of revenge—so I would think long and hard before I took any action at all."

"I know in my heart that you would *never* kill me. You are too good a man, Mr. Hurley."

"Best compliment I ever had," John said as he turned and bounded down the steps, almost falling, as he had tears in his eyes.

It had been a very tough day and he was exhausted, physically and mentally. But he was relieved. His family and friends would now be safe and Mrs. Perez will not lose her other two sons. Hopefully, she will be able to help them follow the straight and narrow path in life.

He doubted it—he knew from a long police career that the only things that persuaded career criminals were gunshot wounds.

Just visiting that prison was depressing. But in his mind, even prison was too good for Jose!

CHAPTER THIRTY-NINE

Everyone got the good news—Susan, Mom, Dad, Gramps, Grandma, Calvin and even Carol.

Calvin and Gramps said that they should still kill the bastards who had beaten them up. Gramps had more than a few harsh Scottish words to say about "the bastards."

"A deal is a deal," John said, laughing and giving a big sigh of relief that the ordeal was over.

John then went to his house in the Sunset District with great trepidation. He did not want anything to happen now, and *someone* may not have gotten the word. He wouldn't be the first cop whose house had a "gas leak," he did not want to be blown to bits in a booby-trapped living room.

The alarm system was not working. The phone lines and power had been cut. The back door was broken in and the place was a bloody mess. The bastards had knocked over every piece of furniture in the house. Every picture on the wall had been knocked down and smashed to little bits, every piece of clothing from his closets was cut into pieces. The only thing that was missing was a horse's head in his bed!

He stood back and took in the whole picture of the damage and the hate that had gone into ruining everything in the house, and surprisingly, he started to laugh.

That's okay, he thought. *I can put it all back together. I never liked those clothes anyway. I needed new furniture as well. And besides, IT IS OVER!*

He sat down where he stood and started to cry hysterically with relief. The tears surprised him. It wasn't that he was mad or afraid—he was just glad that it was over. His family and friend were now safe. And an old lady had saved two of her sons.

He also knew that he would never again let himself be paralyzed by fear. From this day forward, he would not hide, he would not run—he would face danger and threats head on.

All of a sudden, life was good and easy again—he could finally relax his guard. Then he thought of how he had left it with Carol. She had not returned his recent phone calls. He had to admit he had not been honest or fair with her and she had every right to be mad at him.

Then, of course, there was The Castle and all of its mysteries! He had to take care of that next!

CHAPTER FORTY

John woke that next morning not knowing where he was. Looking around the room he realized he was in his grandparents' home. He looked around at the walls and saw pictures of himself that were taken at special events during his lifetime. First communion, confirmation, and high school graduation! Two pictures that must have been his grandparents' favorites were framed in gold. They were of John in his police uniform, and then as a detective. His whole life was right there before his eyes. This is what his grandparents woke up to every day. Before he was able to get too cocky he saw that his cousins' pictures were also displayed all over the walls. All the MacGregor cousins! It brought back a lot of good memories. Those cousins were like his siblings. Since he was an only child he always enjoyed his time with his fun loving, rough cousins.

John rose, put on his pants and sauntered into the kitchen, yawning and scratching his unruly, messed up hair.

"Oh, it's my favorite, Grandma—oatmeal!"

"It's called porridge" she answered curtly.

"Beautiful day Granny, isn't it?"

"Fog is in!"

"We're going to bring Gramps home from the hospital today, right Granny?"

"I know that! Do you think I'm daft?"

"Do you think he will be able to make the stairs?"

"He's no crippled."

"Grandma, why are you so cross with me?" John was not used to his granny acting this way towards him. She usually had a big hug and kiss for him—followed by kind words.

Grandma MacGregor was facing the sink and John saw her reach for her hankie and saw her shoulders shake.

John sprang up from his chair and rushed to the side of his beloved granny. With his arms around her he said very softly, "Granny, what's the matter?"

She did not turn around. John just stood behind her and hugged her tight, not knowing what else to do.

Finally, she whispered, "We almost lost him, Johnny."

John continued to hold his grandmother tightly and kissed the back of her head. He nestled his face in her lovely, soft white hair. It bothered him to see her so upset.

"You cannee kill a grand old Scot like Gramps," said John trying to lighten the situation.

Grandma turned quickly and faced her grandson. "Aye, you can—if you beat him within an inch of his life."

"Granny, he will be as good as new," were the only comforting words he could think of to say.

"Och, aye—I know." She looked at her favorite grandson and saw how upset she had made him. "I'm no mad at you, Johnny."

"Och, aye—I know that." John always fell back into a Scottish brogue when he was with his grandparents. He had grown up around them and he just fell into the brogue when he was with them, or when he was mad or excited.

"I'm going to get dressed," announced Granny as she gently pushed him aside. She did not want him to see that tears were still flowing from her old eyes.

"It's early, Granny. I'm going for a walk. Is that okay with you?" He didn't want to leave his Granny, if she needed him.

"Don't get lost," she just *had* to add, fully knowing that he knew the area like the back of his hand.

"I'll try not to," he laughingly threw over his shoulder as he bounced down the stairs.

John did know the area like the back of his hand. He half grew up there. Twenty-fourth and Lake! He walked through Sea Cliff and started to run as he entered the Presidio. He ran until he could run no more. Gasping for breath, he sat at the edge of a cliff and just gazed out at the ocean.

He had often thought he should have been a sailor, since he loved the ocean so much.

As he sat and enjoyed the scenery, a large cargo ship passed by. Where was that ship going—Hong Kong, Shanghai, Japan, Australia? Wherever it was going, John wanted to go with that ship. What a glorious sight—the ship seemed to be taken by the arm by the tugs that were gently guiding it out to sea.

Then the thought of The Captain came into his mind. *I won't think of that right now,* he thought and went back to enjoying the nature around him. "There must be a God in heaven to have made such beauty," he said out loud as he gazed at the glorious ocean and the eucalyptus trees that surrounded him.

But what kind of God made The Captain?

It was obvious to him that until the situation in Elk Horn and The Castle was straightened out he would have no real peace within himself. He had solved one problem and now he had to solve the other.

As he jogged back to his grandparents' house, he was acutely aware that only half of his problems had been solved. There was still a big mystery up in Elk Horn that had to be solved so that he could have total peace of mind.

It would be then and only then that he would be totally free!

CHAPTER FORTY-ONE

As Grandma was filling out release papers at the hospital, John headed up to Grandpa's room to help him dress. He knew he was near Gramps' room when he heard his voice in song. "Oh, you cannee throw your Granny off the bus." John started to laugh as he had heard that song many times over the years.

Of course the nurses were egging him on by laughing and clapping.

"That's enough, Gramps. We have to get you dressed and home."

"Och, you're jealous Johnny," Gramps said with a twinkle in his eyes.

"Och, that I am," John said as he winked at the nurses.

It was obvious that Gramps was weak. He was wheeled out in a wheel chair and John had a bit of a time getting him into the car.

"Ian, move your bloody feet and get into the car," was Grandma's command. Ian did.

As Grandma went to sit in the car she whispered to John, "We cannee treat him like an invalid. He will become one if we do."

John was getting a different view of his grandmother. Of course she was sweet, loving and gentle. But she was also tough. She had to be to live with Gramps.

John's parents were waiting at the house on Lake Street for Gramps to arrive.

"We thought he was coming home in an ambulance," said John's mother as the car arrived at the house. She was genuinely surprised that her father had come home in a car instead of an ambulance as planned. She knew how weak he was!

"He would have no part of it," John responded while shaking his head.

"Dad, why didn't you let them bring you home in an ambulance?" Laurie asked her dad.

"Laurie, I'll no let the neighbors see me coming home in a death bus."

The Strange Valley

They all just shook their heads and shrugged their shoulders. That was Gramps, and he would never change.

The Marina style house that Gramps and Grandma lived in meant that there was a flight of stairs to climb to get to the living quarters. Granny went up first to open all the doors and to prepare the way for Gramps.

Gramps stood at the foot of the stairs and just looked up. He never thought it was a long climb before, but he did today. Finally he turned to John, who was going to walk behind his grandfather should he falter. "I'm no up to it, Johnny."

John did not respond, he just acted. "Put your arms around my shoulder, Gramps. I'll carry you up."

Surprisingly, Gramps did not resist. "I've carried *you* up these stairs many a time, Johnny."

"That's right, Gramps. Now it's my turn."

John was surprised at how light Gramps was. It was hardly an effort to carry his grandfather. He had carried heavier things at The Castle so he was in great shape.

When John laid his grandfather in his bed, John thought he would hear a thank you from his grandpa.

He had to laugh when the only thing his gramps said was, "Johnny, do you think the neighbors saw?" John reassured him no one did.

As John and his family sat down to a wee cup of tea and scones, John told them he had things to do before going up country again. He was going to stay with his grandparents for a few days and wait until his grandfather was on his feet. His mother was happy that she would finally be able to go home to her own home and not be afraid that she would be attacked.

The previous night, John and his dad had gone to John's house to figure out what had to be done to repair it and what had to be done immediately. He was leaving the whole project in his dad's hands. Michael Hurley was delighted to have a project. To have a reason to get up in the morning!

John was surprised at how much he had missed a good cup of tea. There was always a pot brewing in the MacGregor house. They were all "tea Jennies" as his grandmother would often say.

As he was sipping his cup of tea, John asked his mother, "Mom, where are all the MacGregors?" meaning his cousins.

"You would think they would be here, wouldn't you?"

"They should have been."

"John, I am not going to start a feud over it."

Unbeknownst to everyone John then called his cousins and gave them hell. They were quite contrite. Some said they didn't even know Gramps was in the hospital. Things were left on good terms, but his cousins got the message. His two MacGregor uncles, his mother's brothers, had passed away years ago and although he liked his aunts, they were not blood. John would later be told that the cousins later visited so frequently that they were becoming a pain in the neck to gramps.

Gramps was heard to say, "If they think they are getting my money, they are crazy."

The cousins did not need Gramps' money—they were all doctors and lawyers—wealthy in their own right. They were just glad to see their old grandpa. "The old Bugger" they would say.

CHAPTER FORTY-TWO

Seeing Calvin Wong was very difficult. He was still on crutches. John saw him hobbling down the hospital hallway towards him.

When he neared his friend he threw out, "If you were Irish you wouldn't need those crutches."

"If I were Irish, my father would have drowned me at birth."

"How are you coming along, Cal?"

"Slow, but sure."

"I'm really sorry that this happened to you."

"So am I."

"When do you think you can leave the hospital?"

"I think within the week."

"Are you going back to work?"

"I'll be on disability for a while."

"But will you go back?"

"I wasn't as smart as you, John. I did not prepare for a life after the police force. You can go on and become a lawyer. All I know how to do is be a detective. I'm not rich like you. I blew it all. So yes, I will have to go back to work."

"I'll let you be my caddy," John joked.

"Good of you John. Very good of you!"

"I hear you got together with Susan."

John looked at Cal's face to see if he knew how "together" he had gotten.

"It was good to spend time with her again."

"Do you think we may still be brothers?"

"We *are* brothers, Cal. I told you that."

"I meant brothers-in-law."

"I have a lot of things to sort out, Cal. I have situations up at my house in Elk Horn."

"Where the hell is Elk Horn?"

"I'll have you up soon, Cal—now that the threat of the Perez Brothers is finally over. And when you come, bring your work clothes."

Cal hesitated, then looked at John very seriously. "John—the contract is off. Officially!"

Calvin had heard this through the scuttlebutt on the streets. It was passed on to him by some of the other police officers who worked the streets of San Francisco. The scuttlebutt was rarely wrong.

As John was leaving he waved at Cal and said, "When you come up to visit me, Cal—ring the doorbell with your elbow."

Cal knew this to mean "come with your arms and hands loaded with gifts, so that you have to ring the doorbell with your elbow." John's grandmother had said that to Cal so often during the years. He had been accepted by John's grandparents. They were like family to him.

Seeing Susan was much harder. He went to see her at the courthouse where she worked. He knew Susan still loved him, she had been working hard to get back together with him and he had hurt her.

Entering the courthouse, he realized that he missed it. He missed the smell, the activity, the rush of humanity going to and fro.

As Susan walked toward John she said, "You miss it, don't you, John?" She recognized the look on his face.

"For the minute, I do. I dare say if I was heavily involved again, I would sicken of it."

"Are you going to take the Bar?" she asked hopefully.

"Not right now."

"Are you going to live in that Castle full time?"

"No. I'll be back and forth."

"You are not going to sell the house here in San Francisco?"

"No. I will never sell that house."

"When are we going to see this Castle you have told us about?" she finally asked, ending the probe.

"I'm still fixing it up and I am working out some issues. But you will be one of the first to be invited up to see it."

"How is your grandfather?" she asked, changing to a more personal issue.

"Cranky."

"How long will you be staying with your grandparents?"

"I will probably be there for a few more days. Gramps is getting stronger and stronger. When he can go to the *john* by himself then I am gone. I love them both dearly but they could drive a sane man crazy."

"My grandparents are the same. They are getting paranoid. They think we are after their money."

John laughed. "It's universal. My grandparents think my cousins are also after their money."

"But they don't think that of you, John?"

"No. I'm golden."

"You mean a lot to them," she said smiling at John.

"And they mean a lot to me. They were like second parents to me. Both of my parents worked and more often than not I was with my grandparents. I love them dearly."

Susan and John sat on a bench while eating a bit of take-out lunch and just sat for a while. They enjoyed soaking up some sun and watching the people of that part of the city going about their day.

As John looked around him, he said, "I miss San Francisco, Sue."

"San Francisco misses you."

"There is not a more beautiful City."

"Some would argue that."

"They would lose the argument."

John gave Sue a goodbye hug and thanked her for the help she gave him while he was taking care of the Perez situation.

"I wish we could say goodbye at my condo," Sue whispered in his ear.

"Susan, you don't have to go to that therapist anymore."

She blushed. "I'm not. But now that I know what I was missing when we were together—I want the chance to make it up to you."

"I'll make sure you get your chance," John joked.

"I'm not joking, John," she threw at him as she walked away. "But I won't wait forever."

As she walked away he was reminded again of how beautiful she was.

He did like her very much. Did the feeling in the pit of his stomach mean that he loved her?

CHAPTER FORTY-THREE

The next morning John woke to the sound of Gramps and Grandma having a conversation at the kitchen table.

"You get here by yourself, Gramps?" John asked while sitting down at the kitchen table.

"Aye! I also peed by myself," Gramps happily announced.

"Good job!" and John clapped as his Granny laughed.

"You can go home now, Johnny. I'm all right."

"Are you sure, Gramps?"

"Aye, I'm sure."

John looked at his granny, and she nodded in assent.

"Just make sure you don't make anyone else mad," his gramps added.

"I'll work hard at that, Gramps."

"When will you be leaving?" they asked their grandson in unison.

"Probably tomorrow morning."

Grandma chimed into the conversation. "Have you seen that girl—the Chink?"

"GRANDMA!"

"What?" she said in surprise.

"You can't say "Chink," Granny!"

Grandma looked at John in surprise. "Is it a bad word?"

"Not a curse word, it's a racial slur."

"But you and Cal say that. I have heard you say it often."

"We were just joking, Grandma."

"So I shouldn't say it?"

"No, Grandma—not a good idea in this town."

Poor Grandma! There was not a mean bone in her body. She would not hurt a soul. John laughed at her innocence and made a mental note to tell Cal and Susan what Grandma had said. He knew they would laugh as he had laughed.

CHAPTER FORTY-FOUR

John's ride back to The Castle was a little different this time. He didn't have to constantly look in the mirror to see if he was followed. Although he did divert from his direct route once or twice just to make sure. It would take time for him to feel completely safe.

He even stopped at a couple of the wineries that dotted the land along the way. The local strawberries were ripe and he bought some for himself and some for Maggie and Mountain.

By the time he finished stopping at every winery and fruit stand in sight, his truck was full and he had to stop for a break—he felt a wee bit tipsy.

One last stop at the supermarket for eggs, bread and milk and he was on the last mile to his Castle.

He stopped first at Mountain's house to get Sutter. He laughed as he rang the doorbell with his elbow, as his hands were full of strawberries and wine.

When Mountain opened the door he laughed at the sight of John with his arms full of goodies.

John looked at his friend for a long time and finally truly introduced himself. "I'm John Hurley, and who might you be?"

"Raymond Roth," was Mountain's reply. He realized that his friend was at last introducing his "real" self. "But you can call me Mountain."

John sat with Maggie and Mountain, having many glasses of wine and telling them why he had been so secretive.

. The strawberries were laid onto one of Maggie's glorious cakes and covered with a big blob of newly made whipped cream.

"Better than sex," said Mountain as he shoveled some of the cake and strawberries into his mouth.

"By far," agreed John.

Maggie slapped the two of them as she filled their glasses with more wine.

After finishing explaining the whole story to Maggie and Mountain, he felt drained after going through it all again.

"Now I know *why* you were so secretive. But I always trusted you. I knew you must have had a good reason to keep your past to yourself—and why you disappeared for days on end. And you say you were a detective?"

"I was one of the best in San Francisco! Although I am sure you would get an argument from many of my fellow policemen."

"I'm sure they would lose the argument," interjected Maggie.

"Thank you, my dear friend," and he gave her a quick kiss on the cheek.

"Have you been to The Castle lately?" John asked.

"No. We were waiting for you to return," said Mountain.

"Let's go back tonight. Let's see if the girl comes to me again," suggested Maggie. She seemed concerned about the girl—the light!

In unison, the men said, "No Way!"

"We must! She needs our help."

"You talk as if she was real, Maggie."

"John, she was real at one time. She needs to go home."

"Where is home?" John asked, really wanting to know where his ghost's home was.

"In God's house!"

"Come over tomorrow night. I need one night of rest and a good night's sleep."

CHAPTER FORTY-FIVE

John was still sleeping in the guesthouse. *I don't want to upset the little girl,* he joked to himself. If the truth be known, he was still scared shitless every time he saw the light.

The next morning he took Sutter out for some exercise. Sutter seemed glad to have room to roam. Mountain's property was much smaller than John's property and the dog had been a little confined.

He let the dog go into the woods to chase a squirrel. John knew the squirrel was too fast for his lumbering St. Bernard.

Sutter was gone for a few minutes and then he came trotting back—with another bone! This one apparently a human forearm; it looked like both *radius* and *ulna*.

"Oh Lord! Show me, Sutter! Come on, boy!" John said as he headed towards the woods and Sutter responded to the thought of play. Sutter led him to the spot. A skull! Then a pelvic bone! Obviously a full body of bones!

John ran back to the house and found a tarp and placed it over the bones. Whether dead or alive, John believed humans had to be treated with dignity.

John could not escape the scene. The bones of the dead body were perfectly placed. Each bone was where it should have been when the body was alive. How could it have lain here all these years without being disturbed? Surely the animals would have disturbed the bones after these many years. Could the little ghost have placed the bones there to have John discover them and to then call the police? Or did someone else place the bones so perfectly? Nothing made sense to John. He didn't understand anything about ghosts and what they could do or not do. He was overwhelmed with confusion. He was tired. He did not want to call the police. At least not now!

CHAPTER FORTY-SIX

Mountain and Maggie came over very late that night. John did not say anything about his recent find as yet. He had to think things out. He had to have a plan of action.

They placed themselves as before. Only this time Maggie sat way out in front of John and Mountain. She knew her husband and John were scared to death of the "little light."

"When she comes to me, I am going to follow. Don't hold me back, and don't come after me," Maggie announced.

They did not have to wait very long. The light again went from room to room as if looking for something. Up to the turrets and back down again. Then it exited through the stonewalls and stopped and looked to the left and to the right. Then it proceeded ever so slowly towards them. Mountain grabbed for John's hand in mock fright. John knew that Mountain was just trying to ease the tension—but he also knew that Mountain didn't like this "little ghost" either.

"Come on, Honey. Don't be afraid." Maggie's voice was gentle and enticing. The light came closer.

The light went to Maggie's hand as if to hold it and it started towards the woods with Maggie in tow.

"Don't follow!" Maggie instructed the men.

Maggie disappeared into the woods. She was gone for quite a while. Mountain was getting very edgy.

Suddenly Maggie came out of the woods.

"She has told me a great deal."

"Does she speak English?" John asked with a smile.

Maggie shot him a look and he shut up.

"We will be back tomorrow night, John," Maggie said assertively, and took Mountain's hand and led him to their truck.

The Strange Valley

John wondered why Maggie had not found the bones that he had discovered earlier in the day.

The next day, John was working on the front lawn and trimming the apple trees that bordered the property.

He was annoyed that he could not find his small shears and his small garden shovel. He was mad at himself because he kept misplacing his tools. He hoped they would eventually show up somewhere in The Castle, or the guesthouse, but he made a promise to himself that he would be more careful—tools were very expensive.

He made himself believe that it was the cheeky squirrel or the big raccoon that had spirited the tools away. Certainly, it was not *his* forgetfulness!

He heard a cat's meow—and when he turned to see where the cat was, he almost fell off the ladder he was standing on.

He saw an elderly woman walking a cat on a leash.

Good Lord! What now? John whispered to himself.

"Hello," said the woman.

"Hi."

"Have you seen my cats?"

"No, I haven't seen any cats on the property."

"They were given to me for my sixteenth birthday and I haven't seen them in a few days."

John could see that this woman had not seen sixteen for many years. He could also see that she was quite senile.

"I will keep a sharp eye out for them and if I see them I will let you know."

"Thank you so much," she said and she headed down the road with her cat on the leash.

As the elderly woman was disappearing from view, a horse's whinny turned him around quickly.

"Carol!"

"In person! Who were you talking to?"

John looked down the road towards the disappearing lady and her cat.

"It was Ms. Pussy," he said cheekily.

"What?"

John almost fell on the ground laughing. He knew he should change the name he had given the woman, but he had named the others after their pets, so he chose not to change it; besides it gave him a chuckle every time he thought of it.

Carol instinctively knew what neighbor he was talking about. "Don't you think you could call her 'Ms. Cats'?"

"No. I like Ms. Pussy."

"You are bad!"

"No, I am just being silly and I love it. I need a lot of levity in my life right now, Carol."

"I think The Captain killed most of her other cats. That's why she walks that one with a leash."

John changed the subject by saying, "You didn't answer my calls."

"I was busy. And pissed as hell," she added.

"I guess you had a right to be."

"You are damn lucky I decided to forgive you. Why didn't you confide in me sooner?"

"I didn't want to jeopardize your life."

"I'm a big girl."

"So I noticed."

"Don't be rude!"

"Carol, it's obvious you are still mad. I don't want to fight. Come back when you've really worked this out for yourself. Truthfully, I don't need this shit right now. I still have issues I'm trying to work out and I don't need this grief."

She turned her horse around quickly. "I'm delighted to oblige." Her horse galloped them both home.

That night was even darker than the previous night.

The three assumed the same positions. Maggie sat in front and the men sat in back.

The light started to search as soon as they arrived; as if she were waiting for them and impatient to get going. The light came for Maggie. Maggie was gone for half an hour.

"That's it! I'm going in," Mountain finally announced and he jumped to his feet. He paused. "Aren't you going to hold me back?" he asked John pleadingly.

"I don't want to stop you from being a hero."

Finally, Maggie came forward from the woods. She looked strange. She was visibly shaken, and her face was white as a sheet.

Mountain was glad she was safe and relieved that he did not have to go into the mysterious woods after her.

"Let's go inside," was all she could manage to say.

"Get her some water," John instructed as he helped Maggie onto a kitchen chair.

"What did you see?" Mountain asked, while handing her the glass.

"You would not believe it!" she whispered hoarsely.

John thought he knew what Maggie had found.

"I want to show you something," John announced, and ran to the barn and retrieved the bones he had hidden and presented it to Maggie and Mountain.

"I think this is one of the missing people. It's probably one of The Captain's relatives or one of the others that he killed."

"I know where the others are," Maggie said with a groan.

John and Mountain looked at her wondering what she meant.

"She showed me. At least ten spots—including the bones under the tarp, that you apparently covered, John."

"TEN?" they both said incredulously.

"Maybe more—I lost count."

"I heard it was the parents, brother and sister and maybe the nanny and the officer's wife. That is six. Who are the others?"

"We have to call the police. That's why the girl led me to the bodies. She wanted someone to find them and to do something about it."

"Not tonight," replied John. Although he dreaded the notoriety that would come when they notified the police, he knew it was time to do so. But he also knew he would not divulge *everything* he had found. At least not yet!

"Let's call first thing in the morning. Stay with me tonight guys. Please!" John pleaded.

"She won't hurt you, John. She is happy now. She is at peace."

"Oh, yeah!" said Mountain. "Then why is she back in The Castle?"

Maggie and John ran to where Mountain was looking out the window and there was the light again, going from room to room.

"I guess she's still looking for something in that Castle," Maggie said softly. "There is something else she wants us to find."

"I wish the hell she would find it and go home."

"She will pass over when she is through with her missions, John. She wants to go home but she can't. I believe it is the little girl who fell from the turret."

"How do you know that, Maggie?" John asked.

"Trust me. I just know!"

They looked out the window again and there was the light, stationary up in the turret. The light stayed there all night. Every time John looked to see if the light was still there, it was!

They agreed not to tell the police about the light and to just let Sutter be the hero—Sutter would be the one that found the bodies and he happily received all the attention that was showered on him. You could almost see the strut in his walk.

CHAPTER FORTY-SEVEN

The next day, after calling the police, John, Maggie and Mountain waited patiently for them to arrive.

"I hope they don't send Officer Chesney," said John. "One body could be his mother." They all shivered at the thought.

Sure enough, down the path came Officer Chesney. John gave Mountain Carol's number and told him to call her and to tell her to come down, right away. She would know how to deal with her childhood friend in this situation.

When Carol came running down, John grabbed her arm and filled her in on the killing field of the back woods, and that one *could be* Chesney's mother.

"Oh, shit," she said in horror.

"I know."

"What should we do?"

"That's why I called you. You grew up with him."

She thought for a quick second and said, "Get him into the guesthouse before telling him." She added, "His father is a retired officer; we should notify him as well. One might be his wife."

John met Chesney as he was exiting his police cruiser and led him to the guesthouse door.

"Come inside, Officer, there's a table inside that you can write on if you have to write a report."

"What is the problem?"

"Something we discovered."

Officer Chesney saw Carol enter and smiled, but was still confused as to what this call was about.

Carol waved John away from the table as she sat across from her friend. She took Chesney's hand in hers.

"What's this all about, Carol? You are scaring me."

"Is there another Officer on duty, Robert?"

"Yes, but he's on a call."

Carol took a deep breath and tried to think of the best way to break the news to her friend.

There was no good way!

"Robert—you remember the man that lived here years ago, don't you?"

"You *know* I do, Carol. My mother ran away with him."

"They never found your mother, did they?"

"No, they never did."

She hesitated, trying to find the right words. "We think *we* may have," she said, and she held his hand tightly.

He looked up in surprise. "Where? Where did you find her?" There seemed to be hope in his eyes that his mother might be alive!

Carol took a deep breath and said in a whisper, "In the back woods of this property."

He knew immediately that there was no longer any hope that he would ever see his mother again. "How do you know it is her?" he asked in a husky and dreadful voice.

"We don't know for sure. But there are at least ten other bodies back there as well."

"TEN?"

Carol nodded. "I don't think you should handle this investigation, Robert."

"I'm okay, Carol. If it is her, I want to bring her home," he said as his voice cracked with emotion.

"You are going to need assistance, Robert. This is going to be a big investigation. Call it in. Get help."

After digesting what he had just heard he said, "You are right, Carol—just give me a minute." Then he added, "Does my father know?"

"No, you are the first to know." She then got up and quietly left to give Robert a chance to digest the horror and tragedy that were going to unfold in the next few days.

It was unbelievable the number of police and FBI agents that swarmed The Castle grounds, not to mention the myriad of investigators from several counties and states around.

Maggie led them to each and every body. It was obvious the police were beginning to suspect her. How could she possibly know the exact spot of all the dead bodies?

Maggie laughed and said, "I was in diapers when some of these people were killed. Sutter led me to them."

The last was a lie, but was believable.

John asked Maggie to stop providing muffins and cakes and iced tea to all the investigators. "They will never leave if you don't stop bringing over your goodies."

By the time the diggers were finished, the backwoods were a bloody mess. Fifteen bodies were found so far. Some were buried one on top of the other.

"No wonder he didn't want animals on his property," Carol said. "He was afraid the animals would dig up the bones."

"Right you are, Sherlock Holmes," John said with a wink.

"Can't you be serious?"

"I'd have an ulcer by now if I couldn't find some humor in all this insanity."

"I'm sorry, John. I was a bit too sharp." She was softening a bit. She stood close to him. She put her arm in his as they walked to the entrance gate of the property. She invited him to dinner.

"Just to get you away from all of this," and she waved her arm in a circle to show she meant the whole property of dead people. "Don't expect anything else."

"By the way, Carol, what did The Captain do about the deer around the property? Did he kill them too? Was he not afraid they would dig up the bodies?"

"From what I understand, deer don't eat meat, they are herbivores," she said, and at that, she gagged and ran home.

CHAPTER FORTY-EIGHT

All the investigators were leaving one by one after digging up the property for weeks. The news media were finally losing interest. At least they had lost interest here at the property. They had gotten all they could get, for now. They asked for interviews and John refused them all. He was very polite about it. "I have only been here a short time and I cannot shed any light on these bodies."

The media got tired of asking and finally his new phone died down. He had gotten a permanent house telephone when the Perez situation was settled. Now he did not care who had his number.

The Coroner had a lot of work to do and DNA testing had to be done to try to discover the identity of the bodies. He took samples from Officer Chesney and contacted the nanny's parents and got their DNA as well. Long distance cousins of The Captain were also asked for their DNA. DNA samples were going to be needed to identify all of the bodies—like the nanny, The Captain's parents and siblings and God knows who else.

The lead investigator, Norman McDonald, sat down with John one afternoon, just before he left. There was nothing more he could do here at the "killing field."

"How many bodies did you find, in total?" John asked.

"We believe seventeen—more or less!"

"Jesus!"

"It is going to take a long while to identify them—*if* they can be identified."

"I had thought from rumors that there could be six victims."

"I grew up here Mr. Hurley, and I have also heard that story about the missing people, and the involvement of The Captain. I have to be honest; there is no way we can prove that The Captain did it. He is dead. His death was ruled an accident. We may never know who killed them or him, and why."

"The bodies were found in his back yard! Doesn't that tell you something?"

"The property borders other properties, sir. The Captain was away for long periods of time. Do you see what I mean?"

"I was a detective too, Officer. I know what you mean. But we all know what really happened, and that The Captain was probably a psychopath."

"Give me the proof and I will happily pin it on him, posthumously."

"So you think it will remain a mystery? And all of those families of the deceased and the rest of the people of the Valley are going to suffer for the rest of their lives?" Then he caught himself; he forgot the officer had no way of knowing about The Captain's tape and all the threats.

"Why would they suffer?"

"Oh, I mean the loss of their animals and such," he added quickly, hoping the officer would accept the lie.

"Yes, there *were* a lot of animal bones. Cats, dogs and God knows what else."

"The bastard killed everything in sight."

The officer could hear the frustration in John's voice.

"Mr. Hurley, don't you think I want to close this case and give this community some peace? The man was a devil. He was pure evil. When he was alive I wanted to kill him myself. I think he killed my aunt's cats. He killed my friend's wife. Officer Chesney Senior is one of my best friends"

"Oh, are you related to Ms. Pussy?"

"What?"

"The lady that walks her pussy cat," offered John trying to get the conversation back to where it was, but still chuckling inside.

The officer continued, "We see now that he was probably one of the worst serial killers in the world. Can I prove it? No! Does that bother me? It bothers the hell out of me. Do you think I like to see my young friend Officer Chesney suffering, as well as his father? I was the first one on the scene many years ago when that little girl fell from the turret. It broke my heart. I will never forget the sight of that little helpless child and her mangled body. Do I think it was an accident? Hell, no! Could we prove it? No! He was very smart. He thought he had everyone fooled. But he didn't have me fooled. Could we do anything about it? No! It was all we could do to keep the local population from killing him. Thank God he was found dead. Thank God it was ruled an accident. We thought it was over—now this!"

"I was not implying anything, Officer. I know from experience that you are doing the best you can under the circumstances."

Officer MacDonald rose and extended his hand. "If anything else turns up, and I hope it doesn't, call me."

"I certainly hope nothing else turns up," John said with a sigh as he walked the officer to the door. "This is certainly a very Strange Valley, isn't it Officer."

"You took the words right out of my mouth!!!!!"

CHAPTER FORTY-NINE

Carol came up to Elk Horn again the following weekend.
"Can't stay away from me, can you?" joked John.
"Believe me, you are resistible, John."
"Now is that a way to talk?"
Carol looked around. "It seems quiet up here. Is everyone gone?"
"Just about; they finally sent someone over to fill up the holes in the back woods."
"It's unbelievable isn't it, John? I could have been one of those holes," and she started to shiver uncontrollably.
John put his arm around her to comfort her.
"Will they charge The Captain?" she asked.
"No, they won't," he said hoping it would not upset her too much.
"Why not?" She couldn't believe what John had just told her.
"No proof."
"So they can't prove he did the killings? Which we know he did! And what if they find the tapes? Innocent people could be prosecuted and the Captain would get off *scot-free.*"
"He didn't get off "scot-free," Carol. Remember he *is* dead!"
If they find the tapes they will exhume his body. They will see he was beat to hell. My father described the condition of the body to my mother—I was in the next room, listening. It sounded like a crowd got together and beat him to death and then kept beating him. His bones were probably broken in a thousand places. They would then know it was not the animals that did it. Then someone, or many in the community, could go to jail for murder."
"Great country we live in!!!!!"
"Don't joke, John—we can't let that happen."
"I'm open for suggestions."
"You haven't found anything?" she again asked.
"No," he lied.

"You didn't find anything in the barn, or the guesthouse?"
"No," he lied again.
"What about The Castle?"
"I'm still working on that."
"What's taking you so long?" she asked impatiently.
"The goddamn place is haunted! I'm scared to work or sleep there at night. Mountain, Maggie and I have seen lights in the windows. You saw them too! Remember when we were parked outside in the driveway, and the lights interrupted our lovemaking? They are there *every* night. She roams through the whole Castle—EVERY NIGHT!"
"She likes Maggie. She showed Maggie where the bodies were. She scares the hell out of me and Mountain."
"Who is *she*? Seriously, John, there is no such thing as ghosts."
"Wanna bet!"
"I want to come down and see what is happening."
"You might want to bring extra clothes."
"Why would I want to do that?"
"You'll see!" John said with a cheeky smile on his face.
"Tell me more about *her*, John."
"Maggie thinks it is the little girl."
"Little Emily?"
"Was that her name?"
"Yes. Emily Ann. But I thought Sutter found the bones?"
"He found some. But we could not let on that the girl and the light led Maggie to the sites."
"I want to see the light again. If it is the little girl she will respond to me."
"I don't like ghosts, Carol. I hate going into The Castle anymore."
"I'll come over tonight and we will see if she comes to me. *If* there *are* such things as ghosts!"
"I'll invite Maggie. She likes Maggie."
"She liked me too. She saved my life."
"Do you think she will remember you?"
"If it *is* Emily, she will remember me. We were great pals. I still treasure the time we had together. I miss her friendship. I never had another friend like her. She was a special little girl."
"Aren't you afraid, Carol? We are talking about ghosts here!"
"If it is really my little friend Emily, then I will not be afraid. At least I don't think I'll be afraid. You'll be nearby won't you, John?"
"Yes, I'll be nearby. But I assure you I will be absolutely no help at all. You will be on your own."
"Scared of the Boogie Man, John?"
"No. I'm just afraid of Emily."

CHAPTER FIFTY

So there they all sat that night. Mountain and John sat close to the guesthouse so they could do the usual "count of three" if they had to. Maggie and Carol sat right in front of them.

"Women are the stronger of the species, don't you think?" suggested Mountain.

Thinking of all the women that he knew, John nodded in assent.

"Is she frightened?" Carol asked Maggie.

"She is more mad than frightened," responded Maggie.

"She was my little playmate."

"She is still gentle and sweet."

"How do you know?" asked Carol.

"The way she leads me. She holds my hand and guides me around obstacles so that I don't fall and injure myself."

"She saved my life, Maggie."

"John told me that. She was a brave little girl. I'm sure she will be an angel when she finally passes. Perhaps she will be *your* Guardian Angel."

"I feel her around me all the time. I think she is my Guardian Angel now."

"You are very lucky."

At the stroke of twelve the light appeared. By now, Maggie, John and Mountain were somewhat used to it and sat still and stared.

Carol on the other hand froze in her chair.

"Don't be frightened, Carol," Maggie whispered, "or she may not come to us."

Carol tried to settle down, but she began to shake.

Maggie reached for her hand, and just Maggie's touch was enough to stop Carol's shaking.

They all watched as the light went from room to room and then back again. Then up to the turrets and back down again. Over and over again!

"I hope she doesn't go into the woods again. I'm hoping we have *all* the bodies," John whispered.

"Sssshhh, John!"

Then the light came through the stonewall of The Castle and floated towards the group. She stopped in front of Maggie and Carol.

"Hello, sweetheart," Maggie said, "thank you for leading us to the bodies. You are such a smart little girl. Are you trying to tell us something else?"

Maggie waited for the light to glide to her.

Instead, it went to Carol. The light seemed to go from one of Carol's cheek to the other and then to her hand.

"She kissed you," said Maggie, "now she wants you to follow her."

Carol got up like a zombie and went with the light. It led her to The Castle.

"I can't go in there, Emily."

It touched her hand and continued to lead her to The Castle. They were at the door, ready to enter, when Sutter came running. Barking loudly, he bounded over to Maggie as if to protect her from some danger. The light faded and disappeared. Sutter had broken the moment. They had forgotten to lock him up.

"Thank you, Sutter," said John and Mountain simultaneously.

"I keep on forgetting to bring extra underwear," said Mountain.

"I wear double, just in case!" John threw back.

"She recognized me," Carol whispered to Maggie.

"Yes, she did!"

"What do you think she was trying to show us, Maggie?"

"I don't know, but she won't rest until she leads us to what she wants us to find."

"She died so many years ago, Maggie, and yet you say she is still a little girl."

"Emily will never grow old. She will always be a little girl. She will always be a little angel."

"Well," said Carol, "I'm a believer."

CHAPTER FIFTY ONE

John knew he had to get into The Castle and finish working on it. He did not mind staying or working in The Castle when there were others with him. Being in the Castle alone was a scary situation for John. He did not like all this ghost stuff.

He had discussed his misgivings with Maggie and Mountain. Maggie said the spirit would not harm him. Mountain asked if he could have John's truck if he went missing.

"Very funny, Mountain!"

Everyone would laugh like hell if they saw me now, John thought. He was walking ever so slowly across the yard from the Guesthouse to the Castle.

The hard hat he had borrowed from Mountain was sliding back and forth on his head; he eventually had to stop and adjust the straps to get it to fit. Mountain was at least three head sizes bigger than John. The hard hat made him feel safer somehow. What it would save him from, he did not know.

Maggie had said to talk to the spirit. She said to be kind and gentle to the little one.

John wondered how he could be anything *but* kind and gentle to a little girl ghost.

As he gingerly entered The Castle, he immediately began to talk to the spirit, well, more ramble on than talk.

"Hello, Emily. I've just come to work on The Castle. I won't be bothering you. You can look for things while I am here. I know what happened to you, and I am very sorry."

Then he heard a crash upstairs.

"Oh, shit," was the response from John. "Oh, excuse me Emily, I did not mean to curse, but you are scaring the hell out of me. You know, I didn't have an easy life either. Let me tell you, many a bad person has tried to kill me. So I know how you feel. Then there's the time my cousin held my head under water at Stinson Beach—I almost drowned. Oh, I know I didn't die, but I was scared. Then there's the time my other cousin pushed me off a cable car and I broke my arm. So you see my life has not been easy either. So please have pity on me."

John listened for a response, but didn't hear one. He then continued, "We found the bodies you led us to. That was very smart of you. We are trying to prove that The Captain did it."

Another crash from upstairs!

"Oy Vey!" John had to laugh a little to himself—where did *that* come from? He guessed he had heard it from a fellow Jewish detective. With a trembling voice John continued again, "Emily, we know he pushed you from the turret and God knows what else he did. But please don't punish me. I'm just a nice guy trying to fix up this bloody Castle."

Another crash!

"Jesus, Mary & Joseph!" John knew he had heard his mother say *that* very often. John then remembered Maggie saying, "Follow the signs."

"Maybe she wants me to go upstairs," he said to no one in particular.

He went very slowly, step by step, up the old creaking stairway to the second floor. There did not appear to be anything out of place, and he was about to return to the first floor where he felt safer. There he would be close to the front door should he feel the need to run.

There was another crash above him!

Above him was an old attic. It was a very spooky attic with old empty trunks and an old baby carriage. *Probably Emily's,* he thought.

The flashlight that he carried was trembling in his hand as he climbed the stairs to the attic. He did not like all this spirit stuff, especially when he was alone. He started talking again—again more for himself than for Emily.

"You know, Emily, I'm not use to this supernatural stuff. The plain fact is I'm scared to death. Oh, I know about the little Irish gremlins or whatever they call them. My old Irish Grandmother told me many a story about them. I am still afraid of the Boogie Man. My Scottish Grandmother, who I am sure you would like very much, told me never to walk under a ladder, break a mirror or drop any salt without throwing it over my left shoulder, and never to put my shoes on a bed. These things alone scare me, but *you* walking around is a little more than I can bear. I am a scaredy-cat, Emily. Weren't you ever frightened? How silly of me, how could you live in this Castle with The Captain and not be scared. Oh, and thank you for saving Carol. She knows you probably gave your life for her and . . . what now, Emily? What's that light in the corner?"

He slowly went to the tiny speck of light. He thought it was just a speck of sunlight coming through the window. He noticed there was a piece of baseboard that seemed to be loose and he was about to kick it back into place when he felt

The Strange Valley

a terrible pain in his leg, like someone had kicked him and kicked him hard. The pain was awful!

John was about to run like buggery out of the attic and out of the house, when the door to the attic slammed shut, closed and locked itself—*from the outside*.

"Enough is enough, Emily! LET ME OUT!" John screamed. He pulled and pulled on the door, but it would not open. He kicked the door in frustration.

John looked around the room for a tool that he could use to break down the door when he saw a *much brighter* light at the corner where the baseboard was loose. He realized, at that moment, that there was no sun in the sky. It was a cloudy day. The light in the corner was not sunlight. And there was no electricity in the attic.

John walked to the corner where the light had stationed itself. He didn't see anything except the loose baseboard. He pulled it a little to see how loose it was and it came off the wall in his hands.

Termites, I guess, he muttered to himself.

He spied an object crushed into the wall. He tried to pull it free, but it was coming apart in his hands as he pulled on it. He thought it must be very old. John then very gingerly removed some of the upper wall and was finally able to pull the object free.

Just a book, he thought. Then he saw the name on the front of the book, and he had to sit down before he fell down. His head had gone dark and he felt woozy. It was a diary, The Captain's diary! "Captain Timothy Henson" was the name on the front cover.

"I have it, Emily! I HAVE IT! Now please, open the door," he begged. The door swung open. Similar to the way the front door opened on the day that John entered The Castle for the very first time. That front door was impossible to open—but it opened. Who locked and then opened the attic door? It had to be Emily!

John held the book under his arm for safekeeping. It was literally falling apart.

John laid it on the kitchen table and made a cup of coffee. He wasn't sure he wanted to read "The Devil's Diary." What horrors would it contain?!

The reading of the diary was like reading a Stephen King novel, only even more frightening because what he was reading actually happened. John cringed and almost gagged with every page he read.

It detailed how he had killed his parents, his siblings, the officer's wife and the nanny, and how he had buried them in the back woods.

He named the others that were found, but John did not recognize their names; but he was sure the police would do a thorough investigation *if* he gave them the diary. They would put names to the bodies, or vice versa.

The Captain went on to say that he killed the animals so that they would not dig up the bodies. He detailed how he hated the horse that Carol had ridden as a child, and how mad he was that Carol had gotten away because his *daughter* Emily had helped her to escape.

The word "daughter" sprang out at John. *Was the nanny the real mother,* he wondered?

He sat back after reading most of the diary. He felt sick to his stomach. He wondered how a man could be so evil. The Captain did not just write that he killed the people, but he wrote in detail how he did it, especially how he had killed Mrs. Chesney. He described the sexual acts that he performed on all the people he had killed. His mother, father, sister and brother all had been sexually molested by this killer and sexual deviant. Some acts were performed after the deaths of these poor innocent people. No one was safe from this madman.

The question that was rolling through John's mind was, *should I make this public? It would hurt so many people.*

Upon reading one of the last pages of the diary, he knew that he could not make it public just yet. The Captain showed no remorse for what he had done; he even anticipated the diary being found one day. He indeed wanted it published! The diary ended by The Captain stating again that if he suffered an early death, it would not be an accident; the police should know that one of the neighbors had killed him and that they would find the threats from the murderers in a porno tape cassette case hidden in the barn. He did not mind admitting the evil deeds after his death; indeed he took pleasure in writing about it in his diary. And he definitely wanted his neighbors to be prosecuted and punished for his murder should he be found dead.

The irony was, even though he admitted to committing so many atrocities—he was dead and could not be prosecuted. But someone or many in the Strange Valley could be found guilty of murder, if the right evidence was found, and possibly be put to death. Stranger things have happened!

John yelled at the top of his voice, "I FOUND IT YOU BASTARD! YOUR NEIGHBORS ARE SAFE!"

John found some solace in the fact that The Captain had feared for his life. He was overjoyed that he was the one to find the diary. "Of course it was with your help, Emily. I could not have found it without you." He was sure to give Emily the credit that she deserved—he wanted no problems with Emily!

He did not want to anger the little spirit. He did not know what spirits were capable of, and he certainly did not want to find out.

John went to the local bank and put the diary in his safe deposit box, along with the tape he had found. He decided to bide his time about making it public, if ever. He would tell no one of the discoveries right now; not even Maggie or Mountain. He felt guilty about that, but thought it was the safe and right thing to do.

CHAPTER FIFTY-TWO

Carol stopped by to say hello to John, she was up for the weekend. She wanted an update on events and to see if they had identified any of the bodies. She invited John for dinner that night.

John arrived with some of the wild flowers he had picked from his property.

"You always come with something in your hands."

"My Scottish Grandmother always said if you cannee ring the doorbell with your elbow because your hands are filled with gifts, then you shouldnee come at all."

"I think I will like your grandparents. They seem like a lot of fun. How is your grandfather coming along?"

"He's almost as good as new. He is chomping at the bit to come up and help me work on The Castle. But I want to wait until all this police stuff is over."

"I guess you haven't found anything, eh?"

"Is that why I am here for dinner, Carol? Do you intend to pump me for information, again?"

"Why are you always so suspicious of me? You are always ready for a fight."

"I'm sorry. I'm just jumpy I guess. I've had a horrible few weeks."

"Has the spirit been around anymore?" Carol asked, changing the subject just a bit.

"I think she will always be around. At least until she feels she is no longer needed. She is a sweet spirit, I am told, but I think she should go home. She still scares me half to death."

"You are a big boy; you can handle it."

They were bantering back and forth when the doorbell rang.

"Expecting anyone? Perhaps it is your little friend Emily."

After giving John a quick glance, Carol went to the door and opened it, not bothering to look out the security peephole. John was there, so she felt safe.

"Robert!" It was Robert Chesney. Officer Robert Chesney.

John cringed when he heard the name. All he could think of was the horror of his mother's assault and death that he had read about in the diary. It ran in his mind like a movie and he felt like losing the meal he had been eating.

"Come in, Robert. Have you any news?"

They could see he was visibly upset.

"You have company," Robert Chesney said, after noticing John. "I'll come back another time."

"No, Robert. It's only John Hurley. You know him."

"Hello, Mr. Hurley."

John nodded a hello back.

Officer Chesney sat down at the table and had coffee and cake with John and Carol. You could see he had something on his mind and was thinking of whether or not he was going to share it with Carol while John was there.

Finally he could contain himself no longer. He took a handkerchief from his pocket and slowly unraveled it.

"What's that?" asked Carol innocently.

"It's my mother's locket."

"Where did they find it?" Carol asked amazed, immediately fearing the answer.

"With her bones," Robert choked out.

"They identified her?" asked John.

"Yes. She is finally home."

Wiping his eyes with the handkerchief that had held the locket, he said, "Look Carol, the locket has a picture of me and my sister. She was leaving home, but she took a piece of us with her."

"She loved you, Robert."

"I know." Tears started flowing down his cheeks. "She never went anywhere, Carol. She didn't go on a cruise. She never got to Spain or France or wherever The Captain had those houses. She was so close by all these years. Why did he have to kill her? If he didn't want her anymore we would have taken her back. He didn't have to kill her." Officer Chesney laid his head on his arms on the table, and sobbed.

John stood up quickly and blew a kiss to Carol and hurriedly left. He knew Robert Chesney would need comforting and Carol was the one to do it. They were old friends. Robert didn't need a stranger around at this time.

CHAPTER FIFTY THREE

There was a pall over this Strange Valley. So much death can do that to a population. Most of the people of the Valley were frightened like Carol. One of them had probably killed The Captain and that person was afraid he, or she, would be found out. Or perhaps they all killed him. Perhaps some were innocent and were afraid that they would still be accused of the murder. Everyone seemed to be afraid that the finger would be pointed at them should any evidence be found; like the tapes The Captain had made of all of their calls and threats. They were afraid of the unknown.

John believed he probably had the proof that The Captain was probably murdered—that is what his diary implied. The question was, *by whom?* Just about everyone he had ever met in his neighborhood had motive and opportunity to murder The Captain.

It could even be Carol, he thought sadly. *She had reason enough to kill him. Maybe that is why she is so eager to find those tapes and if she knew there was a diary she would freak out.*

John secretly thought it could very well be Carol's father who did the deed. He was big enough and had good reason to take The Captain's life. The Captain killed his horse and had assaulted his daughter. John secretly thought, *I wonder which one bothered him the most.*

Mr. Lang was a big man and he had a bad temper. He was at least six foot five and built like a battleship.

John wondered if Carol suspected the same thing since she was so interested in finding The Captain's evidence. John suddenly shivered as he remembered one page where The Captain had written *"Pay close attention to that bastard Lang. He threatened me the most."* John wondered why The Captain had not given the diary and tapes to his attorney to keep in the event of his death. That was The Captain's biggest mistake.

John decided it was time for his parents and grandparents to come and visit and help him restore The Castle. It would also help lift the depression off of his shoulders. There was just too much death and destruction around; he needed to have some fun and laughter, and that is what his family could provide.

The spirit of Emily seemed to have died down since he found the diary, so she probably would not appear to his family. At least that is what he hoped.

"The Castle seems to be free of spirits at this time," declared Maggie. "But I don't think she has gone over yet. She is a gentle and loving spirit so she will probably keep out of the way while your guests are there. But being just a child she may try to have a little fun."

CHAPTER FIFTY FOUR

John was expecting his parents and grandparents to arrive any minute. They had said they would be there at 1:00 p.m. That meant that they would be there at 12:30. His parents were never late.

John spent the morning getting everything ready. There was enough food for an army and a wee drop of whiskey for his gramps. He was looking forward to seeing them, but remembered how outspoken and tactless his parents and grandparents could be—the first days of the visit would be full of unwanted advice and pointless criticism. He prepared himself for the worst.

He walked around the property inspecting it for the company; making sure there was nothing his grandmother could trip over and that everything was nice and neat in The Castle for his mother.

As he looked back at The Castle he knew then that he loved this place. Even with all the problems that had come with it. He loved the thousands of pine trees that shrouded The Castle from a view from the street. Total privacy—and that is what he valued the most. He no longer needed to hide from the Perez Brothers, but he still loved the serenity that The Castle provided for him.

The sun was hitting The Castle just right, and it appeared regal and royal. His grandfather had once told him he was related to Bonnie Prince Charlie of old. Right now he felt like a King. No matter what his relatives thought, he would always be glad that he had bought this Castle.

If he had not made this investment he would never have met Mountain and Maggie, and of course his beloved Sutter. Strange, he thought, that he did not think of Carol as well. *Just an oversight,* is what he thought.

As his parent's car turned onto the driveway, he turned to The Castle and said, "Now Emily, no funny business while my parents and grandparents are here. I don't think they could take the fright of knowing you are floating around somewhere in the house. It is just a truce Emily, nothing more."

John felt like laughing when he saw the looks on the faces of his relatives as they got out of the car. His mother said, "I feel like I'm in Disneyland." That was just the start of it.

I guess I'll never grow up in their eyes, he thought as he helped carry all of the "CARE" packages his parents had brought with them.

Mom always brought John extra socks and underwear. Even though John always protested that he had quite enough, she always brought more.

Dad always brought *his* tools and brand new ones for John. At this point, John had enough tools to last him a lifetime, even though many of them were still missing. He hoped they would eventually show up. He secretly wondered if his dad always brought him tools because he did not want John using his.

Gramps always brought John a bottle of Scotch—since that was John's favorite. Gramps' favorite too!

After getting all the luggage and paraphernalia settled in the proper rooms, they all sat for a little lunch around the dining room table that John had bought.

Gramps said, "I feel like I'm at King Arthur's Court."

Grandma asked, "Don't you get lost in this big place, Johnny?"

Mom said, "It's so isolated, John. You can't even see this place from the street."

Dad said, "You have to get rid of some of these pine trees or they will fall and kill someone."

John laughed inwardly. For all the reasons that he had bought The Castle, his family had negative comments.

Only Gramps saved the day by saying something positive and funny.

John had known that his parents would find The Castle a little overwhelming. After all, their houses had almost always been attached to other houses in San Francisco. The house that John had bought from them, which was his childhood home, was detached—which meant that there was perhaps five feet between the adjoining houses. So twenty acres were a bit overwhelming.

And so, that is how the day progressed. They were all giving their advice on how they would do things differently and John knew he would ignore everything they said.

Finally, Gramps came to him and put his arm around his grandson's shoulder and said, "It's a fine place, Laddie. It's a grand place!" Gramps could see that John was a wee bit tired of the criticism. "I would like to redo those built-in cabinets in the dining room. I can restore them like new."

"Go to it, Gramps." John was moved by his grandfather's positive remarks about The Castle. Gramps always knew the right thing to say.

Mom went to work cleaning and reorganizing the kitchen, and John would spend weeks afterward trying to find things all over again.

The Strange Valley

Dad went to work on the outside, pulling weeds and small dead bushes. He tried to advise John what flowers to plant so there could be new life generated around the property at different times of the year. Occasionally his father cut down a bush that John had recently planted!

Grandma sat making him an afghan, since he was going to freeze to death in this drafty old Castle.

John asked his mom why they had all brought so much stuff with them. His mom responded, "It's called 'first footing.' In Scotland you always enter a house for the first time with food and money in your hands or it would be bad luck."

"Well, I should have good luck for many a year then with all the stuff you brought."

Eventually they all grew more at ease with each other and The Castle. They started to joke and laugh and John could hear Gramps singing in the dining room as he worked his magic on the old built-in breakfronts. "Wee chickie birdie, too lo lo, laid an egg on the window sill." A song that Gramps had often sang to John while bouncing him on his knee as a child.

"Johnny, have you seen my little carpenter's level—I need it to make sure everything I work on is straight and even."

"No Gramps, but I am sure Dad will have one."

The moment was interrupted when John heard a truck coming onto the driveway. Upon looking out the window, he saw it was Mountain and Maggie, coming to say hello to John's parents and grandparents.

John knew they were going to come, as he had asked them to come over and break up the day. He did not know what his parents' reactions to The Castle would be.

Suddenly, Grandma came running into the kitchen all upset. "Johnny, there are strangers come to kill us. One is as big as a mountain!"

John laughed and said, "They are my friends Granny. Don't worry."

"Oh, Johnny, he is so big!" Granny whispered.

"But as gentle as a baby, Granny. Just you wait and see."

As they all got to know Mountain and Maggie they began to immediately treat them like family and made them very welcome. They just had to get over the initial shock of the size of Mountain.

Maggie got close with Granny. They could both work wonders with their hands. They spent the day trading ideas on knitting and crocheting.

Gramps took to Mountain. It was amusing to see them together. Wee Gramps and Mountain! Mountain wanted to learn as much as he could about restoring wood and old furniture.

John heard Gramps say, "Get down on your knees Mountain, so we can talk face to face." Then he heard a roar of laughter from Mountain.

Funny how the very young gravitate towards the very old!

John was touched to see how his friends interacted with his family. They treated his grandparents with such respect. His Gramps and Granny were so happy to be the center of attention.

It did not seem appropriate to have a barbeque at The Castle. It just seemed too informal a meal to present in such a grand setting. So Mom cooked a big pot roast with mashed potatoes and string beans. Maggie had brought a huge apple pie, made from scratch. By the time the meal had ended and everyone had consumed a great portion of the wine that John had provided, they were all great friends. It was as if they knew Mountain and Maggie forever.

It was time for his family to retire for the night, so John walked Maggie and Mountain out to their truck.

"Are you going to let them sleep in The Castle?" asked Mountain.

"I've nowhere else to put them. The guesthouse is too small."

"Emily will not frighten them," said Maggie.

"I asked her not to," added John.

Mountain looked at his friend in amazement. "Are you starting to believe in ghosts now?"

"Maggie has made me a believer."

"When do your folks leave?"

"I'm not sure. I hope they don't stay too long. I don't want them to know about what has been transpiring with the police and all."

"I heard they found Chesney's mother."

"Yeah, Mountain! What a bummer! But they gave him his mother's locket that they found with the bones. He seemed genuinely happy that his mother was wearing it when she left, and that the locket was with her all these years."

"Have they identified anyone else?"

"I'm not privy to that information. I'm sure we will find out after awhile. The police are trying to keep everything away from the news. So far, my folks have not put two and two together. I'm sure they have heard on the news about all the bodies being found, but they don't seem to realize that it was my place that all this gore and murder was found on."

"If they ask, John, tell them the truth. Don't try to fool them. Don't let them lose trust in you," Maggie said wisely.

"How did you get to marry such a special woman, Mountain?"

"The stars were shining down on me the day I asked for her hand." Mountain gently kissed Maggie's hand.

"I was the lucky one." Maggie looked lovingly up at Mountain as they were trading compliments.

"Find me someone just like Maggie."

"Can't John, she is one of a kind."

"Let's go, Mountain—before John gets sick to his stomach with all this sugar and spice."

"What do you think of my folks?"

"They are great John, your grandmother and I got along wonderfully. She is going to teach me how to make haggis."

"God help us all, Maggie."

John went whistling back to The Castle, his tread was light. This had been a great day. Having his friends and family surrounding him gave him such joy, even if Gramps never found his level.

CHAPTER FIFTY-FIVE

The days were passing gently. Everyone was busy doing what they thought they had the most expertise in. John felt good having his family around him. For so long, he had been frightened and secretive. Now his family surrounded him. He laughed to himself when he thought of what his MacGregor cousins would say if he ever invited them to The Castle. He decided it would be a cold day in hell before he had his cousins to his Castle. Later he decided it might be great fun to hear their responses and to know that they would be as jealous as hell that he had such a grand place.

John's mother came to him one afternoon and asked what time they were going to Sunday Mass. "It is Sunday tomorrow you know, John!"

He had to think quickly! John had not attended church for years. He knew that if he ever had kids he would go back to Mass, as Mountain had said, but at this time in his life it did not seem important, unfortunately.

His mom thought he attended Mass every week. John would not put her any the wiser.

"I'll check and see what time Mass is being celebrated Mom."

He got out the telephone book and saw that the closest Catholic Church was The Madonna of the Oaks, and saw that Mass was at 10:00 a.m.

Mom had converted to Catholicism when she married Michael Hurley, much to the distress of Laurie MacGregor's staunchly Scotch Presbyterian parents. But they had liked Michael very much and knew that their daughter loved him, so they lived with it. But they would not go to Mass that Sunday.

It was a quaint old church. Sparsely attended. Mostly older people were in the pews.

One "church lady" immediately accosted John and his father.

"We need help with the Mass. The altar boys did not show up."

"John here can do it. He was the best altar boy in his day," voiced his mother.

At that moment John wanted to throttle his mother.

"And we need someone to help with the collection," added the church lady.

"I can do that," offered John's father.

So, unexpectedly, John and his dad became major participants in this particular Sunday Mass.

John was surprised that it all came back to him after all these years. *Like riding a bike*, he thought.

When he watched his mother receiving communion he could see she was beaming with pride. She was so proud of her two men.

After the Mass, an elderly gentleman came up to John. Giving his hand for a handshake he said, "I'm John O'Leary, of the O'Leary and O'Leary Funeral Parlor."

Grasping the undertaker's hand he said, "John Hurley. A pleasure to meet you, sir." John thought the man was just being friendly to new faces at the church.

"You are the one that owns The Castle, aren't you?"

"Yes, that's right."

"I was wondering if you would help me?"

"If I can, I will."

"I was wondering if you had the name of the attorney that handled The Captain's estate."

"I'm not sure if I still have that information. But I will look and if I have it I will call you." John was taken aback at the request. What did this man need that information for?

"That would be great."

"May I ask you why you need the attorney's telephone number?"

"Well, I know it will sound a bit tacky, but we were never paid for the processing of The Captain's body."

"That was a very long time ago," John said. He thought that it *was* a bit tacky for this undertaker to be asking for money after so much time had passed.

"I know. But it *is* a bill owing." The undertaker could feel a little animosity coming from John. And in truth, John thought this man looked like "Digger O'Dell."

"Perhaps the real estate agent would have that information." John really did not want to get involved with this old undertaker. He felt like saying, w*rite it off as a bad debt*, but they were in church and he decided to be pleasant in the presence of his mother.

John turned to leave, but turned back and asked, "By the way, Mr. O'Leary, were you the one that processed The Captain's body?"

"Yes, I was the one. I was very young at the time."

"Can you tell me what condition the body was in?" John was fishing to know if this man knew of the injuries The Captain had allegedly sustained.

"It was hard to tell, he had been dead for a long time. Since it was to be a closed casket with no relatives attending a service, we did not process the body for viewing."

"You saw nothing unusual, then?"

"No, he was dead so long, and the decomposition so great, they could not even do an autopsy. The relatives just said to bury him as soon as you can. We could see that there was no love lost between the living and the dead."

"I see."

The two stood looking at one another for a moment, each wanting to end the encounter, but not knowing how.

"So you did not see anything unusual about the body?" John asked again.

The undertaker paused, and finally said, "Oh, now that I think back, The Captain had something grasped in his hand. I could not get it out of his hand, no matter how hard I tried—rigor mortis had set in the body for a long time before I worked on it. I always wondered over the years what it was. It was in his left hand."

"You didn't try to see what he was grasping?" John asked in surprise.

"Yes, I did try. From what I could feel I knew it was something hard and smooth. But I could not identify what it was. It could have been a large button, or a tooth, or a woman's hairpiece, or a ring. I just could not identify the object."

"You could not pry open his hands?"

"I would have to break off his fingers, and I would not do that. The body is sacred, dead or alive, you know. I did not think it was that important, so I left whatever it was in his tight boney grip."

John began to like this "Digger O'Dell"—he seemed to be a decent human being.

"It would be interesting to know where he is buried." John was still pumping for information.

"The attorney might have that information."

"You did not bury him in a local cemetery?"

"No, we did not."

"What did you do with the body?"

"We delivered the body to The Castle."

"Is he buried on The Castle grounds?" John asked the undertaker and immediately prayed he wasn't. If he was, John knew he would dig up every inch of land until he found him and disposed of him. Then he remembered that every inch of land *had* been dug up.

"I have no idea where he is buried."

John asked how much the undertaker was owed.

"Three thousand dollars," the undertaker very quickly responded, as if it had been at the forefront of his mind all these years.

The Strange Valley

John whipped out his checkbook and wrote the amount the undertaker quoted. He hoped this would close another hole that The Captain had left open.

"For the sake of good will," John said as he handed the check to the undertaker.

"Much appreciated," the undertaker said, very happily taking the check.

John was still sick to his stomach thinking of The Captain's body being "somewhere" on his property. Maybe that is why Emily is still upset!

As they were parting, the undertaker could see the confusion and disgust on John's face.

"Mr. Hurley!" Digger O'Dell shouted after John.

John turned back towards the undertaker.

"Mr. Hurley, you *do* know that The Captain was cremated?"

John stood still in his tracks. CREMATED! NO EVIDENCE! Carol need not worry any more. Nobody needs to worry any more! He almost jumped for joy.

Composing himself, John asked, "Did you deliver the ashes to The Captain's attorney at The Castle?"

"Yes, and it was delivered in a beautiful little antique urn."

John knew there was no more information to be gotten from "Digger O'Dell" the undertaker, and felt it was well worth the three thousand dollars that he had paid to discover the body had been cremated. The community could be somewhat at ease now. The body could not be dug up to see if The Captain was beaten to death. But there was one sticking point. What was in The Captain's hand? Where are those bloody ashes now? Even in his death The Captain was a pain in the ass.

How can I find out where that urn is? John wondered as he drove his parents back to The Castle.

He would not mention anything to Carol right away. He would have to put all the puzzle pieces together. He had to decide how to discover where the remains were, without raising suspicion.

One mystery solved, another mystery jumps into its place. He was cremated—but he had something in his hand. Could it identify the killer?

CHAPTER FIFTY-SIX

His family was beginning to get itchy to get home. His parents missed their little Yorkie dog.

"Why didn't you bring him?" John asked his mother.

"He gets car sick," responded his mother. "With Gramps and Granny in the car it would not have been pretty," and she laughed thinking of her dog and her parents in the same car. "Next time we will bring him."

Gramps had restored the breakfront in the dining room to its original condition. It was now breathtakingly beautiful.

"It's beautiful, Gramps. Thank you."

"It was my pleasure, Johnny. I enjoyed doing it for you."

"There's lots more you could do around here, Gramps."

"Oh, I'll be back. It's a grand old place. It reminds me of a grand old Scottish Castle. I felt right at home here. By the way, what have you named it?"

John had not thought of naming The Castle.

"You name it, Gramps," he suddenly threw at his grandfather.

"You want *me* to name The Castle, Johnny?"

"It would make me very happy if you did."

Gramps thought long and hard and then said very loud and clear in his very Scottish brogue, in a voice as elegant as the grandest King of old, "I hereby name this Castle *HEATHER GLEN*."

John repeated it, "Heather Glen. I love it, Gramps. From here on in it is Heather Glen."

Grandma took John aside before leaving and said she had something important to tell him.

"John hoped it had nothing to do with Gramps or his parents. He prayed that no one was ill!"

The Strange Valley

Granny pulled John's head down so she could whisper in his ear. She looked around to make sure no one was listening, "The house is haunted, Johnny." She said it very secretively. She did not want the others to hear.

"Why do you say that, Grandma?" John asked in pretended surprise. He had thought that Emily had not acted up.

"There was a wee one that crept into bed with me every night. I always felt a wee kiss on my cheek after she settled in."

"That's silly, Granny. And how would you know if it was a boy or girl?"

"It reminded me of how it felt when your mother crept into bed with me when she was frightened or felt lonely when she was a little girl. This wee one needed something. She needed a wee bit of love!"

"Were you frightened, Granny?"

"Frightened of a spirit? Och, no! Nothing frightens me at my age. But don't tell the others about this little spirit. Find out who she is Johnny, and get her help. Find out what she needs so she can pass over."

"How do you know all this, Granny? How do you know about spirits?"

"Lots of spirits come to me, Johnny, my Mother comes to me often. My sister also comes to me frequently." She teared up when she said, "My sons come to me every day."

John took his Granny in his arms to comfort her. "You are just like Maggie."

"I know; we are very much alike."

John was unhappy to see his family leave after their short visit, but was grateful that they did—he had work to do. He had unexpectedly enjoyed their company very much, and because his mother had insisted on attending church, he now knew The Captain was cremated and his ashes were floating around some place on his property. John had to find the ashes before anyone else. One find seemed to lead to another.

John slept an exhausted sleep that night, in Heather Glen Castle.

"Thank you, Emily, for not creating a problem and I hope you enjoyed being with my grandmother. She liked you too."

Good Lord, he thought, *now I am talking to a bloody ghost!*

CHAPTER FIFTY-SEVEN

John awoke the next morning, happy that he did not have to entertain anyone that day, because as his granny would say "*he had a big head.*" He had a pounding headache that was the result of the fine Scotch he had enjoyed the day before. Caffeine and aspirin usually helped, and by the afternoon he was beginning to function.

He decided to go through all the closing papers from the purchase of The Castle to find the name of The Captain's attorney, the same one that handled the sale of the property. He was amazed that he found the papers that he wanted; he was usually careless with those things. He reminded himself to put the papers in his safe deposit box at the bank.

Finally he came up with the attorney's name. Richard Townsend had handled the affairs for The Captain. John decided to call him. The phone rang a long time before anyone answered.

Finally, "Hello!"

"Hello. This is John Hurley calling. I am the purchaser of Captain Henson's Castle. Do you remember me?"

"Oh yes, Mr. Hurley, what can I do for you?"

"Two things—first I need to know what you want me to do with the items stored in the old barn. We had agreed that I would keep them for six months and then I could get rid of them if I did not hear from you."

"Let me get the file," offered the attorney.

Must be a one-man office, thought John. He was waiting on the phone for a long time.

John heard rustling in the background and then he heard the telephone being picked up again.

"Here it is. Oh, yes! I told the two nieces that if they did not call me and make arrangements to move the items in the house that they would be disposed of in six months. From this file it is six months and more. So just toss them out or do whatever you want with the stuff. Is there anything good in there?"

"It is mostly just old trunks and dressers. I need something in writing, Mr. Townsend. I don't want the relatives coming back to me later and suing me for getting rid of the stuff."

"I understand, Mr. Hurley. I'll get something out to you today. My secretary is out sick, but I will type it myself. You said *two* things."

"Yes, I met the undertaker that processed The Captain's body and he said that he delivered The Captain's ashes to you at The Castle. I was wondering if you remembered where The Captain was buried."

"It was not delivered to me. It was delivered to my father who was the attorney at the time. But he is dead! I don't have a clue as to what the relatives did with the ashes. Knowing how the relatives felt about The Captain, they probably found the nearest garbage heap and disposed of him."

"Would it be in the file?"

"Let me see."

John waited, hoping that the ashes were disposed of somewhere very far away. Then every one in the Strange Valley could breathe easy.

"No, there's nothing in the file, Mr. Hurley. Sorry! Why are you so interested in the ashes?"

John had to think quickly. "The Captain hurt a lot of people up here in Elk Horn. No one can bear the thought that an urn containing his ashes is anywhere near where they live. They all hope that the ashes were strewn in the oceans that he sailed."

"Yes, I remember a lot of animosity from the neighbors when I was up there taking care of the sale of the property."

"Thank you anyway, Mr. Townsend. You have been most helpful."

John went to the barn to see what he was going to throw out or give to a charity. Suddenly he was looking at the furniture with a different eye. Once redone, some of the furniture would fit in quite nicely with the décor of The Castle. The rest of the items he would probably give to Mountain or Maggie if they wanted them.

John called his parents that night and asked them if they thought that Gramps was up to doing some refinishing of some old furniture he had discovered.

"His health seems okay, and he has been asking when we are coming to see you again, so I am sure he would love to come. But how would he get up there?"

"I'll pick him up."

"Call him and tell him you need him. He would like that. Tell Granny she is needed too."

"How is everything there? How is my house coming?"

"Dad is working hard on it. He is happy to be busy and appreciated."

"Well, I certainly do appreciate everything you both have done for me, Mom."

"I know Johnny. You are my favorite son."

John always laughed at that, since he was the *only* son, he was an only child. Growing up he had missed having any brothers or sisters.

But he spent a lot of time with his cousins who were like his siblings.

He also liked being the center of attention as an only child. He felt he had the best of both worlds.

CHAPTER FIFTY-EIGHT

Returning home after picking up his grandparents, they unloaded all the delicious strawberries they had bought. They were still in season. Second season!

"What are you going to do with all those strawberries, Granny?"

"I'll can them. Or make jam."

"Fantastic!" said John, wiping strawberry juice from his lips.

They had also stopped at the local hardware store to buy some canning equipment and some material that Gramps said he might need. It took a while to find exactly what Gramps and Granny wanted, and also to listen to the cashier's stories. Gramps bought some tools to replace the ones that he misplaced in The Castle.

The owner of the store had also caught John's eye and motioned for him to come over to talk.

"What is it?" John asked smiling. He knew some more small talk or rumor was coming.

"Remember that story I told you of a husband going to chop up his wife's lover when he got out of jail. And after he got out of jail no one could find the lover?"

"Yes, I remember the story."

"Well, they found him. They finally found the lover."

"Where did they find him?" asked John with a touch of interest in his voice for the benefit of the storeowner.

"In *your* back yard!" the storeowner announced gleefully.

"How do you know that?" John asked, thinking that it might be a made up story.

"One of the policemen told me."

"They definitely identified the body?"

"Yes, they did."

"Well, at least the lover had a lot of company for a long time," John said offhandedly.

Mr. Hardware got a kick out of that.

More death and mystery on his property! *Maybe I should turn it into a cemetery, since everyone seems to like to bury people there,* is a thought that he often had.

John's grandparents were spending the day with Mountain and Maggie. Maggie needed some help in learning how to properly can jam. Maggie's jam often went bad and had to be thrown away. Gramps was helping Mountain restore a small chest that had belonged to Mountain's mother.

John was glad for the respite.

Sitting with a glass of iced tea he was enjoying the animals that were coming and going from his property. There were deer, squirrels, and a myriad of birds that fed from his feeders. He even thought he saw a small fox. He hoped he would never see the mountain lions or bears that the community says roamed the Strange Valley.

Suddenly he heard a tramping noise. Almost like a parade sound. As if people were marching in step. Looking up the driveway he was surprised to see all of his neighbors marching, in step, towards him.

He could identify The Stinker, all the "animal people" and Carol's dad. To his surprise, there were many, many others that he did not recognize. They had never come by to tell him of their experience with The Captain.

Mr. Lang was the first to reach John.

"Hello, John."

"Mr. Lang," John said in acknowledgment.

"May we all speak to you?" asked Mr. Lang.

"Of course you can."

"May we come inside?"

John looked at the crowd and thought he could probably accommodate them all in his huge dining room.

They all marched in; dogs and cat as well. The women settled themselves around the dining room table and the men stood behind them.

Mr. Lang started by saying, "Please introduce yourselves."

It went around the table and finally John heard the names of the people he had called by their animal's names or their state of hygiene.

John acknowledged each with a nod.

John then waited for Mr. Lang to begin.

"My daughter Carol says you are a good man, Mr. Hurley."

"Thank her for me."

"She said we should come and talk to you and you would keep our conversations private."

"I will."

The Strange Valley

"Can I shake your hand on your word?"

"Of course," and John leaned over and shook on his word.

"As you may or may not know, Mr. Hurley, the Captain came to this Valley and affected the lives of everyone in this room. Some were affected in a minor way; others in a catastrophic way. Not one of us evaded his evil."

He continued, "From the killing of our animals; to the abuse and rape of our children and God knows what else—everyone has suffered. It is also believed that he murdered his own parents and siblings and the mother and wife of officers of the County. There are others that were affected that we don't even know about since some were too embarrassed or afraid to come forward."

John thought of The Captain's diary. He knew of all the others that had been harmed by The Captain.

"Finally, we all got sick of it and jointly made a plan that we thought might make him leave and then we would have some peace in the Valley. We decided to bombard him with threatening telephone calls and letters. We now know how stupid it was, but we were desperate. The police could not, or would not, help us. They said their hands were tied. So for a month we bombarded The Captain with calls, threatening his life, or at the very least threatening an awful beating."

"The Captain finally responded by letting us know that he had recorded all of our telephone calls and kept the letters that were sent to him. He told us that should anything happen to him his attorney would immediately turn them over to the police and we would all end up in jail."

"After The Captain died, we all held our breath. We had heard the rumors about the condition of his body and that did not fit with the story that a branch falling from a tree had killed him. But nothing happened. The police apparently decided it was an accident. They found a sawed off branch that they thought had fallen on his head and the saw was grasped in his right hand, so they immediately declared his death accidental and closed the case."

"As the years went by, we breathed a little easier. When you bought the house, we again began to worry. What if you found the tapes? What if you gave them to the police? What if they dug up the body and found he could have been murdered? What would happen to each and every one of us?"

John knew they had nothing to worry about. He had found the tapes and they were safe in a bank vault. They didn't know about the diary, and John had that as well. The only thing left for them to worry about was The Captain's ashes. But they did not know, at this time, that The Captain was cremated, and that there was something buried with The Captain that had been grasped in his dead boney hand that could point a finger at one of them.

Until all the pieces of the puzzle were before him, John could not, and would not, let these good people know what he had. At least not until he found the urn filled with The Captain's ashes, somewhere in the Strange Valley.

John saw they were all waiting for him to speak. "Mr. Lang and to all of you here, I knew there was a tape. Carol and I looked for it. We found nothing. Let me assure you that if I find these tapes the police will not get them and you will be the ones to decide how we dispose of them. If they are here, I will find them and I will make sure all of you are protected. I know The Captain was a very bad man. I will not let him hurt you again."

"Can we help you look?" piped up Mrs. Poodle.

"The tapes are not in The Castle, and Carol and I have already searched the barn thoroughly."

"Please, can we search the barn again?" pleaded Ms. Pussy.

John looked around the table and could see how worried all of these gentle people were. He knew if he allowed them to search the barn again it would give them some comfort and peace of mind.

"If that would make you feel better, I would be happy to let you do that."

They all got up in unison and almost happily marched to the barn. The dogs were barking gleefully, thinking they were off to play somewhere since the steps of their owners were so lively. Even Ms. Pussy's cat pranced towards the barn.

Mr. Lang walked with John. "These are very simple and honest people. Look around and you will see one man who is a Medal of Honor winner, and there are very few of our old warriors who have received that honor that are still alive at this time. There are at least two or three that have received the Purple Heart. So you can see they are good people, brave people—they don't deserve to have The Captain hanging over their heads."

"I understand, Mr. Lang. I understand perfectly and that is why I am willing to help in any way that I can."

The neighbors really went at it. Especially Mr. Lang! John again wondered if *he* did the deed, or maybe Mr. Lang thought perhaps his daughter Carol did it.

The neighbors were extremely thorough, but were careful not to break anything. They searched every nook and cranny. Every drawer on every dresser was opened and turned upside down. But they were very careful to replace everything as they had found it. They were even searching up in the rafters. Thank God John had gotten rid of the bones. The police had them now.

Suddenly Mr. Doberman yelled, "I found a box!"

John and the rest of the searchers ran to the spot and sure enough there was a wooden box with a lock on it.

"Where did you find it?" John asked dumbfounded! John could not imagine where it could have been hidden. Carol had searched so thoroughly.

Mr. Doberman pointed to a false bottom under a dresser drawer.

John knew it could not be the tapes or the diary, as he had them safely put away. Unless there were more in this box!

John picked the lock. He had learned to do this when he was on the police force. He was hesitant to do so in front of all the people in case something awful was in the box.

Inside the box were all sorts of things. There were women's hair barrettes, rings, necklaces, earrings and all sorts of other little objects. There were mostly women's accessories, but unfortunately some children's belongings as well.

"That ring was my sister's," said one man as his voice began to tremble. "My mother gave it to her for her Confirmation," and he started to sob as he cradled the ring in his hand.

"The little necklace belonged to Carol," Mr. Lang choked out.

"It appears he kept a little object from everyone he hurt," said John. From his detective days he knew that these serial killers or abusers tended to keep an object from each of their victims. A trophy! Rummaging through all the items in the box, John knew The Captain had hurt a lot of people.

"Let me hold on to these until we find the tapes and letters, then the curtain can be closed on this whole disaster. Then you can each take what item belonged to you or your loved one. I will put them in my safe deposit box for now. You can trust me. Do you all agree that I can put them away for now?"

They all shouted "YES" in unison. John felt good that they all trusted him. He would not break his word; he would not let them down. Many rings and necklaces were gently replaced by the relatives of the victims. They were a bit reluctant to let go of what was left of their loved ones. It was all that they had left to remind them of their beloved relative or friend.

If the situation was not as serious as it was he would have laughed at the troupe as they almost skipped down the path as they left for home. They were so happy to have found something. One among them was most certainly the killer. He or she had to be. They were all afraid, but one of them was probably petrified with fear. But John could not tell which one it was. He had a strong opinion as to who had done it, but as yet he could not prove it. Very often, his suspicion would shift from one neighbor to another. After all, they all had good reason to murder the man that had ruined their lives. He wondered if the truth would ever be known.

John also knew that although he had his suspicions as to who had committed the murder of The Captain, it could also be the most unlikely person of all the neighbors. This had happened over and over during his career as a policeman and a detective. Many a time, he and his fellow detectives were blown away when they solved the crime and discovered it was the least likely suspect.

Gramps and Granny came home, after visiting with Mountain and Maggie, and Granny berated John for doing nothing all day while *they* were busy at work. He did not tell them about the visit from the community of this Strange Valley and of their search and discovery.

"Go and bring in the jam that I made, it's on the front stoop," Granny ordered John.

"I'll get it later, Granny."

"You'll go and get it now, Johnny, with your lips trembling."

John looked at his grandmother and smiled. She was kidding but she had said that to him many a time when he was a young boy. "With your lips trembling!"

"Aye Granny, just don't beat me!"

John went and hugged his granny and she hugged him back. They had just shared memories of long ago, and it was sweet.

"Did you have a good time with Mountain and Maggie?"

"Och, aye—they are grand people," answered Gramps.

"I showed Maggie how to make some Scottish cakes. She showed me how to make her wonderful muffins."

"I'm glad you both had a good day."

"And how was your day, Johnny?"

"It was a bit strange, Granny. But all in all, it was a good day."

CHAPTER FIFTY-NINE

Granny was making breakfast when John came bounding down the stairs ready for a good workout.

"The 'wee wain' is still here, Johnny," Granny said as soon as he entered the kitchen.

"She is?"

"Aye, she still creeps into bed with me. She will not lie next to Grandpa."

"I don't blame her," John said, knowing what the last man in The Castle had done to her.

"What, Johnny?"

"Where is Gramps?" John asked, changing the subject.

"He is out walking the dog. Or the dog is walking him," she laughingly added.

It was comical to see the wee Scot walking Sutter the St. Bernard. But Sutter knew Gramps was old and weak and the dog was extremely gentle with him.

John saw his Gramps walking down the pathway. Gramps was a grand looking man with a full head of white hair and the biggest, blue eyes set in a handsome Scottish face. John hoped when he got old that he would look like his grandfather.

Gramps walked into the house rubbing his stomach and said, "I'm ready for a good breakfast, Lassie."

"That ye will have, my Laddie," Grandma kidded back. She went to work to cook her two favorite men their favorite breakfast.

She too was a grand looking woman—long, magnificent white hair pulled into a bun. Her green eyes were soft and pure. Her beautiful clear skin was without one wrinkle—even at her advanced age.

John wondered why he had never noticed how handsome his grandparents were. Now he knew he would never forget.

"What are you up to today, Johnny?" Gramps asked.

John ignored the question and announced to his grandparents, "I have a story to tell you. I hope it doesn't upset you."

They both looked at John as if to say, *what could possibly upset them?* After all, they had left family in Scotland and came to a strange country as youths. They had lived through so many wars. They had lost two of their children. What could be so bad that they would be upset?

John sat them down at the kitchen table and proceeded to tell them about The Captain, the bodies that were found on the property and about all of the community and their worries.

"Is that all?" Granny said when John was finished.

"You're not upset or frightened?"

"Och, no," said Grandpa.

John just shook his head.

"But the wee one will not come near me," said Gramps sadly.

Realizing that Granny had told Gramps about Emily, he said, "She was murdered by The Captain who was her father."

"The bloody bastard," whispered Gramps under his breath.

John decided to tell the whole story. "The little girl saved another little girl who lived down the street who was being abused by her father, The Captain, and he killed the little girl for saving her friend."

"Och, away!" exclaimed Granny.

"Mary," said Gramps, "You must cuddle her and talk to her. The wee little girl has suffered so."

"I talk to her every night. I know she is trying to tell me something. But I cannee tell what it is."

Now John thought he had seen it all. His grandparents were talking about a ghost as if it were real. Thank God his parents were not here. They would probably put his grandparents in a nursing home thinking they were daft.

"Let's keep this between just us," begged John of his grandparents.

"Och, don't worry Johnny. We'll no tell your parents. They would put us in a looney bin."

John loved these two wee Scots. He had loved them since the day he was born. He believed he had loved them even before he was born. He was sure of that. Most of his life was spent in their presence. They were not only his grandparents; they were also his pals. They had looked after him so often and bought him many of the clothes that he had worn; especially for Easter and Christmas. They always made sure he was the best-dressed kid on the block. He was their pride and joy.

Granny went to bed early that evening, and John and his grandfather sat in the huge leather chairs in the library, warming their feet in front of the fire in the fireplace and sipping a glass of Scotch.

The Strange Valley

John liked being alone with his Gramps. The old stories usually started after a few drinks. But tonight was a little different.

"Johnny, will you make me a promise?"

"Anything you ask, Gramps."

"Don't let your Mother ever put us in a nursing home."

"That will never, ever happen, Gramps. Never!"

"And if I should go first, you will take care of your grandmother."

"I will always take care of Granny. That goes without saying."

"She has been my love for over sixty years, Johnny."

"I know Gramps, I know."

"I think if she goes first I will follow by my own hand."

"Don't say that, Gramps!"

"I cannee live without her, Laddie," Gramps said, knowing it to be the truth. "When *you* find the right woman, you will know what I mean."

John could not speak. The tears were flowing down his cheeks.

"Och, Johnny, don't cry for us. We have lived a good life." After a pause, Grandpa added, "You have been a joy to us, Johnny."

John's throat was too constricted to reply.

Gramps continued. "I would like to be buried in Glasgow, Johnny. I want to be buried near my parents. In my bonnie Scotland! Och, I know, your mother will have none of it. But that is my wish."

In a raspy voice, John said, "If I can do it Gramps, I will take you back to Scotland. That is a promise."

"Granny *must* be buried with me. She must be right beside me, in death as she was in life."

"She will be beside you."

Gramps did not want his bonnie grandson to be so sad so he said with a sparkle in his eyes, "Don't let those bloody MacGregor grandchildren of mine get a hold of me. They are a bunch of bloody buggers. They never come to see us and that hurts your grandmother very much. But rest assured when we die they will be around like flies."

"I won't let them, Gramps," said John with a little smile.

"Oh, and *when* I go, have a grand party. Have lots of food and drink and lots of singing and dancing. I want to have a real old Scottish Wake."

"I will have the grandest party for you, Gramps."

"Mourners should not know if they have been to a wake or a wedding."

"I know. It will be the best party ever."

"Don't scrimp on the food or drinks like some do."

"That won't happen, Gramps."

"Have the bagpipers playing their tunes all day."

"They will play from morning to night, Grandpa."

Gramps looked at the grandson that he adored. "I thank God every day that you came into our lives, Johnny."

John responded "I would not be the man that I am today without you and Granny. I mean that with all my heart."

Then John saw that his Gramps' eyes were brimmed with tears.

"Gramps, you are feeling okay aren't you?" and John got up and knelt next to his grandfather and put his arm around his shoulders.

"Aye, Johnny—I'm fine. I just wanted to have this wee talk with you, just in case. I'm no a young man you know. God could take me at any time."

"Do you believe in God, Gramps?" John asked while trying to hold back his tears.

"Just look around you, Laddie. Do you think all this beauty just happened? Aye, there is a God and I thank him every day, on my knees, for what he has given me."

"You are such a good man, Gramps."

"I had to be, to be given a grandson like you."

After that, they sat in silence and drank until they were silly and stupid drunk, and started singing all the old Scottish songs.

It was a glorious night. It was a wee bit sad, but still a glorious night.

They half carried each other up the stairs that night singing "I belong to Glasgow," at the top of their lungs. Then they both fell into a drunken sleep, with a smile on their faces.

John was sure he would never love anyone the way he loved his grandfather. To John, the man was like a living Saint. The man had never, knowingly, hurt another soul in his entire life. John unfortunately could not say the same of himself.

Grandpa had been a good son to his parents. He had been a good husband, a good father, a wonderful grandfather. Ian MacGregor was a "good man"—and there was no greater compliment than that.

CHAPTER SIXTY

John and his grandfather came down the stairs the next morning at the same time. The old Scot looking and acting just fine! John's eyes were bloodshot and he felt like hell. But he could not let on to his grandparents how he felt. They would just say it was his Irish blood that was giving him the headache.

Granny looked at them both sternly.

Gramps turned to John and said, "We're in for it now, Laddie." He had a twinkle in his eye.

"You two should be ashamed of yourselves. You were loud enough to wake the dead."

John and Gramps looked at each other and in cheeky unison said, "Oh, did we wake Emily?"

"Don't be sacrilegious," she shot back, but with a slight smile on her face.

"Emily was not with me last night," she continued. "She must have been with you."

"That's okay, right Gramps? I don't think we said anything out of place."

"I hope you two didnee curse?" Granny said with a twinkle in her eye.

Gramps and John looked at one another and Gramps said, "That we cannee say, Mary, my very dear Lassie—that we cannee say."

"Eat up! Eat up! I'm sick of the two of you," she said in mock anger. "Maggie is coming over in a wee while and I want to be ready for her."

"Is Mountain coming too?" Gramps asked hopefully. He had formed a special bond with the big man.

"Oh, I don't know," said Granny as she looked out the window. "Who is that coming down the path, Johnny?"

John went to the window and saw Carol bouncing down the lane.

"It's Carol Lang, Granny. She's a friend of mine!"

Granny looked out the window and said, "I think she is more than a friend, Johnny."

"You always were a wise old bugger, Granny."

After some introductions and some small talk, Carol and John went outside for some air.

"I like your grandparents, John."

"Granny knows we slept together," John said to get a rise out of Carol.

"You told her?" Carol asked incredulously.

"No, she just knew."

"How?"

"I think she is a witch."

"John!"

"A good witch!"

"No such thing."

"Emily sleeps with her."

"Is your whole family nuts?"

"No! Just me, Gramps and Granny! This place has done it to us."

Carol laughed. "I came to thank you for what you did when my father and the neighbors came to talk with you. They were very impressed with you. They trust you and believe in you. My father told me all about it."

"I meant everything I said to them."

"I know you did."

"Now that Granny knows we slept together, can we do it again?" John asked in fun.

"Do you think we can put it all back together again, John?" Carol asked, suddenly serious. "After all that we have been through?"

"That's up to you, Carol. You have been so mad at me for so long."

"I'm trying to put the past behind me."

"All I asked you for was an address."

"You took advantage of me. It was privileged information. I could have lost my license."

John started steering Carol towards the guesthouse. "Let me take advantage of you again," he said smiling.

Carol was weakening; she just could not stay mad at John for very long. Then she said, "Wait a minute, John Boy—I am not that easy."

"I don't mean *right now*. Carol, I have something important to tell you."

Carol eyed John with suspicion, but followed him.

As she followed John to the guesthouse, she said, "I heard one of the neighbors found a box with some items in it."

"They are called trophies. The Captain kept a trinket from all of his victims. You included," he added.

Carol stood stock still. "My father did not tell me that."

"He had your little necklace."

The Strange Valley

Carol's eyes started to water. "He kept my necklace?" she asked with great surprise in her voice.

"You were lucky, Carol. I think he meant to kill you."

Carol just shook her head. "Where did the neighbor find the box? You and I looked everywhere."

"There was a mock drawer in one of the dressers. One of your smart neighbors suspected something, got a knife and forced it open. There, were all the things that The Captain had kept; the things he had kept from each of his victims."

"I'm surprised he didn't get Mrs. Chesney's locket."

"Apparently she would not let it go."

"I must tell Robert that."

"I think that would make him happy."

"Did Robert and his father come with the search party of neighbors?"

"No, they were not there."

"They probably didn't even know about it. I'm sure the neighbors don't want anything to do with the police. Even if Robert is a neighbor and his mother was murdered, he is still a policeman. I'm surprised his father was not there. It was his wife that was murdered. But I guess the neighbors figured an officer is an officer forever and did not invite him either. I guess they were not taking any chances," Carol explained to John.

John sat Carol at the kitchen table and held both of her hands in his.

"I hope this is good news," she said worriedly as she gazed into his eyes.

"I know you have been very worried that The Captain's body would be found and exhumed."

"I heard he was beaten to a pulp, John. And if the tapes are found, we are all in trouble."

"Carol, listen to me very carefully. The Captain was cremated."

Carol's heart skipped a beat. "How do you know?"

"I met the undertaker who had processed The Captain's body, and he said his father delivered The Captain's ashes to his attorney here at The Castle. By the way, it cost me three thousand dollars to get that information."

Carol could not resist jumping up and hugging John. John got up and made it a real hug. She pulled back and looked at him and then gave him a passionate kiss. John slipped his hand under her sweater and rubbed her back. She pulled away sharply.

"I thought that that information was worth a little feel," John joked.

"You make a joke out of everything, John," said Carol as she drew back. "Can't you ever be serious?"

"That's not my style."

Carol just shook her head. As usual, she was confused by John's behavior.

She jumped back to the conversation of The Captain's ashes. "Do you know where the ashes are?"

"No one seems to know."

"But we are out of the woods, right? He was cremated—he is just ashes?"

"Not necessarily. We don't know what might be among the ashes. I never looked at ashes before. Could The Captain have put up a good fight? Did he knock someone's teeth out and they are with The Captain's body? Do teeth burn? Did he grab a button, or someone's glasses? I won't feel at ease until we find the ashes."

He was dancing around the issue—he *knew* there was *something* buried with the Captain's ashes. Something that The Captain had grasped in his hand, but he did not want to make Carol any the wiser, at least not yet!

Carol's face went white.

"What?" asked John.

"My father has been missing a religious medal. He wore it every day. His mother gave it to him. Around the time The Captain was killed it went missing."

John knew what Carol was thinking, so he tried to ease her mind.

"Don't let your mind wander, Carol. He probably lost it at work or working around the horses. Your imagination is running wild."

"Yes, you are probably right. But what about the tapes, we still haven't found them."

John was not going to let on that he had the tapes and the diary.

"Nothing yet," he lied.

"Well, it is a plus that he was cremated, right?" Carol again asked, hoping that John would again put her mind at ease.

"A major plus!"

"What if we find nothing more?"

"Then you have to live with it and go on with your life. And the neighbors have to go on with their lives as well."

"It is a cloud over our heads."

"Right now, it is a cloud with a silver lining."

John knew that without The Captain's ashes the cloud would always be there. Even without the tapes and the diary, if the ashes were found and there was incriminating evidence found, then the case could reopen.

John also knew that Carol had lived with the fear all these years thinking that her father might have had something to do with the murder. He tried to dispel her fear, but he himself was suspicious of Mr. Lang's involvement in the alleged murder. Mr. Lang seemed very capable of killing someone. But then, there were many "old warriors" among the neighbors and these old warriors had killed many an enemy in their lifetime. Many had fought the Germans, the Japanese, the Koreans and any other enemy that was a threat to the United States of America. They might, very easily, be able to kill someone like The Captain, who was certainly "a major enemy." At this point, there were a lot of 'persons of interest.'

Carol put her arms around John's neck again, hoping to get them back on track. John did not need any coaxing and he responded very quickly by picking her up and heading for his bed, kissing her all the while.

As they were busily pulling the clothes off of one another, they heard a knock at the door.

"Who is it?" John asked with a husky voice.

"I've made a nice tea spread. I thought your friend would like a taste of my scones and jam."

"It's Granny," he whispered to Carol.

Carol started to redress herself. "Maybe I won't like your grandmother as much as I thought," she joked.

"Be right there, Granny."

"Okay, the kettle is on."

"First it is Robert, now it's your Granny. There is something working against us, John."

"We will have to find the right time and the right place."

"Perhaps you should come to my place in Redwood City."

"That sounds like a plan."

They promised each other that they would make a date and meet at her place where they would have uninterrupted privacy—where they might be able to resurrect the closeness that they had once shared.

As John and Carol ate the strawberries and cream that Granny had prepared for them, they held hands under the table.

"In Scotland, we call this a *High Tea*," announced Granny.

"You make the best High Tea in the world," John told his Granny.

Granny looked knowingly at John and Carol and knew they wanted to be alone.

"I'm off to find the old bugger," announced Granny, "before he kills himself. Gramps thinks he is still a young man and takes on too much."

John smiled. "Go to it, Granny." He knew that she had sensed that he and Carol were more than friends. She was definitely a good witch.

He suddenly felt a strange sadness. He did not know why. Perhaps it was because he realized his grandparents were quite old and he couldn't bear the thought that they might, one day soon, pass from this life. Suddenly the thought of that loss was just too much for John to bear.

But the sadness passed quickly because he knew his grandparents were not afraid of death. They had told him that quite often. They both felt they had lived a good life here on earth and were ready for the next journey. They always said they would go gently and willingly into the next life.

CHAPTER SIXTY-ONE

Where the hell did that attorney put those ashes, John was thinking as he worked around The Castle. *Did he bury it somewhere on the property?*

So much of the property had been dug up while retrieving all the victims of The Captain, that surely if it was on the grounds of The Castle, it would have been found.

I wonder if the attorney just dumped the ashes out somewhere. No, I don't think he would do that. John just kept working and thinking and talking to himself.

Strangely enough, he got a call that afternoon from the undertaker. It was as if they had been on a mental link.

"Mr. Hurley, I want to thank you again for that repayment of three thousand dollars. When I told my brother of your generosity he was dumbfounded. I also asked him if he knew anything about The Captain's ashes. He remembers our father telling him that *now* The Captain is a part of The Castle forever."

"What do you suppose he meant by that?"

"Who knows? That is all he remembers. I hope that helps you."

"Thank you so much for the information. I really appreciate it."

John thought to himself, *I don't know what prompted me to pay that bill, but it was the best investment of my life.*

At least now John knew The Captain was not buried on the grounds. He was somewhere in The Castle—but where? John believed he had searched every nook and cranny. Where could it be?

John decided to bring his grandparents in on the search for the ashes. They seemed delighted to be part of the mystery and the hunt. Somehow, before his eyes, his grandparents seemed to be getting younger.

"He's not in the bedroom we sleep in," Granny announced wisely.

"How do you know that?"

"Emily would not sleep in the same room as he."

So John crossed that bedroom off his list.

The Strange Valley

"Emily showed us where the bodies were buried, Granny. Do you think she could tell us where The Captain is?"

"I'll talk to her tonight."

The work on The Castle was really progressing. Gramps was restoring the woodwork in The Castle beautifully. Granny was busy canning food that would last John the rest of his life. Gramps wanted to start on the wainscoting in the dining room. It was the beautiful wood half paneling that lined the dining room walls. The wood was becoming dried out after all these years. Gramps said he could restore it like new.

"Go to it, Gramps."

Gramps was working very diligently. "You cannee rush these things, Johnny."

The smell of the materials Gramps was using was overwhelming. John would open the windows every day so that Gramps would not be overcome by the chemicals.

"Don't you smell that, Gramps?"

"At my age, I cannee smell a thing," and he closed the windows every time. "You are freezing my arse off, Johnny. Leave the windows closed."

John could not convince his Gramps that the window had to be open.

"And stop borrowing my tools, Johnny."

John worried that Gramps was getting very forgetful. He was forgetting where he put his tools and that was very unlike Gramps.

While closing the window that day Gramps noticed a change in the color of the wood below one of the dining room windows and pointed it out to John.

John stood back and looked at the window. "Can you fix it, Gramps? Can you match it?"

"Aye, Johnny, I can."

It wasn't long before John heard his grandfather ripping apart the paneling in the dining room. John wasn't worried. His grandfather was a master carpenter.

John busied himself in the library. He thought this would be his favorite room. Wood throughout, and wood shelves on all four walls that John would eventually fill with books of his desire. He had bought the greatest desk he had ever seen and it dominated the room. Yes, he would enjoy this room.

"Hey, Johnny!" he heard his Gramps call.

John went to the dining room as he knew his Gramps' hearing was not so good these days.

"What is it, Gramps?" John could see that Gramps had already ripped out the bad wood from beneath the window.

"There is something in there, Johnny." Gramps was flat on his stomach looking into the hole that he was working on.

"Move over, Gramps. Let me see what's in there."

John went to the window and got on his knees and stuck his arm into the hole and fished around until he hit something hard. He lay flat on his belly and stuck both arms in the hole in an effort to pull the object out of its hiding place.

He finally pulled it out and placed it on the dining room floor.

"What is it, Johnny?"

John looked at the object in disbelief. "I think it *is* The Captain. I think you found The Captain, Gramps."

"God's truth!" exclaimed Gramps. He was as shocked as John.

John brought it into the kitchen and placed it on the kitchen table.

"Get that bloody thing off my table!" screamed Granny.

"You are right, Granny" and John took the urn out to the guesthouse.

He turned to see if his grandparents were following him.

"We don't want to be anywhere near that devil," his Granny yelled after him.

John placed the urn on the kitchen table in the guesthouse. He got a cloth and wiped the outside of the urn. It was a beautiful urn. It was probably worth a lot of money in today's market. He just sat back and looked at it.

After all this time the mystery and misery of The Captain might be solved. Somehow he could not bring himself to open the urn. He was shocked to realize that his hands were shaking. He realized he could not open it right now. He had to digest the whole situation. He had to get use to the idea that he had finally found the urn and that the mystery might finally be solved.

The undertaker was right—The Captain *was* part of The Castle for many a year. And if not for his gramps he would have been there for eternity.

He sat and just stared at the urn. It was beautiful, but it contained such evil. The Captain did not deserve to be resting in such beauty.

John placed the urn in the bathtub where it belonged and covered it with a towel. Although he felt like flushing The Captain down the toilet he could not bring himself to do it.

He wondered if he should put it back where it was found and seal it in the wall forever.

When he returned to the main Castle, his granny asked, "Did you open it, Johnny?"

"No, Granny, I did not open it yet. I don't know why, but I am very nervous about what I might discover."

"You know, Johnny, Emily kept bringing me downstairs towards the dining room, but I kept bringing her into the kitchen for a cup of tea and a chat."

Johnny looked at his granny to see if she was going senile.

"Oh, she didnee talk back," Granny said after seeing the look on her grandson's face. "But I think she needed a granny who would talk and listen to her. I believe she was trying to lead me to The Captain's urn."

"Tell her thank you," John said cheekily.
"She needs to go home, Johnny. Back to God!"
"I'm doing my best to help her pass over, Granny."
"I know you are, Lad."
Gramps added, "She's a wee angel. She will be with the angels."

John as usual was surprised at his gramps' comments. He was seeing his grandfather in a whole different light. He was always a kind and gentle man despite his tough talk and rough exterior. But as he aged, he was getting kinder and gentler. He was a real gentle soul. John was again glad that he had bought this Castle. He was delighted that he got to know his "real" Gramps.

He vowed to spend more time with his grandparents. Maybe he could take them on a trip back to Scotland and they could travel to the Highlands that his grandfather so often talked about.

Yes, he would do that—he would take them back to Scotland now, while they were alive and well.

CHAPTER SIXTY-TWO

John was sleeping fitfully. He was having nightmares about what he would find in the urn.

He woke with a start in the middle of the night. He sat straight up in bed.

There was *the light* at the foot of his bed.

He rubbed his eyes and decided it was just a trick of the moon coming through the window.

He pulled the covers up over his shoulders, and then over his head, and tried to go back to sleep.

There was a tug at the sheets. John looked up and there was the light, still at the foot of the bed, getting brighter every second.

"What is it now, Emily?" he wearily asked. He was not afraid. He was totally used to Emily at this point and he knew she would not hurt him. At least that is what Maggie had told him.

The light started out of the room and down the stairs. When John did not follow, she returned and this time her light blinded him.

John got the message and grabbed his pants and tried to put them on while hopping and falling and trying not to break his neck by falling down the stairs. He was trying very hard to keep pace with Emily. He knew from the urgency of her walk and the brightness of her light that she wanted him to follow her and to follow her quickly.

Emily floated through the wall of The Castle and seemed to stop and wait for John to follow.

"Sorry, Emily, I have to use the front door," and he ran to keep up with her after closing the door behind him, keeping Sutter from following him.

The light went straight to the guesthouse. John opened the door and waited for Emily's light to enter. At this point, Emily's light did not enter the guesthouse, and she did not float back to The Castle—she went back like a streak of lightning!

The Strange Valley

Emily would not go near The Captain. She would not go near that devil. She would not go near his ashes.

"So you want me to open the urn, eh, Emily? Well the least you could have done was to stay with me." John laughed at that. He was berating a ghost.

John retrieved the urn from the bathroom and put it on the table. He did not want to open it. He had dreaded this moment. But it had to be done sometime and now was as good a time as any. It's what Emily wanted.

He had a hard time getting the top off of the urn. His hands were shaking. After all, it had been over twenty years since the top had been sealed.

Finally it broke free. John peeked in the urn to see what was in there. Just ashes! After donning a pair of gloves he dug into the ash and he coughed as the dust of the ashes flew up. "Damn you, Captain. You are a pain in the ass even now." It sickened John to think that he was inhaling some of The Captain's ashes. He knew now that he should have worn a mask—but it was too late. He tried to spit out the taste of the ashes but they were still floating, polluting the air.

He rifled through the ashes very gingerly. He knew it was a human body and even though it was the ashes of the devil, he would show it respect.

John was beginning to feel confident that there were only ashes in the urn. No teeth, buttons, or glasses from The Captain's killer were among the ashes. There was nothing among the ashes that would point to anyone in this Strange Valley. Nothing at all! John felt relief flow through his body.

Then his hand hit something hard. "Dear Lord, let it just be a bone," he prayed out loud.

He fished out the hard object and brought it over to a better light and wiped away twenty years of dirt, grime and ashes.

John looked at the object in the full light of the lamp.

Oh shit, John whispered to himself. John's hands shook. Was the mystery solved? Did he now know the killer of The Captain? Perhaps!

He gripped the object in his hand and thought of all the people that would be hurt by this discovery. People that he had grown close to! People that he had come to like and indeed love very much. This discovery would cause a cloud to descend upon the Valley, never to lift for decades.

The owner of this object was a murderer. But should there be punishment for murdering the filth of the earth like The Captain?

John knew that he had spent his life defending the public from murderers and bringing them to justice. But what should he do now? He knew he would lose many a good night's sleep trying to decide on the moral issues of reporting the discovery and the human decision to not report the discovery. In his mind, he thought he knew the answer.

But a question came into his policeman's mind. Could it have been a set-up? Could the murderer have placed this object in The Captain's dead hand to take the suspicion off of him or her? He had been a detective long enough to know that *nothing* is ever what it seems.

John knew the mystery was not really solved—as yet. At first he had been so sure. Now he was as confused as ever.

He made a vow to himself and all the surrounding neighbors, that somehow, he would discover the true killer.

CHAPTER SIXTY-THREE

The next morning John swore his grandparents to secrecy. They were to tell no one about the discovery of the urn.

He immediately went to the bank and put the object he had found in the urn with the diary and the tapes. The object that had been clutched in the death grip of The Captain's hand!

As he sipped a cup of tea later that day he wondered what he should do.

It's all there, he thought. *I have almost everything that is needed to solve the mystery of the Strange Valley. Now what the devil do I do?*

His thoughts were interrupted by the call of his grandfather.

"Come here, Johnny, I have something to show you."

"Where are you?"

"I'm in the dining room with your grandmother."

John walked into the dining room and asked, "What's up, Gramps?"

"Look at the dining room table, Johnny."

There on the table were all the tools that had been lost by John, his father, his grandfather and Mountain.

"Where did they come from?"

With a smile, his grandmother said, "It could only have been Emily. You have found everything that she wanted you to find—and now you can have your tools back!"

John had time to think about what he should do with the urn, tapes and diary. His grandparents wanted to go back to San Francisco to check on their wee little house. So he drove them back, and he had a chance to check on his own house.

As he entered his house in the Sunset, he was amazed at the transformation. His old house was now almost brand new.

"It's beautiful, Dad. You did a great job. It is better than new."

"I enjoyed doing it for you, John. I even did some of the work myself. Maybe I'll do a little job here and there and make some extra money."

"Once word gets around, Dad, you won't have a minute to yourself." That pleased his father.

"I like being busy. This retirement business isn't all it is cracked up to be."

Later that day, visiting Calvin, he was overjoyed that he was totally well, and back on the job.

He met Susan in Chinatown for dinner. "I still miss you, John!"

"You must come up to The Castle soon, Sue. It's almost finished."

"Why do you call it a Castle, John?"

"Because it is," and he whipped out a picture.

"Oh, my Lord, what in the name of Heaven made you buy such a big place?"

Thinking of what had transpired in the last few weeks he replied, "It was my destiny."

"Will you come to my condo for a nightcap?" Susan asked hopefully.

John cupped Susan's chin in his hand. "Not tonight."

"Am I too much for you, John?"

John smiled, understanding the inference of the new Sue.

"It's a challenge, but I'm game to take you on; just not tonight."

After leaving Susan, he thought of calling Carol. But he did not want to blurt out anything about the urn and what he had found among The Captain's ashes; and of course, he didn't want her to find out about the diary and tapes. They were always on his mind and he did not want to slip up.

He had asked her not to tell anyone that The Captain had been cremated and he was sure she would keep her word. She did not know that John had found the urn with The Captain's ashes, and he would not tell her—not yet!

He was still not sure of what to do. This was a murder! The murderer, he assumed, was still alive.

John tried to envision what happened that night of The Captain's alleged murder.

The murderer could have gone into the woods earlier and sawed off a large limb of a tree so that The Captain would be intimidated when he saw him with the huge limb in his hand. Did he put the saw into The Captain's hand?

But how was The Captain lured into the back woods?

Did he go willingly? Was he forced?

Was there an altercation? Apparently, there must have been a struggle if The Captain had ripped something off of the attacker's clothes.

What did the murderer want? Did he or she want The Captain to stop the murders of the animals? Did he or she want him to stop the abuse of the children of the Valley? Did he or she want him to stop the murders of their loved ones? Did he or she want to find their loved one? Did they just want The Captain to move out of their Valley and to let them breathe freely once again?

Could it have been a simple accident?

The Strange Valley

Another thought entered John's mind. Did each of the neighbors come by once The Captain was discovered dead either by accident or murder, and each give him a good wallop? Was the word of The Captain's death passed from neighbor to neighbor, and then one by one they had their revenge by beating the hell out of the corpse?

Perhaps the inhabitants of the Valley were just trying to protect the real murderer—so they each took a turn in beating him, not really knowing if he was dead or alive. Apparently, at the time, they didn't care.

Is that why they were all so anxious to have the mystery settled? Did they all have a guilty conscience? Were they afraid that the truth would come out once the body was found?

There were so many unanswered questions. Would the truth ever be known?

Then he remembered. *He was cremated*, he said to himself. *They will all be happy to know that The Captain was now just ashes and no longer a threat to most of them. But one among them was still in danger.*

So many scenarios went through his mind, but it was all speculation. The truth would only be known when he confronted the murderer—whoever that was!

He had always been a good and honest detective. He still wondered if it was his moral responsibility to turn in the urn and the object he had found among the ashes. If it *was* a murder—it was wrong! Maybe he should let the authorities sort it out!

Then the thought of all the bodies that were found on his property and all the alleged sexual attacks came into his mind. He wondered why The Captain had not been killed much earlier. Why had this Strange Valley waited so long to stop that evil man?

He had sympathy only for the residents of Elk Horn. He had never met The Captain, but he hated him, for all the horror and damage he had done in his short life.

CHAPTER SIXTY-FOUR

It was two full weeks before John decided how he would handle the discoveries that he had made. These were simple and gentle people that he was dealing with. Most of them now closer to death than life, and he did not want to scare them. He wanted to give them peace of mind for the rest of their lives, however long that might be.

He had to decide the best way to divulge all the information about the tapes, diary and the urn.

The people of this Strange Valley did not know John very well. He was a stranger to them. He was a new resident. Not really one of them! He couldn't be trusted one hundred percent. At least not yet!

If he just told them that he had found the items and disposed of them, he knew they would not be satisfied. They would still worry, all of their lives, that the truth would be discovered.

John had to prove to them, without a shadow of a doubt, that the items would never, ever, be found, and they were safe for the rest of their lives.

He had gone through many scenarios but finally settled on one scenario that would be gentle and easy on the people of this Strange Valley.

He called Carol and told her that he had made some discoveries and he wanted to gather together all the neighbors that were involved in the atrocities that were committed by The Captain. He wanted to have a big gathering, to have a big party. And all the neighbors involved *must* attend. *Every one of them must attend!*

They must come dressed in their very best clothes. It would be an "affair to remember" for the rest of their lives and they must dress for the occasion.

"You want them to come dressed up, as if for a wedding?" asked a bewildered Carol.

"Exactly!"

"Okay, but I don't understand why. Besides many of these people may not have dress-up clothes."

"Then they must buy them or borrow them or just wear the very best that they have. But this is going to be a fancy dress-up affair."

"What discoveries have you made, John? Can't you share them with me?"

"I am going to share them with everyone at the same time. Please trust me!"

"Okay, I guess I *have* to trust you. Let's get together and make a list. We don't want to forget anyone. But I have to tell you, I'm not sure about this whole idea of yours. I don't understand what you are trying to do."

"I'm asking you again to trust me, Carol."

"Okay, I'll get going on the list."

"Good idea," he responded.

There were close to seventy names on the list once it was finished. All the people on the list were personally notified of the date and time to meet at The Castle for the party and an important announcement.

They were also sent a written invitation so that they would know it was an "important" event. It was a formal invitation! Much like a wedding invitation, and there were reply cards that had to be returned.

None of the people that were invited balked at the dress code. As a matter of fact they loved the idea. They did not know why there was to be a big party, but they were more than happy to attend. They would have preferred that the party was held somewhere else—most of them hated The Castle, for good reason.

John laughed at the date of the meeting. Friday, the Thirteenth!

The day finally arrived, and John looked out the window at the tables and chairs he had set up for the big party. He had rented plates and silverware. Only the best for this important occasion!

He had rented everything from a local store and Mountain had helped him set up the tables and the formal settings. There was a head table and two side tables on either side. A total of seventy seats, set up like a wedding reception. That made John a little nervous. He hoped Carol didn't get any ideas.

Mountain and Maggie would come later with food and drink once the big show was over. They would wait for John's call. They too were in the dark as to why this affair was being held. John felt it better that they too did not know.

The disc jockey that John had hired to play music was also waiting at Mountain's house. He too would come right over when called.

Everyone arrived on time. They were all very curious, excited, and very nervous; and some had looks of dread on their faces.

Carol was still in the dark as to what John's plans and discoveries were. She was just following his directions, putting pads and pencils by everyone's seat.

She was dressed beautifully with a flowing satin dress. John was handsome in his formal tuxedo.

It was a beautiful day, thank goodness! The sun was shining, it was eighty degrees. It was the start of a perfect day and John hoped it would end that way.

John could hardly recognize the people as they arrived at The Castle, one by one, without their animals.

Ms. Pussy wore a wide brimmed hat and a beautiful flowing chiffon dress; complete with long white gloves. She probably wore it as a young girl, but she looked lovely now as well.

Mr. Stinker had on a tuxedo. He looked very dapper.

Mr. Lang looked like a local banker with his three-piece suit and tie.

He could not put a name to the woman who came in her wedding dress.

Mr. Bird came in his old Marine uniform. It still fit and there were many medals pinned to his chest.

Many other men also came in their military uniforms. Some came in their Navy blues with the bell-bottom trousers. The buttons around the fly area gave away the era in which the men served. Others were dressed in their old khaki uniforms. He could see the Medal of Honor medal and the Purple Heart medals—they were all shining brightly.

John could see that most of the men had served during the Second World War. Some he believed served in the Korean War and perhaps one or two had served in Vietnam.

They all wore their uniforms with great pride, as they should—they were our warriors of our past!

One woman was wearing a nurse's uniform with the Purple Heart pinned proudly to her chest.

One gentleman was wearing a WWII German uniform. And he too wore it proudly! His country had lost the war but he had fought the good fight. He also held an American flag in his hand to show his neighbors where his allegiance now lay.

This was not only a Strange Valley but possibly the most patriotic group of people he ever had the privilege to meet.

There were a lot of stories that these people could tell. John vowed that after the mess of The Captain was settled he would make sure he heard them all.

Yes, they all marched in, one by one, in their finery. The Chesneys, father and son, came in their police uniforms. One still active, the other proudly retired.

Once they were all seated, John got started. "Just under a year ago, I bought this Castle. I felt it was here that I could have the privacy and solace that I felt I needed at the time. The truth was I was in hiding. I could not admit it at the time, but that was one of the reasons I bought this place. I am a retired detective and I had sent a killer to jail for life and he had threatened to kill me. I was

The Strange Valley

scared! So I hid! Every time a car pulled into my driveway I thought it might be my killer. Every time someone came down my driveway I was sure they were there to kill me. I thought that every car that drove in back of me on the streets and highways was my enemy. I lived in fear! Then I faced up to the danger and settled it once and for all, and now I am free."

"All of you, like me, have been living in fear. There has been a threat hanging over all of your heads for a long time. I have seen it in your faces and in your voices. I believe it is time you had some peace."

Everyone seemed to be nodding their heads at that last statement.

He said strongly and loudly so everyone could hear. "I have found the tapes that The Captain made of all of your threats." There was a nervous murmur throughout the crowd. "I have listened to them and I recognized each and every one of you."

No one in the crowd moved. Some hardly breathed. They were frightened! They did not know this man very well and he had their future in his hands.

"Now, it is against the law to tamper with evidence. If we destroy the tapes we are all breaking the law. You must all understand this. If we agree to destroy them then it must be unanimous. There is a pad and pencil in front of you. I want you to write "yes or no" and fold the paper. In the meantime I am going to play the tapes for all of you to hear so you are sure I am telling the truth."

John had decided on this type of vote so that if just one person voted "nay" he or she would not suffer the anger of all the others. If there should be *one* "nay," then the afternoon event would be over. A unanimous vote was needed.

As the tapes were played, you could hear the anger of the then younger voices spewing out over the tapes. The voices were older now, but still recognizable. Some of the residents of The Strange Valley were wiping away tears. It was bringing back all the memories of the horror and anger of the past.

Carol gave him an "I can't believe you are doing this" look of disbelief. She was also frightened as she recognized very clearly the voice of her father.

John had set up a burning barrel that he usually used for leaves and pine needles. He had set it up in the middle of the tables and he ceremoniously pulled out the ribbons of the tapes and threw them into the fire. The crowd simultaneously rose and erupted into applause and cheers as they kissed and hugged one another.

"I need your attention," John yelled to quiet down the crowd. They all turned their attention to John. "There are three parts to this ceremony!"

Everyone looked at each other in puzzlement.

"I also found a diary of The Captain's. I have read it. It is sickening. It tells in detail what he has done to you or your loved ones or your beloved animals. Do any of you want to read it?"

In unison, they all said, "NO!"

"Then I need each of you to come up and tear out a page and put it in the fire. We all have to be a part of this decision. This too is against the law! We are tampering with possible evidence!"

One by one they rose and eagerly went towards John and some gently tore out a page and threw it in the fire and clapped their hands up and down as if to say "finished!" Others ripped out the pages in anger. One person, tellingly, tore out two pages. John knew that that person had suffered more than the others. When the last person threw his page in the fire, John tore out one for Emily and threw the entire book in the fire. Again there was applause and cheers. They were beginning to unwind and enjoy the celebration.

"A little kindergartenish, isn't it, John?" whispered Carol. Although she was overjoyed at the events of the day she was also a bit peeved. "Why did you not fill me in on the discoveries before this?"

"I believed it was the best way to handle it. They are simple, good people. I needed a simple solution and I believe this is the best way. I didn't tell you or anyone beforehand, in case the secret leaked out."

John then pointed to what seemed like a piñata hanging from a nearby tree.

"My friends," John said looking from one neighbor to the other and he pointed to the urn. "That is the urn that contains The Captain's ashes! HE WAS CREMATED!"

Once again, they all rose in unison and again there were cheers and sustained applause. They would not stop clapping and they would not sit down. They were high-fiving each other. Some were hugging and indeed some were kissing. One or two of them were doing a little jig. No one could now prove that The Captain was murdered and mutilated.

John still wondered how they all knew the condition of The Captain's body when it was found. It was not a matter of record, just a rumor. His death certificate stated "accident." He again wondered if they could *all* be guilty in some major or minor way.

Upon looking at the faces of the crowd of people cheering and applauding, John was almost sure that each and every one of them had gotten in a "good lick" once The Captain was found in the woods. Perhaps no one would ever know who gave the final, fatal blow. Then again, the one who gave the first blow could have been the one who gave the fatal blow, and that person probably knew it—or perhaps he didn't know it! Well, *now*, no one would ever know!

He again looked at the neighbors who were dressed in their service uniforms. They, especially the ones with the Purple Hearts and Medals of Honor, were certainly used to death, had probably killed many an enemy during their service. They could have killed The Captain very easily and with no remorse. The Captain had been hated more than any foreign enemy.

The Strange Valley

"Each of you is allowed a swing at the urn." He handed the bat to Mr. Lang to start. It almost did a complete loop around the branch he hit it so hard. Mrs. Poodle had quite a swing as well. Ms. Pussy surprised everyone with her strength. And so it went; they were each getting a swing at The Captain and it was releasing a lot of emotion and anger. They seemed to be enjoying it.

John cringed as the expensive urn was beaten and battered. He probably could have sold it for quite a bit of money. But it was better this way. It helped to release some of the anger that the neighbors had harbored in their souls for so long. It would give them closure.

As the last person swung the bat at the now heavily dented and almost unrecognizable urn, John again addressed the crowd.

"There is one last thing. How shall we dispose of the ashes? Let's take a vote. Write it down on your pads."

Everyone sat with pen and paper and gave it serious thought. Some wrote down an answer very adamantly; some had their pencils resting between their teeth as they thought of a good answer. John thought it was a bit like *Jeopardy* on TV. Who would write the right answer?

John was enjoying the day. He was getting satisfaction from the fact that he was giving a lot of people a new lease on life.

John read the answers that everyone had written. He then read them out loud. "Flush him down the toilet." That brought a cheer. "Feed him to the pigs." That brought a bigger cheer. "Throw him in the ocean." "Bring it to Lake Tahoe. The water is cold and deep there." Some were so disgusting he decided not to read them out loud.

"This one is the best," he finally said. Indeed John had decided a long time ago how the ashes would be disposed of. None of the neighbor's suggestions would be used. He believed his idea was the best and would long be remembered. But the neighbors would now think that one of them had chosen the way The Captain's ashes would be disposed of.

Just then, Maggie and Mountain arrived with the food and drink and began setting up the tables with knives and forks and platters of food that they themselves had prepared. Real plates were used. No paper plates for this event. Almost like a wedding! It was a special occasion!

A neighborhood disc jockey from one of the local bars came and set up his paraphernalia. He had been instructed to play songs of the twenties, through to the eighties.

Everyone was milling around the tables, admiring the flowers and settings. Eventually, they made their way to the delicious food and began to wolf it down. John took down the urn and went to his cellar.

He filled seventy little canning jars of Granny's with The Captain's ashes. He mentally apologized to Granny. *I'll buy you more jars Granny, don't worry.*

He put each jar into a brown paper lunch bag and brought them up to be given to each of the attendants of the party as they left the celebration.

As he came back to the reception with the little brown bags and some extra wine he had grabbed from the huge wine cellar, he heard the music of Glenn Miller floating through the air. Some of the neighbors were dancing cheek to cheek and swaying and humming along with the tune.

John just stood back and admired the dancers. Ms. Pussy's chiffon dress was flowing in the wind. Others were doing the Peabody, a dance that was becoming an endangered species. The Charleston had the elderly huffing and puffing but they did it with a smile on their face. He had never seen the classic Tango danced before, but two guests were dancing it today, at this special party.

John was sorry that his grandparents weren't there to do a Highland Fling or an Eightsome Reel. At this point that was the only thing missing.

When a slow two-step came on, he took Carol's hand and led her to the dance area. They danced very close to each other to a very old romantic song. The words of the song had been sung by many great singers for many, many years. Many lovers had hummed the tune as they swayed to the music in anticipation of what could follow.

John felt that a good song and a good dance partner were sometimes better than sex.

They did not speak; they just swayed with the magical song.

After the dance, Carol and John sat and had a drink and watched the festivities.

It was as if a Somerset Maugham or an F. Scott Fitzgerald novel had come to life. He could see the look on Maggie and Mountain's faces and he knew that the moment was magic for them as well.

Mountain and Maggie had catered a marvelous event. They were naturals at this. "They should open their own place and cater to the public," said John.

"This was a great idea, John, even though you kept me in the dark."

"Thank you, Carol. And thank you for the dance."

"I didn't know you could dance so well."

"I was the best dancer in George Washington High School."

"Well, you haven't lost your touch."

"Are you happy you won't have to worry about your father anymore?"

"What do you mean by that?"

"You thought that perhaps your father had killed him, didn't you?"

"I was desperately worried that perhaps he had killed him after finding out about the abuse that I had sustained at The Captain's hand. The fact that he could not find his religious medal made me a nervous wreck. But he is not the type of man to murder anyone."

"Now you don't have to worry one way or the other. No one has to worry anymore."

"Yes, thanks to you! I'm most grateful."

"Well there is a way you could make it up to me," John said with a sly grin.

"Do you think about nothing but sex?"

"I have to admit, it has occupied my mind since I was fourteen."

"You did it at fourteen?" she asked incredulously.

"No! But it wasn't for the lack of trying."

"You are bad, John!" Carol said with a slight chuckle in her voice.

"Yes, I know!"

Carol just smiled. She whispered, "Come by tonight and I will see what I can do."

John just nodded in anticipation.

They continued to watch the festivities with a smile on their faces.

Young Officer Chesney was now dancing with Ms. Pussy. She seemed to be leading him in the dance.

The Stinker and Mrs. Poodle were doing the Twist.

Everyone had a partner for at least one dance.

It appeared that they had not enjoyed themselves for a very long time. They had spent so many years in distress. Now they were making up for lost time.

Mr. Castle had found and gotten rid of the tapes that could send them to jail. Mr. Castle had found a diary that they didn't even know existed and had destroyed it. And finally, Mr. Castle had found The Captain's ashes and pretty soon those ashes would disappear as well. They would all now be free!

John believed this is what the guests were all thinking about on this glorious day.

CHAPTER SIXTY-FIVE

As everyone was leaving, they all shook John's hand or kissed him and hugged him and thanked him for all he had done for them. Some of them were walking arm in arm down the path. This affair had apparently ignited a passion in them that had been silent for many years.

Good for them, John cheered to himself.

As he handed each of the neighbors their little brown bag, he had to laugh as they almost skipped down the driveway with their little gift bag they were given to take home; just like little kids.

In the bag they would find a note that said, "Do as you wish with your little piece of The Captain."

John knew what to do with his little jar. He would keep it in a prominent place in his home to remind him of what evil there can be in this world.

As the last guest approached, John gave him one mighty handshake. John looked him straight in the eye to see his reaction. The look on the face of the guest went from total surprise to recognition. The guest looked down at what John had pressed into his hand. His old police badge.

Finally, after looking at it for what seemed like ages, he whispered hoarsely, "Where did you find it?"

Officer Andrew Chesney, Sr. seemed to have aged twenty years in the last few minutes.

"It's a long story."

"Can we go somewhere and talk?" asked Andrew Chesney, looking around, hoping that all of his neighbors had left and were not within earshot.

John now knew that his guess was correct—Officer Andrew Chesney Sr. was the murderer!

John took the officer's arm and led him to the guesthouse. Even though Chesney was retired, John respectfully referred to him as Officer Chesney.

John handed Officer Chesney a can of beer as they settled on the couch.

The Strange Valley

Chesney was waiting for an answer to his first question. Again he asked, "Where did you find it?"

"I found it among The Captain's ashes. Before that, I believe The Captain had it grasped in his hand. The undertaker that took care of him when he died said that The Captain had something held tightly in his hand but he could not remove it. Because there were no relatives interested in having a ceremony, he just cremated him."

"I have worried myself sick over the loss of this badge for the last twenty years. I had hoped it had just dropped in the woods somewhere."

"Why don't you tell me what happened."

"Are you the only one that knows about this badge?"

"I'm the only one."

"My son does not know?"

"No."

Andrew Chesney sighed in relief. He had been waiting for this day for years. He had lived in dread for so many years. His only concern now was for his children. Although they were now adults, he did not want them to suffer the loss of another parent. They had suffered quite enough.

CHAPTER SIXTY-SIX

Chesney sat silent for a minute and then began. "I went to The Captain to find out where my wife was. That's all I intended to do. I wanted to find my wife. She had been gone too long and she needed to come home to me and the children. The Captain just ranted and raged and cursed at me. I grabbed him by the shirt and dragged him into the woods to scare him. I picked up a broken branch and threatened to hit him with it."

"*You* didn't saw it off?"

"There was no sawed off limb there at the time."

"We started to scuffle, and he hurt me more than I hurt him. I was surprised at his strength. Then he said the most awful things about my wife. Sexual things! Things he said they had done to and for one another. I went wild! I hit him on the head with the heavy branch. He lunged at me and I guess that is when he got my badge. Then he fell, bleeding. I got scared and ran."

"I didn't hear anything for days. I half expected some of my fellow officers to come and arrest me, but nothing happened. No one came."

"A few nights later I went back to see if he was still there. I hoped he wasn't there. I hoped he had gotten up and went home. I could not believe my eyes. He was beaten to a pulp. I swear, Mr. Hurley, I only hit him once. I don't know who did the rest. I didn't think I hit him hard enough to kill him."

"Finally, after many weeks he was found. I was off duty that day, thank God, and two fellow officers responded to the call. They called it an accident."

"How could they call it an accident?" John asked.

"Apparently, someone had gone back and laid a saw in The Captain's hand and a sawed off branch lay right by his head, it was covered in blood."

"What about the condition of the body?"

"They said the animals did it. They say the animals tore him apart."

"Did you ever think that maybe you *did not* actually murder him? Perhaps you just stunned him."

The Strange Valley

"I didn't mean to really hurt him. I just wanted to scare him and get answers about my wife. But all these years I did believe that I *might have* been the one that caused his death."

"Someone may have found him, realized he was not dead and finished the job," offered John.

"I don't know. I guess I will never know."

"It seems to me that it was a joint effort. Perhaps they thought it was you and they tried to protect you. Or perhaps they just hated him so much they all had to get a shot at him. Just like today—or maybe the animals *did* get him."

Chesney looked again at his badge. "Are you going to turn me in?"

John shook his head no.

"As a fellow officer, it is your duty to turn me in, you know that."

"I am no longer an officer. I will not turn you in. Any other time I might have. But I believe you might have done the world a favor. You might have saved a lot of lives. The Captain would never have stopped his criminal ways. Besides, we don't know if *you* actually killed him."

"How can I be sure that you won't turn me in because of this badge?"

"It is the word of one officer to another."

With a sigh, Officer Chesney said, "That's good enough for me."

"Besides, would I have had the big event of today if I were going to turn you in? I don't agree with what you might have done, but I believe if you did it, it was a crime of passion. In my career as a police officer and a detective I have seen real bad murderers go free. I believe you rid the world of an evil man." He then gave the old officer a slight grin. "But don't do it again!"

Chesney looked at John, and said, "Thank you for my life."

John looked at Chesney and saw the lines that had almost completely taken over his face. Not one laugh line. Just frown lines. Like the lines of a sad clown.

"I'm sorry for the loss of your wife," John finally said.

"I don't think I will ever get over it," Andrew Chesney said ever so sadly.

"Just go and enjoy your grandchildren. They deserve to have you around. Don't let The Captain take that away from you as well."

John walked down the path with him and shook his hand once again.

As John turned and started to walk back towards The Castle, Officer Chesney called after him, "One last thing, Mr. Hurley!"

"Yes?"

"When I went back to the body the first time, I found . . . this." Andrew Chesney rummaged around in his pocket and drew out a metal object. John looked at the officer's hand and there lying in Officer Chesney's hand was a religious medal.

John was stunned. Mr. Lang's medal! It had to be!

"You found *this* by the body?"

"Yes. I went back, hoping The Captain would not be there. That I had not really killed him! I found The Captain and this medal, lying by his body."

"You kept it all these years?"

"I have *worn it* all these years. I saw it as a sign of forgiveness. Perhaps as a Catholic I read meaning into it that was not true. But it has kept me going all these years. Can you understand that, Mr. Hurley?"

John could. He had a St. Jude's medal that his mother had given him when he was a teenager, and he carried it with him all the time. His friend Cal was a Buddhist and he carried something of his religion with him as well. His friend, Officer Bernard Swartz, a Jew, wore a Star of David around his neck. So yes, he could understand that the medal gave Chesney some peace of mind.

John took it in his hand and asked if he could keep it, as he thought he knew who it belonged to.

Chesney nodded in assent. "Don't tell me whose medal it is Mr. Hurley, I don't want to know."

Chesney wanted to thank John again, but the tears streaming down his cheeks embarrassed him and he turned quickly toward home.

As he neared the end of John's driveway he stopped and shouted back, "If I can ever do something for you . . ."

John shouted back, "You are the first one I will call."

CHAPTER SIXTY-SEVEN

After such a long and eventful day, John was ready for a good night's sleep and turned in early.

He settled into bed, and not long after, Sutter sauntered in, jumped up onto the bed, walked around in circles a few times and snuggled in for the night.

John was exhausted and thought he would nod off right away, but he couldn't sleep—he was over-tired. He tossed and turned for a long while, then gave up, got out of bed, pulled on his robe and went down to the kitchen to forge through some of the day's leftover food. The refrigerator was crammed full of the food that Maggie and Mountain had prepared. John found some cold chicken drumsticks, and a container of milk. He sat down at the kitchen table and dug in, not bothering to get a glass for the milk—he drank straight from the container knowing his mother would have a major fit if she saw him.

As he ate, John pondered the last secret the Strange Valley had. John vacillated back and forth, just a little, about who he thought really murdered The Captain. Was it Andrew Chesney or one of the neighbors of the Strange Valley. There was no definite proof as to what happened that night. He could not fault anyone who had given the killing blow. If he was in the same position, he might have murdered The Captain as well.

John finished off the chicken, took a last swig of milk from the carton, and headed back to bed.

He climbed back into bed, careful not to wake Sutter.

Even though he was a very gentle natured dog, if you woke him unexpectedly, he would let you know his displeasure with a growl.

John got himself comfortable, and after still not being able to drift off to sleep, it finally came to him the reason why. It was his old detective instincts kicking in. Whenever he worked on a case, as a detective, it would always bother him if there were any loose ends.

Someone, one of his neighbors, was a murderer, and he could not prove who.

John thought the way he had handled the burning of the tapes and diaries and the bashing of the urn was the best way to close the chapter on The Captain. He wanted to handle the situation in a very simple way that everyone would understand. But he was beginning to have second thoughts. The Captain deserved a painful, prolonged death, but was *he* letting a murderer *go free* to possibly kill again?

Well John, he thought to himself, *it is what it is. You gave your word to 'all' the people of the Strange Valley that you would forever keep their secrets. There is nothing you can do now. Your word is your word—just put it out of your mind. The subject is closed.*

He finally started to drift off to a very uneasy sleep. He always had the ability to totally remove a subject from his mind, if there was no way he could change the outcome. This was one of those times.

John was not a fan of all the cable crime channels, or the flashy criminal procedure shows, that were on TV all the time, but he thought the situation he was in would make a good script for one of those shows.

Or at least a Hollywood movie, of that he was sure.

CHAPTER SIXTY-EIGHT

Everything was different the next morning. The air was clearer. The sun shone brighter. The flowers started to blossom. The birds chirped chirpier. The squirrels played their games and squeaked in apparent joy. The dogs pranced higher, the cats meowed a pleasant song; and there were herds of deer on his lawn instead of just a few. Everyone seemed to walk faster, even The Stinker. And the Stinker didn't even stink anymore. The pall had lifted from this Strange Valley.

John surveyed The Castle and all of his land, and he knew he was close to finishing the upgrades and repairs that were needed.

Then what? he thought. *What am I going to do up here once I finish working on The Castle?*

John decided to spend some time in San Francisco. He had not been home for a while. He enjoyed the drive to San Francisco.

He was delighted with his almost brand new home in the Sunset, and he missed the fog and the salt in the air. He had missed his beloved San Francisco.

He walked for hours on Ocean Beach. Back and forth! Then he sat and watched the large ships heading out to sea.

He did a ride-along with Calvin for a day just to renew his friendship. Just one day chasing after crooks convinced him he did not want to be a detective again.

He spent a couple of days with Susan. They had a ball down in Santa Cruz. They were like little kids on the rides, and Susan hugged the stuffed animals John had won for her. They swam in the ocean, and ate the calamari that he had bought on the pier. The rest of the day they fed on popcorn, corn dogs and just about every other junk food the boardwalk could offer. John loved the beach and the ocean. He had missed it!

John also spent a couple of days with Carol. After thinking it over, she was angry that he had not let her in on the "big secret" beforehand. "You should have told me about the tapes and diary."

"Seems like you are always mad at me," he replied.

They spent some time in Monterey. They toured the Aquarium and had picnics on the beach. John just sat, many times, just gazing out at the ocean and horizon.

"A penny for your thoughts," she would say.

John came back to the moment one time and said, "I would love to take a long cruise. On my own boat! Just to sail with nothing and nobody around."

"Do you know how to sail?"

"I'll learn."

"And you will sail all alone?"

"I hope someday to have a significant other."

"Live all oats and you'll get grass."

John looked at Carol. "What the hell does that mean?"

"My mother use to say it. I think it means have high dreams and you will be disappointed."

"That would be a helluva way to live. Stop dreaming just in case you might be disappointed!"

"It's just a saying, John, don't get so riled up."

John knew he had overreacted and he put his arm gently around Carol's shoulder. They watched the beautiful sunset, kissed under the stars and made love under their blanket.

On their last day together, he gave her a special gift. It was in a beautiful jewelry box. Carol held her breath. She knew it must be an engagement ring. She slowly opened the box and gasped. It contained *her father's religious medal*. She recognized it from long ago. She remembered the unusual chain that the medal hung from. It *was* her father's!

"Where did you get this?" she asked as the tears brimmed in her lovely eyes.

"I can't tell you. But I believe you have nothing to worry about for the rest of your life."

"Was it with The Captain's body?"

John took her hand in his and kissed her. "No more questions, Carol. It's over! I don't ever want to talk about The Captain ever again."

"But . . . !"

"Sshhh!" He quieted her as he gently kissed her and drew her to their hotel bed. They made love quietly and passionately and with a sense of some urgency from Carol. Did she suspect something? Was John ever going to commit to her?

After the loving they walked on the beach arm in arm. Suddenly Carol left John's side and waded into the ocean as far as she could. She took her father's medal from around her neck and threw it as far into the waves as the strength in her arm could throw it.

She walked back to John, soaked from head to toe, but standing proudly, and defiantly. "NOW it is over! Thank you, John."

CHAPTER SIXTY NINE

The next few days John spent with his parents.
He also spent two full days on the golf course with his dad.
"I have missed this, Dad."
"Not more than I have, son."
His mother made all of his favorite foods. "Mom, you are going to kill me with all this good food."
"Then come more often."
"I will," he said as he kissed his mother's forehead.
And of course he had to spend some time with his grandparents. He could not explain it, but when he was in his grandparents' home, he felt at ease and safe. Just as he did as a child!
"How's the wee Castle?" asked Gramps.
"It's not a wee Castle, Gramps" he responded. "It has over twenty bedrooms and twenty bathrooms."
"Och, away! I didnee see all of them. Why would anyone need twenty bathrooms? How much can one person pee?"
John laughed as he reminded his grandfather that they had only stayed in the north section of The Castle. He had closed off the south section while restoring the north section. He was now near to completing the south section.
"Is it almost finished, Johnny?"
"Aye, Gramps, it is."
"Did you like the work I did up there?"
"It was spectacular, Gramps."
"Did anyone else like my work?"
"Anyone that saw it was amazed at the quality of the work."
Gramps just smiled with pride.
"How is Emily?" asked Granny.
"She is still with us, Granny."

"How do you know that?"
"That's what Maggie tells me."
"Well then, Maggie would know."
"I think you and she are good witches."
Granny just laughed. "How about a wee cup of tea and I'll read the tea leaves for you. I'll tell your fortune."

John knew better, he could and would not refuse. He laughed inwardly at Granny's past tea leaf readings. No one ever got a bad reading. Everyone was going to lead a long life and be rich.

Granny began to read his tea leaves. "You are at a crossroads," she began. John looked up at his granny. This was not the usual reading!

"I see you are going far away," read Granny.
"The Castle is far away, Granny."
"I see a new path."
"Where does the path lead, Granny," he asked, deciding to play the game.
"You have a foot in two roads at once. I see two hearts. One is broken."
"You are scaring me, Granny."
"You may need medical attention in the near future!"
"What does *that* mean?"
"You'll probably fall and skin your knee, like you did as a wee boy."
"That is all there is!" ended Granny.

Despite John's pleading, Granny would read no more.
"Granny, did you just make all that up?"
"I read it as I see it."
"Maybe you are going to take me back to Scotland," Gramps said with a wink.
"Don't even kid about a thing like that," said John, remembering his promise to his grandfather.

After he stood for measurements for a new sweater his Granny was making for him, and being scolded for staying away for so long, John hugged them tightly and promised to come more often.

CHAPTER SEVENTY

John was happily putting last minute touches to his front garden. He was planting some bushes and pulling out some weeds.

His mind was finally at ease after all that had transpired during the past year.

He did not have to worry about the Perez Brothers and he settled, as best he could, the mystery of The Captain, and the worries of the people of this Strange Valley.

As he was bending down to pick up his gardening tools, he heard someone call his name.

He turned and saw Officer Chesney Sr. walking out of the woods with a backpack on his shoulders and a rifle in his hands.

"Hello, John."

"Hello—what on earth are you doing walking through my woods? You scared the hell out of me."

"I was told there was an injured doe out there in the backwoods. I wanted to find her and if need be put her out of her misery."

"I guess you didn't find her—I didn't hear a gun shot."

"No, these animals are very resilient. The doe probably found a safe place to hide and heal, or die in peace."

"John, I am very thirsty. May I have a glass of water, or a beer? Tramping through these woods took a lot out of me at my age."

"Oh, sure, Mr. Chesney, I could use a beer myself." John rose to go into The Castle. Then he remembered what Chesney had gone through and said, "I guess you would prefer not going into The Castle?"

"I don't mind. I would like to see what you have done to the place."

They settled themselves in the kitchen and John got each of them a beer, and he was gracious enough to put out some nuts.

There was little talk as they sat and drank. John did not know this man very well, so the conversation was a little stilted.

The telephone rang, and John asked his leave to answer it.

"Certainly," said Chesney. "I have to go to the *can*."

"Use the one just down the hall."

John was on the telephone longer than he thought he would be, but when he hung up, Chesney had not returned.

"Mr. Chesney," he yelled, "Are you lost?" John had to chuckle a little. Most people did get lost in his big, old Castle.

"I'm here. I was just looking around a little. I hope you don't mind," he said as he looked at his watch.

"No, I don't mind." But something triggered his cop instincts. "Where is your backpack, Mr. Chesney?"

"Oh, I must have left it in the bathroom. I'll get it before I leave."

Why would he have taken it with him to the bathroom, John thought?

They sat and drank the rest of their beers, and again there was not much conversation between them. John was becoming uneasy—he was hoping that Mr. Chesney would soon leave. He had nothing in common with this man, except what had happened at The Castle, and John was sure Chesney didn't want to talk about that again. He noticed Chesney was continually either looking at or fumbling with his watch and beginning to sweat profusely.

"Mr. Chesney, do you have an appointment to go to somewhere? You keep looking at your watch."

"No, it's just a habit I have."

"There is something I think you should know, John. I think I owe it to you."

"And what would that be Mr. Chesney?"

Chesney took a last swig of beer and lifted his eyes to the ceiling and yelled, "I KILLED THE CAPTAIN!!!!" It came so suddenly and he shouted it so loudly that it almost knocked John off of his chair.

John finally found his voice. "We went over all that Mr. Chesney. No one knows who really killed that evil man." John tried to speak in as calm a voice as he could, to settle the man down.

"I KNOW!!! I KNOW WHO KILLED HIM! IT WAS ME!!! I took the bastard into the woods and bashed in his head with a baseball bat. I hit him again and again! I couldn't stop hitting him—I was out of my mind. I checked for a pulse many times and there was none—he was dead. But even then, I kept hitting him—over and over again. I HIT HIM—I KICKED HIM—I BASHED IN HIS HEAD AND FACE."

John couldn't move—he could hardly believe what he was hearing.

The Strange Valley

Chesney continued, "I was exhausted, covered in sweat and I was crying. I don't know why, but I was crying, and yet I could not stop hitting him. It was as if the devil had worked his way into my soul."

John still could not believe what he was hearing. But looking into the eyes of Andrew Chesney as he told his gory story, he knew he was looking into the eyes of a killer.

"Believe it or not, at the time, I was glad that I killed him. I felt I should have killed him many years before."

Chesney could hardly stop to take a breath—he wanted to get it all out into the open. "Then I heard some noises in the woods; it frightened me, and I ran. When I returned days later, it was then that I found the saw in The Captain's hand and the branch by his head. He was unrecognizable. *I* had beaten him badly, but now he was beaten to a pulp. Someone else had gotten to him—but it was me that killed him."

"I couldn't help myself. Even in the condition that the body was in at the time, I started to hit him again, *and again.*"

Andrew Chesney started to giggle, then laugh, then the laugh became maniacal—and he couldn't stop.

John realized the man had gone mad. Years and years of worrying about his wife and then carrying the guilt of the murder of The Captain had driven him out of his mind.

"It's time for you to go home, Mr. Chesney," John heard himself say in a very gentle voice. He slowly rose from the chair and walked slowly towards the door.

Just as he reached the door, he felt the cold steel barrel of a pistol pressed against the back of his head.

John stiffened. "You don't want to do this, Mr. Chesney!"

"I can't let you live—you are the only one that now knows I killed The Captain."

"I told you I would not tell anyone about your badge being found in The Captain's hand—I gave you my word."

"Now that you know the real truth, that I *killed* The Captain, you could slip up, and my grandchildren would know that their grandfather was a murderer."

John again tried to placate this distressed man. "I gave you my word—policeman to policeman. Your secret is safe."

Chesney just shook his head back and forth, and then he began to sob.

John knew from experience that he would not be able to talk sense into this man. He had gone off the deep end.

Chesney whispered in John's ear, "I left a bomb in one of the rooms of The Castle, loaded with C-4 explosives. In less than an hour you and this Castle will no longer exist."

John now knew why Chesney had left his backpack behind. If it was packed with C-4, the explosion would not only wipe him and The Castle off the face of the Earth, the collateral damage it would generate could kill or seriously hurt many of his neighbors in the general area.

He had to find that bomb, *fast*—and the madman's clock was ticking.

"Why would you do that?" John asked as calmly as he could.

"This is an evil place and it must be destroyed."

"What room did you leave it in?" John asked, fully knowing he would not get an answer from this man who had finally lost his mind.

Chesney laughed. "You will never find it—besides you won't even know when it blows up. You will be on your way to heaven or hell."

Many scenarios of what he should do at that moment were rushing through John's mind.

Suddenly, he turned and tried to grab the pistol from Chesney's hand.

The gun went off!

John grabbed for his left shoulder and the blood gushed through his fingers. He waited for the final bullet that would end his life.

Through a haze of pain, he saw Chesney rush past him, crying hysterically and John tried to roll out of his way. He knew in the state that he was in, with a bullet in his shoulder, or worse, that he could not wrestle the gun from the hands of this mad man. He let the man pass. He hoped the man would keep running and not turn and shoot him again. Blinded by tears, Chesney fell out the door and then down the steps. When he fell at the bottom of the stairs, he picked himself up and ran to the backwoods.

When he felt it was safe to move, John summoned all the strength that he could muster and crawled to the door. He managed to pull himself up by the doorknob and lock the door—he didn't want Chesney to have second thoughts and come back and shoot him again.

He got to his feet, and staggered towards the phone. Before he could dial 911 and summon the bomb squad, he heard a shot from the direction of the back woods. He instinctively knew that Mr. Chesney had taken his own life.

It was a sad ending to a sad life that was caused by a miserable slice of humanity—The Captain!

The mystery was finally, *definitely* solved. There was no more wondering about *who* in the Strange Valley had killed The Captain.

Now, he had to find that bomb—he didn't know how much time he had left to do it and he was in a Castle with thousands of places to hide an explosive device.

John ran from room to room looking for the backpack; or any other sign of a bomb.

The Strange Valley

He knew he was running out of time. His left shoulder was immobilized and he was getting weaker by the minute. He was losing a lot of blood.

"EMILY—HELP ME!" he shouted into the air.

As he was running towards the kitchen, he saw a bright light by the basement door.

"EMILY—IS IT DOWN THERE?" The light got brighter. It was so bright it almost blinded him.

John ran down the basement stairs, following the light. It led him to the wine cellar that was full of racks that held hundreds of bottles of wine, new and old. Even with Emily's light shining, it was hard to see more than a few feet in any direction. He frantically ran up and down the aisles of the wine cellar, searching for the bomb, grabbing large bottles of wine off the racks and flinging them aside to see if the bomb had been hidden behind or under them.

As he threw one bottle after another off the racks lining the basement wall, Emily's light circled his head to get attention, then darted away. John followed the light to a wall, and once there he saw the single globe of light that was the usual form of Emily's manifestation split into seven smaller globes that formed into a straight line and began to flash sequentially—like the runway approach lights at SFO—pointing to a dark corner behind the compressor for the wine cellar's air conditioner. It was a tight squeeze, but John managed to work his way into the corner and hit something with his foot—with Emily's light flashing he could see that it was Chesney's backpack. He reached for it, then stopped, realizing that Chesney may have booby-trapped it. He looked at his watch—it was close to an hour since Chesney had planted the bomb. He would have to take the chance that Chesney was an amateur bomb maker and that the bomb didn't have any sophisticated detonation circuits.

Very gingerly, John picked up the backpack with the bomb in it, and wormed his way out from behind the compressor. He carried the bomb very carefully, not knowing if it would explode at any moment. Emily lit the way to the stairs, he ran up them as quickly as he could, then through the kitchen and out the door.

He was weak from the loss of blood, he felt like passing out, but he managed to run across the backyard towards the woods. As he went, John remembered all those movies that he and Calvin had howled at where the bomb timer would beep 3 times before the bomb went off, to give the doomed hero an "Oh, Shit" moment before the poor guy was blown to smithereens. He didn't think those movies were so funny now.

He reached the woods and ran deep inside, dodging trees and branches as he went through, until he thought he had ran far enough to make sure that The Castle would be outside the blast radius of the bomb, then ran 50 feet more. He gently put the bomb down, then turned and limped back as fast as he could to the protection of the thick stonewalls of The Castle.

In less than two minutes the bomb went off—just as he flung himself into the back door of The Castle. The concussion of the blast shook The Castle, breaking some of the windows that Mountain had so painstakingly installed, and John knew it probably shook the whole Strange Valley.

John tried to wrap his shoulder to stop the bleeding until the paramedics arrived. He was grateful to be alive and not badly hurt.

Days later, he went back to look at the crater that the bomb had caused.

Well, I always wanted a swimming pool, he said to himself. It was then that he didn't know whether to laugh or cry.

John shared Mr. Chesney's confession with the Amador Police and it flew through the Strange Valley like wildfire.

It was only now that the fear was totally gone. Nothing could ever hurt the people in this Strange Valley again. It took a long time, but the fear about The Captain was gone. The Captain was murdered by Andrew Chesney Sr., and *everyone* said Chesney had every right to do so!

The people of the Strange Valley were the Judge and Jury, and their verdict was that Officer Andrew Chesney was posthumously "not guilty," even though he had jeopardized all their lives. The Captain had driven him mad, they determined, and that was the final, sad end of it.

And Grandma MacGregor was right—John did need medical attention—for his shoulder.

CHAPTER SEVENTY-ONE

John had made his final decisions before returning to his Castle. He had convalesced at his grandparents' house until his shoulder was almost healed.

He had a lot of time to think as he was healing.

For a long while he had been torn between his two houses, his two walks of life and his two lady friends.

But he finally knew what he wanted to do. It took a month to work out the plans in his mind and then he put the plans down on paper. Then they were solidified.

The Castle was sold very quickly and this was the day he was to leave. In a way it was sad. A lot had happened in such a short time. He would miss the magnificent Castle, Heather Glen, and he would miss the people of the Strange Valley. Not so strange anymore!

It had served a purpose for John. He had needed to get away—to hide for a while. He had settled the matter of the Perez Brothers. He felt good about solving the mystery of the death of The Captain and easing the minds of the people of this Strange Valley. It was almost as if he had been destined to buy The Castle and to help all these wonderful people. It was now time for him to move on.

The day had come when he was to leave The Castle and to start on his new life's journey.

He had just tossed the last of his belongings in the car. There wasn't much. Just his clothes and a few mementos! He had sold The Castle furnished.

He ran back to The Castle at the last minute to retrieve one last item. The jar filled with The Captain's ashes.

He took one last look before starting the car. Yes, he would miss this Castle, Heather Glen, but the new owner said he could come back any time and stay for free.

He looked up at the turret from which Emily had fallen and he saw her light, shining brightly. She was no longer afraid and she would stay on in The Castle. She was not ready to *go home*. The light moved up and down as if she were waving goodbye to John. He couldn't help it—he waved back.

The new owners of The Castle were at the front door, waving goodbye to him as well—Maggie and Mountain! Sutter, sitting beside them, looked as if he was waving, too. The dog was happy to be left with Mountain and Maggie, but would miss John—a little.

The Castle, Heather Glen, was now a "haunted" Bed and Breakfast, and already booked for one solid year. Everyone had heard of Emily, the gentle ghost—and the good food, good cheer and entertainment that Maggie and Mountain provided. The new proprietors had already made The Castle a success.

Emily now loved living in The Castle! She did not miss a chance to scare the hell out of all the visitors, and they loved it.

Emily was finally "at home," and enjoying herself as any child should. She was having fun, the fun she had missed as a child. It was as if she stayed around to help Maggie and Mountain, and she would stay as long as she was needed. She now felt safe in The Castle, and Maggie and Mountain were almost like her parents.

John had sold The Castle to Maggie and Mountain at the same price that he had bought it. He held the loan; interest only. Maggie and Mountain were more than grateful for the opportunity that John Hurley had given them. But more than that, they were good friends. Mountain was now like a brother to John.

John was asked to be the godfather of the child that Maggie was now expecting!

As he turned out of the driveway and drove down the street, he couldn't believe his eyes. All of the neighbors of the Strange Valley had lined the street and were waving American flags.

Then they started throwing confetti at John in his Corvette Convertible and they were yelling, "Thank You."

There was so much of it that John's hair was completely covered with confetti, to the point that you could hardly tell what color it was.

Beautiful bouquets of flowers were thrown on his car.

John felt "Royal"—just like a conquering hero, home from the wars—like Eisenhower and Gen. MacArthur. Or like the President of the United States.

He knew he did not deserve the accolades and tributes, but he was delighted that the people thought enough of him to come out and give him a good send off.

The street was lined with people all the way down to Route 88. At the very end of the line stood Carol! When he saw her, he slowed down, and Carol tossed a dozen roses that landed on the hood of the convertible. She gave him a wink and they shared a knowing smile.

John would never forget that tribute. It was a perfect end to a perfect day.

A last wave and John was now headed back to the City that he loved. SAN FRANCISCO!

Carol soon followed, as she had a full day in Court in San Francisco. She was part of the defense team that was handling another one of those awful murder cases that always seemed to be part of the daily news.

As he drove west, he would glance often at the wedding ring on his left hand. They had a wonderful wedding and reception up at The Castle, and they were now ready to start on their new lives together.

They were first married in the Catholic Church, Madonna of the Oaks, in a traditional Scottish ceremony—complete with a lone piper. All the residents of The Strange Valley were in attendance. His bride wore a simple white gown that made her look more beautiful than he had ever seen her before. John looked handsome in his Scottish regalia. His grandmother had made his kilt and she was so proud of the grandson that she had helped to raise. Ian MacGregor, John's grandfather was the Best Man. John did not want to hurt Calvin's feelings since he had always said that when he got married Cal would be by his side—but John felt that gramps, his sentimental Old Scottish Grandfather would find the honor of being best man very meaningful, and indeed his old eyes were never without tears the entire day.

And besides, Calvin would soon get his chance.

Susan Wong was his soul mate, and before she agreed to marry him, she made John promise that they would also have a traditional Chinese ceremony to show respect to her parents.

Susan was absolutely breathtaking in her traditional Chinese wedding dress for the second ceremony, and Calvin was standing right next to John when he and Susan took their vows. All of the parents were now happy, and John had to laugh at his Scottish family, experiencing their first Chinese wedding in San Francisco. The reception was held in the best restaurant on Grant Street in Chinatown.

Their honeymoon was going to be a trip around the world on the biggest cruise ship sailing the seas.

It was the best John could do until he learned to sail the Seven Seas on his own.

He had met with Carol at her parent's place in Elk Horn and told her of his decision days before the first wedding. It was awkward and uncomfortable for them both. As they went into the living room and sat on the couch, he delivered the news, as gently as he could.

Carol's reaction took him by surprise. "I think I always knew it, John. We were great in bed together, but I always had doubts that we would ever make it as a couple."

John honestly had to admit, "That is what I had thought as well."

"It's not that I don't love you, but sometimes love is just not enough."

"I agree." John wanted to say something thoughtful or profound, but the words escaped him. All he could think to say was, "You're taking this a lot better than I had thought you would."

"I wish you well, John. And thank you for all you have done for my family, and all of my neighbors."

"It *was* one hell of an adventure, wasn't it, Carol?"

They kissed, and parted for what they thought was the last time.

John's heart was now filled with hope and happiness.

He knew he had chosen the right path and the right woman.

As he and his new bride waved goodbye to their friends and relatives on shore, from their place on the deck of the luxurious HMS Queen Diana, John was sure there could not have been a better ending to the events of the past year.

He turned to his bride and kissed her hair and hugged her tight. He then turned and looked towards the horizon and the unknown. He wasn't frightened anymore. He was sailing into the unknown future with his beloved, his soul mate.

Together they would travel the world and together they would handle life's joy or tragedies. *"Till death do you part"* is what they had promised and as they held hands they knew it was a promise they intended to keep.

THE END